No one writes r...-
land.

Miss Cartland was originally inspired by the best of the romantic novelists she read as a girl—Elinor Glyn, Ethel M. Dell, Ian Hay and E. M. Hull. Convinced that her own wide audience would also delight in her favorite authors, Barbara Cartland has taken their classic tales of romance and specially adapted them for today's readers.

Bantam is proud to publish these novels—personally selected and edited by Miss Cartland—under the imprint

BARBARA CARTLAND'S
LIBRARY OF LOVE

Bantam Books in Barbara Cartland's Library of Love

Make sure you haven't missed any of Barbara Cartland's own unforgettable novels of love. Ask your bookseller for all the Bantam titles of Barbara Cartland romances.

Barbara Cartland's Library of Love

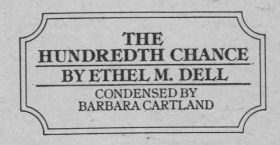

THE HUNDREDTH CHANCE
BY ETHEL M. DELL

CONDENSED BY
BARBARA CARTLAND

BANTAM BOOKS · TORONTO · NEW YORK · LONDON

THE HUNDREDTH CHANCE
A Bantam Book / June 1977

ISBN 0–553–10925–1

Published simultaneously in the United States and Canada

Bantam Books are published by Bantam Books, Inc. Its trade-
mark, consisting of the words "Bantam Books" and the por-
trayal of a bantam, is registered in the United States Patent
Office and in other countries. Marca Registrada. Bantam
Books, Inc., 666 Fifth Avenue, New York, New York 10019.

PRINTED IN THE UNITED STATES OF AMERICA

Introduction
by Barbara Cartland

The Hundredth Chance is one of Ethel M. Dell's most passionate and dramatic tales. Maud, her sensitive, unhappy heroine, who adores her crippled brother, Lord Saltash, the aristocratic, mocking villain, and Jake—the strong, silent, deeply passionate hero—are all animated with pulsating, often primitive emotions which I found enthralling sixty years ago, and still do.

Only this compelling writer could keep us on tenterhooks until the very last few pages in case the tale does not end happily.

Read this book and you will find, like me, that you cannot put it down.

▼

THE HUNDREDTH CHANCE

Chapter One

"My dear Maud, I hope I am not lacking in proper pride. But it is an accepted, though painful, fact that beggars cannot be choosers."

Lady Brian spoke with plaintive emphasis.

"I cannot live in want," she said, after a pause. "Besides, there is poor little Bunny to be considered."

Lady Brian's daughter made an abrupt movement without taking her eyes off the clear-cut horizon. They were beautiful eyes of darkest, deepest blue.

Her smile was not very frequent, but when it came it transfigured her utterly, like a burst of sunshine over a brown and desolate landscape.

"Bunny would sooner die of starvation than have you do this thing. And so would I," Maud said.

"You are so unpractical," sighed Lady Brian. "And really, you know, dear, I think you are just a wee bit snobbish too, you and Bunny. Mr. Sheppard may be a self-made man, but he is highly respectable."

"Oh, is he?" said Maud.

"I'm sure I don't know why you should question

it," protested Lady Brian. "He is also extremely kind, in fact, a friend in need."

"And a beast!" broke in her daughter, with sudden passionate vehemence. "A hateful, familiar beast! Mother, how can you endure the man? How can you for a single moment demean yourself by the bare idea of . . . of marrying him?"

"It isn't as if I had asked you to marry him," Lady Brian pointed out. "I never even asked you to marry Lord Saltash, although it was the one great chance of your life."

"We won't discuss Lord Saltash," Maud said, with lips that were suddenly a little hard.

"Then I don't see why we should discuss Giles Sheppard either. Of course, I know he doesn't compare well with your poor father. Second husbands so seldom do. But, as I said before, beggars cannot be choosers."

Lady Brian was forty-five, but she looked many years younger. She was a very pretty woman, and put her daughter in the shade; but then Maud never attempted to charm anyone.

All her being seemed to be bound up in that of her young brother, ten years younger than herself, who had been a helpless cripple from his babyhood, and dependent upon her care.

She had lavished a mother's love upon him during the whole of his fifteen years, and he filled all the empty spaces in her heart.

But now that they were practically penniless, who was to provide for Bunny?

Lady Brian had lived more or less comfortably upon credit for the past five years. It was certainly not her fault that this bruised reed had broken at last.

There had always been the possibility that Maud might marry Lord Saltash, who was extremely wealthy and, by fits and starts, very sedulous in his intentions.

It was, of course, unfortunate that he should have been connected with an unfortunate scandal in the Divorce Court; but then everyone knew that he had led a somewhat selfish life both before and after his succession to the title.

Besides, nothing had been proved, and it was really too absurd of Maud to treat it seriously.

Of course it was very sweet of her to devote herself so unsparingly to dear little Bunny, but Lady Brian was privately of the opinion that she wasted a good deal of valuable time. She was twenty-five and, now that the crash had come, unlikely to find another suitor.

They had come down to this little South Coast resort to rest and look round. Obviously something would have to be done, and done very quickly, or they would end their days in the workhouse.

Lady Brian had relations in the North, but they were not inclined to be kind to her. Her runaway marriage with Sir Bernard Brian in her irresponsible girlhood had caused something of a split between them.

The wild Irish baronet had never been regarded with a favourable eye, and her subsequent sojourn in Ireland had practically severed all connections with them.

Sir Bernard's death had not healed the breach.

She was still regarded as flighty and unreliable.

Lady Brian had stayed at Fairharbour before, at the Anchor Hotel, down by the fishing-quay.

It was not a very high-class establishment, but Lady Brian had favoured it on a previous occasion because Lord Saltash had a yacht in the vicinity, and it had seemed such a precious opportunity for dear Maud.

Nothing had come of the previous visit, however, save a pleasant, half-joking acquaintance with Mr Sheppard, the proprietor. But matters had not then come to such a pass, and she had finally extricated herself with no more than a laughing promise to return as soon as the mood took her.

Maud had been wholly unaware of the passage between them, which had been of a very slight and frothy order.

Not until she found herself in some very shabby lodgings within a stone's throw of the Anchor Hotel did her mother's reason for choosing Fairharbour as their city of refuge begin to dawn on her.

"So you see, dear, it really can't be helped," Lady Brian said, rising and opening her sunshade with a dainty air of finality. "Why his fancy should have fallen upon me I cannot imagine. But . . . all things considered . . . it is perhaps very fortunate that it has.

"He is quite ready to take us all in, and that, even you must admit, is really very generous of him."

Maud's eyes had a look in them as of a caged thing yearning for freedom. Sharply she turned and said:

"Mother, I shall write to Uncle Edward. This is too much. I am sure he will not condemn us to this."

Lady Brian sighed a trifle petulantly.

"You will do as you like, dear, no doubt. But pray do not write on my account! Whatever he may be moved to do or say can make no difference to me now."

"Why not?"

"Because," said Lady Brian plaintively, "it will be too late, so far as I am concerned."

"What do you mean?"

Lady Brian began to walk along the beach.

"I mean, dear, that I have promised to give Mr Sheppard his answer tonight."

"But . . . but . . . Mother." There was a cry in the words. "You can't . . . you can't have quite decided upon what the answer will be!"

"Oh, do let us have a little common sense!" she said, with just a touch of irritation. "Of course I have decided. The decision has been simply thrust upon me. I had no choice."

"Then you mean to say Yes?" Maud's voice fell suddenly flat. She turned her face to the open sea, a glint of desperation in her eyes.

"Yes," said Lady Brian very definitely. "I mean to say Yes."

"Then God help us!" said Maud, under her breath.

"My dear, don't be profane!" said Lady Brian.

* * *

"I say, Maud, what a dratted long time you've been! What on earth have you and Mother been doing? You swore you wouldn't be long."

"I'm sorry, I couldn't help it, Bunny," Maud said. "I haven't been enjoying myself."

"Oh, it's never your fault," Bernard Brian said, with dreary sarcasm.

Maud said nothing. She only laid a smoothing hand on his crumpled brow, and after a moment bent and kissed it.

"I wish to goodness we could get away from this place," the boy said restlessly. "Even the old Anchor was preferable."

"Did you really like the Anchor better?" Maud asked, after a moment.

"Yes."

"You would like to go back there?" she asked.

He looked at her sharply. She met his look with steady eyes.

"Mr Sheppard has offered to take us in."

"What! For nothing?"

"No, not for nothing," she replied. "Nobody ever does anything for nothing."

"Well? What is it!" Bunny's eyes suddenly narrowed and became shrewd. "He doesn't want you to marry him, I suppose?"

"Good gracious, Bunny!" Maud gasped the words in sheer horror. "Whatever made you think of that?"

Bunny laughed, a cracked, difficult laugh.

"Because he's bounder enough for anything; and you're so beastly fond of him, aren't you?"

"Oh, don't!" Maud said. "Really, don't, Bunny! It's too horrible to joke about. No, it isn't me he wants to marry. It's . . . it's . . ."

"Mother?" queried Bunny, without perturbation. "Oh, he's quite welcome to her. It's a pity he's been such a long time making up his mind. He might have known she'd jump at him."

"But, Bunny . . ." Maud was gazing at him in utter amazement. "You can't be pleased!"

"I'm never pleased," said Bunny sweepingly. "I hate everything and everybody except you, and you don't count. The man's a brute, of course; but if Mother has a mind to marry him, why on earth shouldn't she? Especially if it's going to make us more comfortable!"

"Comfortable on his money!"

"But why not?" said Bunny, with cynical composure. "We shall never be comfortable on our own. If the man is fool enough to want to lay out his money in that way, why, let him!"

"Live on his . . . charity!" Maud added bitterly.

"We've got to live on someone's," he said.

"Bunny, Bunny darling!" she whispered passionately. "I would give all the world to make life better for you!"

"No, you wouldn't!" he said unexpectedly.

"Indeed I would!" she said very earnestly.

"You wouldn't!" he reiterated, with the paralysing conviction that refused to hear any reasoning. "If you would, you'd have married Lord Saltash years ago, and been rich enough to pay one of the big men to put me right."

"Bunny!" She winced sharply. "You're not to talk to me of Lord Saltash. It isn't kind. He is the one man in the world I . . . couldn't marry."

"Rot!" said Bunny. "You know you're in love with him."

"I know I couldn't marry him," she said, a piteous quiver in her voice. "It is cruel to . . . to . . ."

"All right," said Bunny, waiving the point. "Find some other rich man, then! I don't care who it is. You'll have to pretty soon. We shall neither of us stand this Sheppard person for long."

"If I could only, somehow, make a living for the two of us!"

"You can't! You're not clever enough, and you haven't time, unless you propose to leave me to the tender mercies of the Sheppard. It would be a quick way out of the difficulty as far as I am concerned, anyway."

"Of course I could never leave you!" Maud said quickly.

"All right, then. Marry and be quick about it!" said Bunny.

He turned his drawn, white face to the window.

"Maud!" he said suddenly. "There's a fellow down there trying to make his horse go into the sea! Let's go down and watch."

Bunny's long chair was in a corner of the room. It was no light task to get it in and out of the house; but Maud gladly wheeled him down the hill to the sun-bathed shore.

That hill taxed her physical powers to the uttermost. Secretly she dreaded the ascent, but not for worlds would she have let Bunny know it.

They reached the sunny stretch of parade in time to see a young chestnut coaxed along the edge of the water by his rider. The animal was covered with froth, and evidently in a ferment of nervous excitement.

The man who rode him sat loosely in the saddle as if the tussle in progress were of very minor importance. He kept the fretting horse's head turned towards the water. He patted the streaming neck and spoke words of encouragement.

At the edge of the parade Bunny and Maud watched the progress of the battle. It was undoubtedly a battle of wills, though there was nothing in the man's attitude to indicate any strain.

"Wonder if he'll do it," said Bunny.

"He'll be thrown if he isn't careful," Maud said.

"Hope he'll tumble into the water," said Bunny, who enjoyed dramatic situations.

The pair had passed them. The man was still preoccupied, the horse half-frightened, half-mischievous.

An odd little thrill went through Maud. It was almost a sensation of foreboding. Then, clean and grim as a pistol-shot, she heard the crack of a whip on the creature's quivering flank.

It was a well-earned correction, deliberately administered, one stinging cut, delivered with a calculation that knew exactly where to strike.

The horse leapt into the air as if he had been shot indeed, and began forthwith to buck-jump.

The whip descended again with absolute precision. It looked almost like a feat of jugglery to Maud's fascinated eyes. The horse uttered a furious squeal.

He was being forced into the hated water, and he set himself with all the fiery unreason of youth to resist.

As for his rider, he became relentless. From that moment she knew with absolute certainty that there could be but one end to the struggle.

Some dim suspicion of the same thing must have penetrated the animal's intelligence, for he seemed to lose heart. He still bucked away from the water and leapt in futile frenzy under the unsparing whip, but his fury was past.

He no longer tried to fling his rider over his head. He seemed to be fighting to save his pride rather than for any other reason.

But endurance had its limits, and his smooth, clipped flanks were smarting intolerably. Very suddenly he gave in and walked into the water.

It foamed alarmingly round his legs, and he started in genuine terror and tried to turn; but on the instant a hand was on his neck, a square, sustaining hand that patted and consoled.

"Now, don't be a fool horse any longer!" said his conqueror. "Don't you know it's going to do you good? Go on and face it!"

He went on, splashing his rider thoroughly, first in sheer nervousness, later in undistinguished content.

He came out of the water some five minutes later, wiser and considerably less headstrong than he had entered it, and walked serenely along the edge.

"A beastly tame ending!" said Bunny in frank disappointment. "I hoped the fellow was going to break his neck."

The horseman was passing immediately below them. He looked up, and Maud coloured a guilty scarlet, realising that he had overheard the remark.

He had the most startlingly bright eyes she had

ever seen. They met hers with a directness that seemed to pierce straight through her, and passed on unblinkingly to the boy.

There was something lynx-like in the straight regard, something so deliberately intent that it seemed formidable. His clean-shaven, weather-beaten face had an untamed, primitive look about it, as of one born in the wilderness.

Bunny, who was not easily daunted, looked hard back at him, with the brazen expression of one challenging a rebuke. But the horseman refused the challenge, passing on without a word.

"I'm tired," Bunny said, in sudden discontent. "Let's go back!"

"Yes, of course," Maud answered.

"You puff like a grampus," he complained as she pushed him up the hill.

There came a quick fall of a horse's hoofs behind them, and Maud bent her flushed face a little lower.

She did not want to meet those piercing eyes again. But the hoof beats slackened behind her, and a voice spoke.

"Say! That's too heavy a job for you."

She paused, and looked round.

In the same moment he slid to the ground, and again those bright, red-brown, intensely alive eyes met hers. She felt as if they saw too much; they made her vividly conscious of her hot face and labouring heart. They embarrassed her, made her resentful.

"You take my animal!" he said. "He's quiet enough now."

She might have refused, had she had time to consider. But he gave her none. He thrust the bridle into her hands, and the next moment he had taken her place behind the invalid-chair and begun to push it briskly up the hill.

Maud followed, leading the now-docile horse, and felt divided between annoyance and gratitude. Bunny also seemed to be struck dumb.

At the top of the steep ascent the stranger stopped and faced round.

"Thanks!" he said briefly, and took his horse back into his own keeping.

Maud stood, feeling shy and awkward, while he set his foot in the stirrup. Then he mounted, and with a desperate effort she spoke.

"It was very kind of you. Thank you very much."

"You've nothing to thank me for," he said. "As I said before, it's too heavy a job for a woman. You'll get a groggy heart if you keep on with it."

There was no intentional familiarity in the speech, but it made her stiffen instinctively.

"It was very kind of you," she repeated.

She gave him a bow that was even more freezingly polite than her words, and she turned, prepared to walk on.

But at this point Bunny suddenly found his voice in belated acknowledgment of the service rendered.

"Hi! You! Stop a minute! Thanks for pushing me up this beastly hill!"

The stranger was still standing with his foot in the stirrup; but at the sound of Bunny's voice he took it out again and came to the boy's side, leading his horse.

"What a beauty!" said Bunny admiringly. "Can I touch him!"

"Oh, don't," said Maud nervously. "He looked so savage just now."

"He's not savage," said the horse's owner.

He pulled the animal's nose down to Bunny's eager, caressing hand.

"He's not savage," the rider said. "He's only young and a bit heady; wants a little shaping, like all youngsters."

Bunny's shrewd eyes flashed him a rapid glance, meeting the red-brown eyes deliberately scrutinising him. With a certain blunt courage he asked:

"I say, did you hear what I said down on the parade?"

The man smiled a little.

"Did you mean me to hear?" he enquired.

"No," said Bunny, staring back, half-fascinated and half-defiant.

"All right, then, I didn't," the horseman replied.

Bunny's expression changed. He smiled.

"Good for you! I say, I hope we shall see you again sometime."

"If you are here for long, you probably will," the man replied.

"Do you live here?" Bunny's voice was eager. His eyes sparkled with interest.

The man nodded.

"Yes, I'm a fixture. And you?"

"Oh, we're going to be fixtures, too," said

Bunny. "This is my sister, Maud. I am Sir Bernard Brian."

Maud's ready blush rose burningly. Bunny's swaggering announcement made her long to sink through the earth. She dreaded to hear his listener laugh, even looked up in surprise when no laugh came.

He was surveying Bunny with that same unblinking regard that had disconcerted her. The slight smile was still on his face, but it was not a derisive smile.

After a moment he said:

"My name is Bolton, Jake Bolton."

"What are you?" said Bunny, with frank curiosity.

"I?" The faint smile suddenly broadened, showing teeth that were large and very white. "I'm a groom."

"Are you?" The boy's eyes opened wide. "Then you're not a 'mister'!"

"Oh no, I'm not a 'mister'! I'm plain Jake Bolton. You can call me Bolton or Jake, whichever you like. Good-day, Sir Bernard!"

He backed his horse with the words, and mounted, and with relief Maud heard him turn his horse and trot down the hill.

*   *   *

"Hark to the brute!" Bunny said.

A long, loud peal of laughter was echoing through the house. Maud shuddered at the sound. The noisy wooing of her mother's suitor made her feel physically sick.

But for Bunny, she would have fled incontinently from the man's proximity.

Because of Bunny, she sat at a rickety writing-table in a corner of the room and penned an urgent, almost a desperate, appeal to the bachelor uncle in the North to deliver them from the impending horror.

Again came that loud coarse laugh, and with it the opening of a door on the other side of the passage.

"Watch out!" warned Bunny. "They're coming!"

There was a hint of nervousness in his voice also. Maud heard it, and rose. When their door opened, she was standing beside him, very upright, very pale, rigidly composed.

Her mother entered, flushed and smiling. Behind her came her accepted lover.

Lady Brian ran to her daughter with all a girl's impetuosity.

"My dear, it's all settled! Giles and I are going to be married, and we're all going to live at the Anchor with him. Dear little Bunny is to have the best ground-floor rooms. Now isn't that kind?"

It was kind. Yet Maud stiffened to an even icier frigidity at the news, and dear little Bunny's nose turned up to an aggressive angle.

"I hope you and Mr Sheppard will be very happy," Maud said, after a distinctive pause.

Giles Sheppard laughed and seated himself on the edge of the table to contemplate her.

"We shall have to try and find a husband for

you, young woman," he said. "I wonder who'd like to take you on. Jake Bolton might do the trick. We'll have Jake Bolton to dine with us to-morrow. He knows how to tame wild animals, does Jake. It's a damn pretty sight to see him do it, too!"

He chuckled grimly with his eyes on Maud's now-crimson face.

"Now, Giles," protested Lady Brian, "you've promised to be good to my two children. Dear Maud has a good deal to learn yet, so you must be patient with her."

She smiled ingratiatingly.

"Now I think we all know each other, and my little Bunny is looking rather tired. I think we won't stay any longer."

"Wait a minute!" interposed Bunny. "That man you were talking about just now, Jake Bolton. Who is he? Where does he live?"

"Who is he?" Giles Sheppard slapped his thigh and rose. "He's one of the best-known fellows about here, a bit of a card, but none for worse for that. He's the trainer up at the stables, Lord Salt-ash's place."

"Oh, he's Lord Saltash's trainer, is he?" Lady Brian said. "Lord Saltash is a very old friend of ours. Does he ever come down here?"

"I don't see him if he does," Giles Sheppard answered as they both left.

"What a disgusting beast!" said Bunny as the door closed.

Maud said nothing. She only went to the window and flung it wide.

Suddenly the house seemed to stifle her, and she ran out for a breath of air. Then something about the moaning shore seemed to draw her.

She reached the edge of the parade. The hour was late; the place deserted. She stood facing the drift of rain that blew in from the sea.

How dark it was! The nearest lamp was fifty yards away! The thought came to her suddenly, taking form from the formless deep; how easy to take one single step in that darkness!

What a fool she was to suffer so, when there was nothing in life worth living for!

Nothing? Yes, there was Bunny. She was an absolute necessity to him. That she knew. She was firmly convinced that he would die without her. And though he would be far, far happier dead, poor darling, she couldn't leave him to die alone.

She lifted her clenched hands above her head in straining impotence. For one black moment she almost wished that Bunny were dead.

And then, very suddenly, with staggering unexpectedness, two hands closed simultaneously upon her wrists, and she was drawn into two encircling arms.

She uttered a startled outcry, and in the same moment began a wild and flurried struggle for freedom. But the arms that held her closed like steel springs. A man's strength forced her steadily away from the yawning blackness that stretched beyond the parade.

"It's no good kicking," a soft voice said. "You won't get away."

Something in the voice reassured her. She ceased to struggle.

"Oh, let me go!" she said breathlessly. "You ... you don't understand. I ... I ... only ..."

"Came out for a breath of air?" he suggested. "Of course, I gathered that."

He took his arms away from her, but he still kept one of her wrists in a strong grasp. She could not see his face in the darkness, only his figure, which was short and stoutly built.

"Do you know," he said, "when people take the air like that, I always have to hold on to 'em tight till they've had all they want. It's damn cheek on my part, as you were just going to remark. But it's easier than mucking about in a dark sea looking for 'em after they've lost their balance."

He led her to a shelter. She sat down rather helplessly, and she spoke after a moment with slight hesitation.

"I shouldn't have lost my balance. And if I had meant to jump over, as you imagined, I shouldn't have stood so long thinking about it."

He bent down, and she was sure that his eyes scrutinised her and took in every detail.

The next moment he released her wrist.

"All right, I believe you. But don't do it again! Accidents happen, you know. You might have had one then; and I should still have had to flounder round looking for you."

Something in his tone made her want to smile, yet she wanted to resent his familiarity at the same moment.

She rose at length and faced him with such dignity as she could muster.

"I am obliged to you, but I fail to see why your responsibility should extend so far. If I had fallen over, the chances are that you could never have found me, or saved me if you had."

"Ninety-nine to one!" he said coolly. "But do you know, I rather count on the hundredth chance. I've taken it, and won on it, before now."

She felt her face begin to burn in the darkness, and she turned abruptly.

"Good-evening," she said, and began to walk away.

He fell in beside her. "I'm going your way. May as well see you past the bar of the Anchor. They get a bit lively there sometimes at this end of the day."

As she reached her door, she paused.

"You're going in now?" he asked.

"Yes," she said.

He came a step nearer, and laid one finger on her arm.

"Look here. You take a straight tip from me! If you're in any sort of trouble, go and tell someone! Don't bottle it in till it gets too big for you! And, above all, don't go step-dancing on the edge of the parade in the dark. It's a fool thing to do."

He emphasised his points with impressive taps upon her arm. She felt absurdly small and meek.

"Suppose I haven't anyone to tell?" she said after a moment.

"Tell me."

She had not expected that. He seemed to disconcert her at every turn.

"Thank you," she said, taking refuge in extreme frigidity. "I think not."

"As you like," he said. "I daresay I shouldn't in your place. I only suggested it because I can't see a girl in trouble and pass by on the other side."

He spoke quite quietly, but there was a quality in his voice that stirred her very strangely, something that made her for the moment forget the man's dominant personality.

She put out a groping hand to him, obeying a curious impulse that would not be denied.

"Thank you," she said again.

He kept her hand for a second or two, holding it squarely, almost as if he were waiting for something.

Then, without a word, he let it go. She turned back, and he went on.

Chapter Two

Maud and Bunny had spent all day settling into their new quarters at the Anchor Hotel, and it had been a tiring task.

The bride and bridegroom had arrived from the registry-office barely in time to receive the guests whom Sheppard had invited to his wedding-feast.

Neither Maud nor her mother had been told much of the forthcoming festivity, and the girl's dismay upon learning that she was expected to attend it was considerable. She was feeling tired and depressed.

Bunny was in a difficult mood, and she knew that another bad night lay before them. Still, it was impossible to refuse. She could only yield with as good a grace as she could muster.

Giles Sheppard watched her enter the drawing-room behind her mother, and a bitter sneer crossed his bloated face. He was utterly incapable of approaching that innate pride of race.

He read only contempt for him in the girl's still face, and deep resentment began to smoulder within him with an ever-increasing heat.

How dare she show her airs and graces here?

She, a penniless minx, dependent now upon his charity for the very bread she ate!

With an ugly jest at her expense upon his lips, he turned to the man with whom he had been talking at her entrance; but the jest was checked unuttered. For the man, square, thick-set as a bull-dog, abruptly left his side and moved forward.

The quick blood mounted in Maud's face as he intercepted her. She looked at him for a second as if she would turn and flee. But he held out a steady hand to her, and she had to place hers within it.

"You remember me, Miss Brian? I'm Jake Bolton, the horse-breaker. I had the pleasure of doing your brother a small service yesterday."

Both hand and voice reassured her. She had an absurd feeling that he was meting out to her such treatment as he would have considered suitable for a nervous horse. She forced herself to smile upon him! It was the only thing to do.

He smiled in return, a pleasant, open smile.

"So you and your brother are going to live here?" he said.

She answered him in a low voice:

"We can't help ourselves."

"What's the matter with that young brother of yours?" he asked.

"It is an injury to the spine. He had a fall in his babyhood. He suffers terribly sometimes."

"Nothing to be done?" he asked.

She shook her head.

"No one very good has seen him. He won't let a doctor come near him now."

"Oh, rats!" exclaimed Jake Bolton unexpectedly.

She felt her colour rise as he turned his bright eyes upon her.

"You don't say that a kid like that can get the better of you?" he said.

"Bunny has a strong will. I never oppose it."

"And why not?"

"I try to give him all he wants. He has missed all that is good in life."

He wrinkled his forehead for a moment, as if puzzled, then broke into a laugh.

"Say, what a queer notion to get!"

She stiffened but he did not seem to notice it. He leaned towards her, and laid one finger on her arm.

"Will you let me see him presently?" he asked.

"I am afraid that is impossible," she replied.

"Why?"

She raised her dark brows.

"Tell me why!" he insisted.

"It is not good for him to see strangers at night. It upsets his rest."

"You think it would be bad for him to see me?" he questioned.

His voice was suddenly very deliberate. He was looking her full in the face. A curious little tremor went through her. She felt as if he had pinioned her there before him.

"I don't say it would be bad for him, only inadvisable. He is rather excited already."

"Will you ask him presently if he would care to see me?" said Jake Bolton steadily.

She bit her lip, hesitating.

"I shan't upset him," he insisted. "I won't excite him. I'll quiet him down."

"I will ask him, if you wish."

"Thank you, Miss Brian."

"Hullo, Jacob!" blared Sheppard's voice suddenly across the room. "What are you doing over there, you rascal? Thought I shouldn't see you, eh? Ah, you're a deep one, you are!

"I daresay now you've made up your mind that that young woman is a princess in disguise. She isn't. She's just my step-daughter, and a very cheap article, I assure you, Jake, very cheap indeed!"

The roar of laughter that greeted this sally filled the room, drowning any further remarks. Sheppard stood in the centre, swaying a little, looking round on the assembled company with a facetious grin.

Jake Bolton rose and went to him. Maud, shivering in her corner, wondered what he said. It was only a few words, and they were not apparently uttered with much urgency. But Sheppard's grin died away, and she fancied that for a moment, only for a moment, he looked sheepish.

Then he clapped a great hand upon Bolton's shoulder.

"All right. All right. It's for you to make the running. Come along, ladies and gentlemen! Let us feed!"

There was a general move, and Jake Bolton pivoted her through the crowd.

They reached the dining-room, and people began to seat themselves round a long centre table.

There was no formal arrangement, and therefore some confusion.

"Fight it out among yourselves!" yelled Sheppard above the din of laughter and movement. "Make yourselves at home!"

"There's a table for two in that alcove," Jake Bolton said. "Shall we make for that?"

"Anywhere!" Maud said desperately.

He elbowed a way for her. The table was near a window, the alcove draped with curtains. He put her into a chair where she was screened from the eyes of those at the centre table. He seated himself opposite her.

"Don't look so scared!" he said.

She smiled at him faintly in silence.

"I gather you don't enjoy this sort of bear-fight."

She remained silent. The man disconcerted her. She was burningly conscious that she had not been too discreet in taking him even so far into her confidence.

He leaned slowly forward, fixing her with those relentless, lynx-like eyes.

"Miss Brian," he said, his voice very level, faultlessly distinct, "I'm rough, no doubt, but please believe I'm white!"

She looked at him, startled, unhappy, not knowing what to say.

"Don't you forget it!" he said. "There are plenty of beasts in the world, but I'm not one of 'em. You'll drink champagne, of course?"

He got up to procure it, and Maud managed in the interval to recover some of her composure.

When he came back, she mustered a smile and thanked him.

"You look tired out," he said, as he filled her glass. "What have you been doing?"

"Moving into our new quarters," she answered. "It takes some time."

"Where are your rooms?" he asked.

"It is really only one room," she said. "But it is a fine one. I have another little one upstairs; but it is a long way from Bunny. Of course I shall sleep downstairs with him."

"Do you always sleep with him?"

"Yes."

"Is he a good sleeper?"

He had moved round and was filling his own glass. She watched his steady hand with a touch of envy. She would have given much for as cool a nerve just then.

"Is he a good sleeper?" he repeated as he set down the bottle.

"No, a very poor one."

"And you look after him night and day? I guess that accounts for it."

"For what?" She met his look haughtily, determined to hold her own.

But he smiled and refused the contest.

"For a lot," he replied. "Now, what will you eat? Lobster? That's right, I want to see you started. What a filthy racket they are making! I hope it won't upset your appetite."

*   *   *

"Oh, Maud! I thought you were never coming!"

Bunny's face, pale and drawn, wearing the irritable frown so habitual to it, turned towards the opening door.

"I have brought you a visitor," his sister said.

Her voice was low and nervous. She looked by no means sure of Bunny's reception of the news. Behind her came Jake Bolton, alert and self-assured.

His thick mat of chestnut hair shone like copper in the brilliant electric light, such hair as would have been a woman's glory, but Jake kept it very closely cropped.

"What on earth for?" began Bunny querulously; and then magically his face changed and he smiled. "Hullo! You!"

Bolton came to his side and took the small, eager hand thrust out to him.

"Yes, it's me. No objection, I hope?"

"I should think not!" The boy's face was glowing with pleasure. "Sit down! Maud, get a chair!"

Bolton turned sharply, found her already bringing one, and took it swiftly from her. He sat down by Bunny's side, and took the little thin hand back into his.

"Do you know, I've been thinking a lot about you."

Bunny was vastly flattered. He liked the grasp of the strong fingers also, though he probably would not have tolerated such a thing from any but this stranger.

"Yes," pursued Jake, in his quiet, level voice. "I reckon I've taken a fancy to you, little chap, I beg your pardon, Sir Bernard. How have you been today?"

"Don't call me that!" said Bunny, turning suddenly red.

"What?" Jake smiled upon him, his magic, kindly smile. "Am I to call you Bunny, like your sister, then?"

"Yes. And you can call her Maud," said Bunny autocratically. "Can he, Maud?"

"I don't think I dare," Jake said.

"Maud!" Peremptorily Bunny's voice accosted her. "Come over here! Come and sit on my bed."

It was more of a command than an invitation. Maud straightened herself and turned. But as she did so their visitor intervened.

"No, don't," he said. "Sit down right there, Miss Brian, in that easy chair, and have a rest!"

His voice was peremptory too, but in a different way. Bunny stared at him wide-eyed. Jake met the stare with an admonitory shake of the head.

"Guess Bunny's not wanting you," he said. "Don't listen to anything he says!"

Bunny's mouth opened to protest, remained open for about five seconds, and finally he said:

"All right, Maud. You can stay by the fire while we talk."

And Maud, much to her own surprise, sat down in the low chair on the hearth and leaned her aching head back upon the cushion.

She had her back to Bunny and his companion, and the murmur of the latter's voice seemed to possess a soothing quality. Very soon her heavy eyelids began to droop and the voice to recede into ever-growing distance.

For a space she still heard it, dim and remote as

the splash of the waves on the shore; then very softly it was blotted out. Her cares and her troubles all fell away from her. She sank into soundless billows of sleep. . . .

*   *   *

She awoke at length with a guilty start. The fall of a piece of coal had broken the happy spell. She sat up, to find herself only with the firelight.

Her first thought was for Bunny, and she turned in her chair and looked across the unfamiliar room. He was lying very still in the shadows. Softly she rose and went to him.

He was asleep, lying amongst his pillows. The chair by his side was empty, the visitor vanished.

Very cautiously she bent over him. He had been lying dressed outside the bed. Now, with a thrill of amazement, she realised that he was undressed and lying between the sheets. He was breathing very quietly, and his attitude was one of easy rest. Surely some magic had been at work!

She dared not switch on the light, but as the fire burned up again she held her watch to the glare. Half past two!

In amazement she began to undress.

There was no second bed in the room, only a horse-hair sofa that was far less comfortable than the chair by the fire.

She lay down upon it, pulling over her an ancient fur travelling-rug belonging to her mother, while another quiet hour slipped away.

Then there came a movement from Bunny.

"Are you awake, Maud?" asked his voice out of the shadows. "Has Jake gone?"

"Yes, darling," she made answer. "Are you wanting anything?"

"When did you wake up?"

"About an hour ago."

"Weren't you surprised to find me in bed?" He chuckled a little.

"Yes, I was," she said. "How did you get there?"

"That fellow Jake, he went over and looked at you, came back and said you were fast asleep, and asked what I generally had done and if he couldn't do it for me. He managed very well and was jolly quick about it, too."

"But, Bunny, didn't he hurt you at all? You nearly always cry out when you're lifted."

"I didn't that time," said Bunny proudly. "I told him I should probably squeal, and he said if I so much as squeaked he'd throttle me. He's a brick, do you know, Maud, and he seemed to know how to get hold of me without being told."

Maud's amazement was growing. The man must be a genius indeed to manage Bunny in that fashion.

"He's a brick," the boy said again, "and do you know he's done almost everything under the sun? It was out in the wilds somewhere that Lord Salt-ash came on him and brought him home to be his trainer. But he's British-born all the same. I knew he was that the first time I saw him."

He was evidently a paragon of all the virtues in Bunny's estimation, and Maud did not attempt to express her own feelings, which were, in fact, very complex.

Very deep down in her woman's soul, a warning

voice had begun to make itself heard, but she could not tell Bunny that. Scarcely even to herself dared she admit that the straight, free gaze of those red-brown eyes possessed the power to set her heart a-fluttering in wild rebellion, like the wings of a captive bird.

*   *   *

In many respects the change from their lodgings up the hill to the Anchor Hotel by the fishing-quay was for the better, and as the days went on and winter drew near, Maud realised this.

Bunny and Maud lived their lives apart from the rest of the establishment, an arrangement which Mrs Sheppard deplored, although she knew it to be an eminently wise one.

Her husband never lost an opportunity to revile the girl who always treated him with the same aloof distance of manner.

He hated her with the rancorous and cruel hatred of conscious inferiority, savagely repenting his undertaking to provide for her. They did not often clash, because Maud steadfastly avoided him. And this also he resented, for he was in effect simply biding his time to drive her away.

Towards Bunny, Sheppard displayed no ill feeling. He had small cause to do so, for the boy was kept rigorously out of his way, and his mother was more than willing to leave the entire care of him to Maud.

Jake Bolton was a frequent visitor to Bunny's room and came and went as he pleased, but on those occasions while he was with Bunny, Maud took advantage to get out on her own.

It was on an afternoon in late November that she went down to the shore during one of his visits to her brother, to watch the fishing-fleet come in through a blur of rain.

She walked the length of the parade twice, and finally turned homewards.

She reached the entrance of the Anchor Hotel, and was stretching out a hand towards the swing-doors when one of them opened abruptly from within, and Jake stepped out.

He was smoking a cigarette, and he did not in the first moment perceive her. She drew back in an instinctive effort to escape notice. But he stopped.

"Is that you? I was just wondering where you were."

"Am I wanted?" she asked quickly, as her thoughts immediately flew to Bunny.

"No, the lad's all right. It's I who want you. Can you spare me a minute?"

It was impossible to refuse, but she did not yield graciously. Somehow she never could be gracious to Jake Bolton.

"I ought to go in," she said. "It is getting late."

"I shan't keep you long."

She noticed that it was plainly a foregone conclusion with him that she would grant him what he asked.

She turned back into the misty darkness with a short sigh of impatience.

"Walk to the end of the parade with me!" he said, and fell in beside her. "I am sorry to have brought you out again into the wet. Will you come into the shelter?"

She stepped within it and stood waiting.

"I want to speak to you about your brother," he said. "And, by the way, before I forget it, I've promised to trundle him up to the stables next Sunday, to show him the animals. You will come, too, won't you? I can give you tea at my house. It's close by."

Maud's eyes opened a little. The suggestion somewhat startled her.

"You are very kind. But I don't think we can either of us do that."

"I am not in the least kind," said Jake. "And will you tell me why you are offended with me for suggesting it?"

"I am not . . . offended," she said, feeling herself grow uncomfortably hot over the assertion. "But . . . I think you might have proposed this to me before mentioning it to Bunny."

"But what's the matter with the proposal?" he said. "The boy was delighted with it."

"That may be," Maud said.

"Don't take fright at nothing!" Jake said, in an admonitory tone. "If you're going to shy at this, I reckon you'll kick up your heels and bolt at my next suggestion."

"Perhaps you would be wiser not to make it."

"Very likely," agreed Jake. "But, as you object to my mentioning things to your brother first, I don't see how you can refuse to listen."

This was unanswerable. She bit her lip. "I am listening."

"And the answer is No, whatever it is," rejoined

Jake, with a whimsical note in his soft voice. "Say, Miss Brian, play fair!"

"I have said I will listen," she said.

"With an unbiased mind?"

"Of course."

She spoke impatiently; she wanted to get the interview over, and she more and more resented his attitude towards her. There was something of the superior male about him that grated on her nerves.

"All right," said Jake. "I'll go ahead. If you will condescend to come up to my place on Sunday, I will show you a man, one of our jockeys, who was injured in just the same way that your brother is injured, and who is now as sound as I am.

"He was operated upon by an American doctor called Capper, one of the biggest surgeons in the world. It was a bit of an experiment, but it suc-ceeded.

"Now, what has been done once can be done again. I happen to know Capper, and he is coming to London next spring. He makes a specialty of spinal trouble. Won't you let him try his hand on Bunny?

"There would be a certain amount of risk, of course. But wouldn't it be worth it to see that boy on his legs, living his life as it was meant to be lived instead of dragging out a wretched existence that hardly deserves to be called life at all?"

He stopped abruptly, as if realising that he had allowed his eagerness to carry him away. But to Maud, who had begun to listen in icy aloofness, that same eagerness was as the kindling of a fire in a place of utter desolation.

"Oh, if it were only possible!" she said. "If it only could be!"

"Why can't it be?" said Jake.

"Because doctors, great surgeons, don't perform big operations for nothing."

"I don't think Capper would charge an out-of-the-way amount if he did it for me," said Jake.

"Perhaps not." Maud spoke in the dead tone of finality.

"Aren't you rather easily disheartened, Miss Brian? Wouldn't your people scrape together something for such a purpose?"

"No."

"Are you quite sure?" he urged. "Won't you even ask 'em?"

"It's no good asking," she said, her voice low and reluctant. "The only relation we possess who might help won't even answer when I write to him."

"Why don't you go and see him?" said Jake. "Put the thing before him! He couldn't refuse."

She shook her head.

"It wouldn't be any good. Besides, I couldn't get to Liverpool and back in a day, and I couldn't leave Bunny for longer. And . . . in any case . . . I know . . . I know it wouldn't be any good."

"I wish the little chap were my brother."

Maud was silent. Somehow his vehemence had upset her; she had an outrageous desire to cry.

Jake was silent, too, for a few seconds; then abruptly he squared his shoulders and spoke with aggressive decision.

"Miss Brian, a good friend is nearer than a

dozen beastly relations. With your permission I'll see this thing through."

"Oh, no, no!" she said quickly. "No, no!"

"For the boy's sake!"

"No!"

"Bunny told me, only today, with pride, that there was nothing in the world that you wouldn't do for him," Jake said in an odd voice.

She made a sharp movement of protest.

"I can't take . . . what I could never repay," she said, speaking almost below her breath. "Neither shall Bunny."

"There are more ways than one of paying a debt," said Jake.

"I am afraid I don't understand you," she said.

"Shall I explain?" said Jake. "Can't you see I'm making a bid for your friendship? You've never contemplated such a fool idea as marriage with me, I know; but go home and contemplate it right now! Ask yourself if you wouldn't find a husband like me less nauseating than a step-father like Giles Sheppard!

"Ask yourself if the little chap wouldn't stand a better chance if you brought him along to me! I reckon we'd make his life easier between us even if Capper couldn't make him walk.

"He's too much for you to carry alone. You weren't created for such a burden as that. Let me lend a hand! I give you my solemn oath I'll be good to you both!"

A tremor of passion ran through his last words, and his voice took a deeper note.

Maud, upright and quivering, felt the force of

the man like the blast of a tearing gale, carrying all before it. She would have left him at the commencement of his speech, but he blocked the way.

She stood imprisoned in a corner of the shelter, steadying herself against the woodwork, while the full strength of his individuality surged round her. She felt physically exhausted, as if she had been trying to stand against a tremendous wind.

"Please let me pass," she said, when she could trust herself to speak without faltering.

He stood back instantly and she was conscious of a lessening of that mysterious influence which had so overwhelmed her.

"Are you angry?" he asked.

She gathered her strength, though she was trembling from head to foot.

"Yes, I am angry," she said. "I have never been so insulted in my life!"

"Insulted!" He echoed the word in unfeigned astonishment; then, as she would have left him, he put a detaining hand upon her arm.

"Say, Miss Brian! Since when has a proposal of marriage constituted an insult in your estimation?"

"A proposal of marriage from you could be nothing else."

"I offer you a way of escape. It mayn't be the way you would choose, but there are worse, many worse. I'm not a bad sort, and I've got a soft spot in my heart for that little brother of yours."

"It would be quite useless for me to consider it," Maud said. "I am sorry if I was rude to you just now, but your suggestion rather took my breath away. Please understand that it is quite, quite impossible!"

"All right," he said. "Still, you won't dismiss it quite entirely from your mind? That is to say, you'll hold it in reserve just in case a way of escape becomes essential to you.

"The offer remains open day and night, just in case the emergency might arise which would make you willing to avail yourself of it."

He took his hand from her arm, and she felt that the interview was over. Yet he walked beside her as she began to move away, and crossed the road again with her to the entrance of the hotel.

"One thing more," he said, as they reached it. "I have no wish or intention to force myself upon you, so if, to please Bunny, you can bring yourself to accompany the pair of us on the Sunday expedition to see the stud, you need not be afraid that I shall attempt to take advantage of your position."

The colour flamed up in her face. He seemed to possess the power of calling it up at will.

She stood on the first step, looking down at him. He moved close to her, and by the lamplight that streamed through the glass doors she saw his frank, disarming smile.

"And look here!" he said. "Don't fling cold water on that other scheme for Bunny that I broached to you yet! You never know what may turn up."

The smile decided her. She held out her hand to him.

"But, you know, I couldn't . . . I really couldn't . . ."

He gave the hand a firm grip and released it.

"No. All right. I understand. But think about it! And don't run away with the idea that I planned it just for your sake! I'd like to be of use to you. But it's the lad I'm thinking of. You do the same! After all, you put him first, don't you?"

"He always will come first with me," she said. "But I couldn't . . . I can't incur such an obligation . . . even for him."

"All right," said Jake, unmoved. "Class it with the impossibles—but, all the same, think about it!"

He was gone with the words, striding away down the street without a backwards glance.

Maud was left alone with an odd feeling of uncertainty at her heart. She felt baffled and uneasy.

*   *   *

That Sunday of their visit to the Saltash Stables was a marked day with Maud for the rest of her life.

Jake had brought them up the long, winding private road which, though smooth enough, was a continual ascent. Maud had wanted to help with the invalid-chair, but he had steadily refused any assistance.

She marvelled at the evident ease with which he had accomplished the journey, never hurrying, never halting, not even needing to pause for breath.

She remembered the nickname he bore on the Turf, and reflected that it fitted him in more than one respect. He was so supple, so tough, so sure.

Suddenly those bright eyes flashed round on her.

"Say, you're tired," he said in his lilting voice. "We'll have tea first."

He wheeled the chair into a great gateway that led into a wide, stone courtyard. Whitewashed stables were on either side of them and at regular intervals large green tubs containing miniature fir trees. At the further end of the courtyard stood a square, whitewashed house.

"That's my shanty," said Jake.

It was a very plain building; in former days it had been a farm. There was a white railing in front and a small white gate flanked by another pair of toy firs. The whole effect was one of prim cleanliness.

"There's a bit of garden at the back," said Jake. "And a summer-house, quite a decent little summer-house, that looks right away to the sea. Now, Bunny lad, there's a comfortable sofa inside for you. Think I can carry you in?"

"Can't you take in the chair?" Maud asked nervously.

Jake looked at her.

"Oh, yes, I can. But the passage is a bit narrow. It's not very easy to turn."

"Of course he can carry me, Maud. Let him carry me!" broke in Bunny, in an aggrieved tone. "You make such a stupid fuss always."

Jake had thrown open the door of his home.

"You go in, Miss Brian! Turn to the right at the end of the passage, and it's the door facing you."

She passed down the passage and turned as Jake had directed.

The door that faced her stood open, and she entered a long low room, oak-panelled like the

passage, with a deep old-fashioned fireplace in
which burned a cherry-wood fire.

Two windows, diamond-paned, and a door with
the upper panels of glass occupied the whole of the
further side of the room. The sunshine slanting in
threw great bars of gold across the low window-
seats.

Tea had been set on a table in the middle of
the room, to the corner of which a sofa had been
drawn. There were bed-pillows as well as cushions
on the sofa. Evidently Jake had ransacked the
house to provide comfort for Bunny.

"There you are, my son!" he said as he carried
Bunny in. "Make yourself as much at home as you
can!"

Bunny looked at him with keen interest.

"Oh, I say, what a ripping room! You're lucky
to live here, Jake."

"Oh, yes, it's a decent little crib," said Jake.
"Those doorsteps were just made for an evening
pipe."

He indicated the closed, glass-panelled door.
Maud went to it and found that the ground sloped
sharply away from this side of the house, necessi-
tating a flight of several steps.

They led down into a sunny space that was
more orchard than garden, fruit trees and grass
spreading down the side of the hill towards the
magic, pine-screened grounds of Burchester Castle.

Jake came and stood beside her for a moment.
He was being studiously impersonal that day, an
attitude which curiously caused her more of uneasiness than relief.

"The arbour is at the end by those apple trees," he said. "You can just see the roof from here. It looks over the field where we train. It's fun to watch the youngsters learning to run. Lord Saltash calls it the grandstand."

"Do you know Lord Saltash?" broke in Bunny. "He used to be a great pal of ours once."

"Oh, that was years ago, in London," said Maud quickly. "No doubt he has quite forgotten our existence by this time."

She spoke with unwitting sharpness, hotly aware that the lynx-like eyes of her host were upon her.

Bunny took instant offence.

"I'm sure it wasn't years ago, Maud; it isn't more than two since we saw him last, if that. As to forgetting all about us, that isn't very likely, considering Mother was one of his bad debts."

"Bunny!" Maud began in rare anger.

But in the same moment, Jake swung calmly round.

"Bunny, do you like shrimps? I got some in case. Miss Brian, I hope shrimps are good for him, are they?"

"She doesn't know," said Bunny irritably. "What's the good of asking her? Of course I like shrimps! Aren't we going to begin soon? I want to go and see the horses."

"You seem to be in an all-fired hurry," observed Jake. "Left your manners behind, haven't you?" He took out his watch. "Half past three. All right, my son, we'll go at four. Miss Brian, do you mind pouring out?"

He set a chair for her facing the window, and sat down himself next to Bunny.

It seemed to Maud that, seated there in his own house, she saw him under a new aspect. He played the host with ability and no small amount of tact.

He talked mainly about the stud, interesting her in the subject until finally he took them to see the horses.

It was among the horses that Maud at length saw Jake Bolton in his true element. They were all plainly very dear to his heart. He introduced them as friends.

His pockets were stuffed with sugar, which both she and Bunny helped to distribute, and not till dusk came upon them did they realise the lateness of the hour.

It was at the last minute that Jake suddenly summoned a little man who was lounging in the gateway.

"Here, Sam! I've been telling the lady about your tumble, and how they put you together again. It interested her."

Sam approached with a sheepish grin.

"I thought I was a goner. But Mr Bolton," he looked at Jake, and his grin widened, "he's one of the never-say-die sort. And the American doctor, well, he was a regular knock-out, he was. Mended me as clean—well, there, you wouldn't know I've had a smash."

One eye wandered down to Bunny in his long chair as he spoke; but he discreetly refrained from comment, and it was Bunny who eagerly broke in.

"What happened to you? Was it your spine?"

Sam was only too willing to oblige. He settled down to his story like a horse into its stride, and for nearly a quarter of an hour Maud stood listening to the account of the miracle which, according to Sam Vickers, the great American doctor had performed.

Bunny drank it all in with feverish avidity. Maud did not like to watch his face.

She did not want to glance at Jake either, though after a time she felt impelled to do so. His eyes were fixed upon Bunny, but on the instant they came straight to hers as if she had spoken.

She avoided them instinctively, but she felt them nonetheless, as if a dazzling searchlight had suddenly and mercilessly been turned upon her, piercing straight to her soul.

It was soon after this that he quietly intervened to put an end to Sam's reminiscences. It was growing late, and they ought to be moving.

Maud agreed; Bunny protested, and was calmly overruled by Jake. They started back through a pearly greyness of dusk that heralded the rising of the moon. They spoke but little as they went. Bunny seemed suddenly tired, and apparently it did not occur to either of his companions to attempt to make conversation.

Only as they descended the winding road that led down to Fairharbour, and a sudden clamour of church bells arose through the evening mist, Jake glanced again at the girl who was walking rather wearily by Bunny's side, and said:

"Wouldn't you like to go to church now? I'll see to the youngster."

She shook her head.

"Thank you very much; I don't think so."

"Oh, go on, Maud!" exclaimed Bunny, emerging from his reverie. "I don't want you if Jake will stay. I'd sooner have Jake. He doesn't fuss like you."

"I'll get him to bed," Jake went on, as if he had not spoken. "You can trust me to do that, you know. I won't let him talk too much, either."

She heard the smile in the words; and because of it she found she could not refuse.

"But I don't like to give you so much trouble."

"You give me pleasure," he answered simply.

"I'll say good-bye," he said, at the gate of the churchyard. "But don't hurry back! I shall stay as long as I am wanted."

She knew that she could rely upon him in that respect as upon no one else in the world. She gave him her hand with another low word of thanks.

"May I walk to the door with you?" he said, and drew Bunny's chair to one side.

It would have been churlish to refuse. She suffered him in silence, and, suddenly, Maud heard the beating of her heart in the silence, and was conscious of an overwhelming sense of doom.

With an effort that seemed to tear at the very foundations of her being, she turned and walked down a narrow path between the tombstones. He followed her till, in breathless agitation, she turned again.

"Mr Bolton!"

Her voice was no more than a whisper. She was thankful that her face was in shadow.

He stood silently, his eyes, alert and bright, fixed intently upon her.

"I must ask you," she said, "I must beg you . . . to regard what I said the other day as final. If I am friendly with you, I want you to understand that it is solely for Bunny's sake . . . no other reason."

"That is understood."

She drew the quick breath of one seeking relief.

"Then you will forget that . . . that impossible notion? You will let me forget it too?"

"I shan't remind you of it."

"And you will forget it yourself?" she insisted.

He lowered his eyes suddenly, and it was as if a light had unexpectedly gone out. She waited in the dark with a beating heart.

And then with a great clash the bells broke out overhead, and further speech became impossible. Jake wheeled without warning, and walked away.

She stood and watched him go, still with that sense of coming fate upon her. Her heart was leaping wildly like a chained thing seeking to escape.

As for Jake, he rejoined Bunny, and squarely resumed the journey back to the town, without the smallest sign of discomposure.

He seemed somewhat absent, however, trudging along in almost unbroken silence; and it was not until he laid the boy down at length in his own room that he said:

"Now, look here, youngster! If you can't be decently civil to your sister, I've done with you. Understand?"

Bunny turned impulsively, and buried his face in Jake's sleeve.

"All right. Don't jaw! But it's so beastly being managed always by women."

"You don't know when you're lucky," said Jake.

Bunny's emotion passed. He looked at his friend shrewdly.

"I suppose you're in love with her," he remarked after a moment.

Jake's eyes met his instantly and uncompromisingly.

"I'm the head of the family."

The man's face softened to a smile .

"Yes, I reckon that's so. Well? What has the head of the family to say to the notion?"

Bunny turned rather red.

"She might have married Charlie Burchester."

"Who?" said Jake.

"Lord Saltash," explained Bunny. "We thought, everyone thought, five years ago, that they were going to get married. He was awfully keen on her, and she, of course, was in love with him. And then there was that row with the Cressadys.

"Lady Cressady got him into a mess, and Sir Phillip always was an obnoxious beast. And afterwards Charlie sheered off and went abroad. He came back after he came into the title, but Maud, she's awfully proud you know, she wouldn't look at him.

"She vows she never will again, though I'm not so sure she won't. He's sure to come back someday," he went on. "He's such a rattling good sort, and he's jolly fond of her."

"And the rest!" Jake said dryly.

"You don't like him?" Bunny's eyes opened wide in astonishment.

"Yes, I like him." Jake's tone was enigmatical. "But I shouldn't call him a marrying man. Anyway, he won't marry your sister, so you can make up your mind to that! Any other gentleman in the running?"

"No, no one. She never sees anybody now."

"Except me," said Jake. "And I'm not genteel enough, eh?"

"You're a brick!" said Bunny, with enthusiasm. "But you know, women don't see that sort of thing. They only care about whether a man opens the door for 'em or takes off his gloves to shake hands."

Jake broke into a laugh.

"Say, sonny, what a thundering lot you know about women! Anyway, I conclude I am right in surmising that you personally could swallow me as a brother-in-law?"

Bunny's eyes began to shine.

"You're the best fellow I know. If—if it weren't for Lord Saltash, I wouldn't say a word!"

"Well," said Jake, very deliberately, "I refuse to be warned off on his account. That's understood, is it?"

Bunny hesitated. The red-brown eyes were looking full and unwaveringly into his.

"I'm not thinking of myself, Jake," he said, with sudden pleading.

Jake's hand closed squarely upon his.

"All right, old chap, I know; and I like you for it. But I'm taking odds. It's ninety-nine to one. If I win on the hundredth chance, you'll take it like a sport?"

Bunny's hand returned his grip with all the strength at his command. He was silent for a moment or two; then said impulsively:

"I say, Jake, you're such a sport yourself! I think I'll back you after all."

"You won't be sorry," said Jake.

Chapter Three

Christmas was drawing near, and several visitors had already arrived. There was generally a short season at Christmas, during which the Anchor Hotel had its regular patrons.

Its landlord was in an extremely variable state of mind, sometimes aggressive, sometimes jovial, frequently not wholly sober. Maud avoided all contact with him with rigorous persistence.

But the state of affairs was such as was almost bound to lead to a climax sooner or later. Giles Sheppard's hectoring mood was not of the sort to be satisfied for long with passive avoidance.

Every glimpse he had of the girl, who ate his bread but disdained to do so in his company or the company of his friends, inflamed him the more hotly against her.

One day about a week before Christmas he unexpectedly presented himself at the door of Bunny's room.

"Look here!" he said harshly. "You've got to turn out of this. The room is wanted."

Maud, who was dusting the room, turned swiftly round with something of the movement of a tigress.

"What do you mean?" she said.

He looked at her with insult in his eyes.

"I mean just that, my fine madam. This room is wanted. The boy will have to go with the rest of the lumber, at the top of the house."

"I understood that we were not to be disturbed at any time," she said, meeting his look with that icy pride of hers that was the only weapon at her command. "Surely some other arrangement can be made?"

Sheppard growled out a strangled oath; she always made him feel at a disadvantage, this slip of a girl whom he could have picked up with one hand had he chosen.

"I tell you this room is wanted," he reiterated stormily. "You'd better clear out at once."

"Bunny can't possibly be moved today," Maud said, quickly and decidedly. "He is in pain. Can't you see for yourself how impossible it is? I am quite sure no visitor who knew the facts of the case would wish to turn him out."

Sheppard stamped his foot and Maud saw that he had been drinking.

"Go!" she said, in tense, frozen accents, pointing to the door. "Go at once! How dare you come in here in this state?"

Before her withering disdain he drew back, as it were involuntarily. He even half-turned to obey. Then, suddenly, some devil prompted him, and he swung back again.

With one gigantic stride he reached the sofa; and before either brother or sister knew what he intended to do, he had roughly seized upon the boy's slight body and lifted it in his great arms.

Bunny's agonised outcry at the action mingled with his sister's, but it ceased almost immediately.

He collapsed in the giant grip like an empty sack, and Sheppard, now wrought to a blind fury that had no thought for consequences, carried him from the room and along the passage to the stairs, utterly unheeding the fact that he had fainted.

Maud, nearly beside herself, went with him, striving to support the limp body where long experience had taught her support was needed.

They went up the stairs so, flight after flight, Sheppard savage and stubborn, the girl in a dumb agony of anxiety, seeking only to relieve the dreadful strain that had bereft Bunny of his senses.

They reached at length a room at the top of the house, a bare garret of a place with sloping ceiling and uncarpeted floor. There was a bed under the skylight, and on this the man deposited his burden.

Then he turned and looked at Maud with eyes of cruel malevolence.

"This is good enough for you and yours."

"You drunken brute!" she said. "You loathsome coward! You hateful, tipsy bully!"

The words pierced him like the stabs of a dagger too swift to evade. He was sober enough to be cowed. But he had borne with her too long—too long! Now matters had come to a head. She would either have to humble herself or go.

As for Maud, she spent the rest of the day in trying to make Bunny's new quarters habitable. She hoped with all her heart that Jake would come in the evening, so that they could move him into the room she occupied a floor lower, which had at least a fireplace.

But for once Jake disappointed her, and so the whole day passed in severe pain for Bunny and misery for her.

Towards evening, to her relief, he began to doze. She watched beside him anxiously. He had been very plucky, displaying an odd, protective attitude toward herself that had gone to her heart; but she knew that he had suffered intensely.

It would be days before he would shake off the effects of the rough handling he had received, and she dreaded the future with a foreboding that made her feel physically sick.

The evening wore away, and when the meal was over Bunny looked at her with a faint smile under his drawn brows.

"Look here, Maud! There's that bed in the corner. Can't you make it comfortable and get a good night for once?"

She looked back at him in surprise. It was very unusual for Bunny to give a thought to her comfort.

"Yes, I want you to," he said. "Go and undress, and then bring your blankets up here! You can't sit up all night in a straight-backed chair, so you may as well be comfortable. Don't stare! Go and do it!"

The bed in the corner was a thing of broken springs and crippled frame-work, and bedclothes were lacking.

But Bunny's suggestion seemed feasible, and since it was plain that he would not be content unless she followed it, Maud yielded without demur.

Her own room was only a flight of stairs away, and she had already fetched several things from it for his comfort. She hoped to get him down to it on the following day, if only Jake would come.

It was neither warm nor spacious, but it was preferable to this fireless attic.

She brought the blankets and arranged the bed.

"I don't think I'll undress, Bunny," she said.

"You are to," said Bunny. "Jake says no one can possibly rest properly without."

She was inclined to resent this assertion of Jake's teaching, but again yielded. Bunny was in a mood to work himself into a fever if his behests were not obeyed.

She went down and undressed, therefore, and presently slipped up to him again, hoping to find him asleep. But he was wide-eyed and restless.

"It's so beastly cold," he said. "I can't sleep. My feet are like stones. Where's the fur rug?"

She looked round for it.

"Oh, Bunny, I'm so sorry. I have left it in your room downstairs. Never mind! Here's a blanket instead!"

She was already pulling it off her bed when Bunny asserted himself once more.

"Maud, I won't have it! I will not have it! Do you hear? Put it back again. Why can't you go and fetch the fur rug?"

"My dear, I can't go down like this," she objected.

"Rot!" said Bunny. "Everyone's gone to bed by now. If you don't get it, they'll be turning the room out in the morning, and it'll get lost. Besides, you look all right."

She was wearing no more than a light wrap over her nightdress; but, as Bunny had said, it was probable that everyone had retired, for it was late.

Only a few dim lights were left burning in the passages. There would be no one about, and it would not take two minutes to slip down and get the rug. She dropped the blanket he had refused and went softly out.

The whole house was in silence as noiselessly she stole down the stairs. It was close upon midnight, and she did not meet or hear anyone. The place might have been empty it was so still.

The room was just as she had left it, the sofa drawn up by the burnt-out fire. She found the rug, pushed the sofa back against the wall, and began a quiet search of all the drawers and other receptacles the room contained.

She had almost finished her task, and was just closing the writing-table drawer, when a sudden sound made her start. A creaking footstep came from the passage beyond the open door.

She turned swiftly with a jerking heart to see her step-father, bloated and malignant, standing on the threshold.

For a single instant he stood there looking at her, and a great throb of misgiving went through her at the savage triumph in his eyes. He had been drinking, drinking heavily, she was sure; but he did not seem to be intoxicated, only horribly sure of himself, brutally free from any trammels of civilisation.

He closed the door with decision, and moved forward.

In the same moment she moved also towards the sofa over which she had thrown the rug she had come to fetch. Her heart was beating hard and fast, but she would not address a single word to him, would not so much as seem to see him.

Supremely disdainful, she prepared to gather up her property and go. But as she turned to the door, she found him barring the way. He spoke, thickly, yet not indistinctly.

"Not so fast, my fine madam! I've got to have a reckoning with you."

She drew herself up to the utmost of her slim height, and gave him a single brief glance of disgust.

"Be good enough to let me pass!"

But Sheppard did not move. He had been fortifying himself against this all day long.

"Not so fast!" he said again, with a gleam of teeth under his dark moustache. "You made a mistake this morning, young woman; a very big mistake. Don't make another tonight!"

Maud froze to an icier contempt. The steady courage of her must have shamed any man in his sober senses.

"Stand aside instantly, or I shall ring the bell and rouse the house!"

He laughed at that, a cruel, vindictive laugh.

"Oh, you don't come over me that way! You mean to have your lesson, I see, and p'raps it's as well. It's been postponed too long already. There's a deal too much spirit about you, and too much lip, too.

"Think yourself much too high and mighty to associate with the likes of me? Think you can call me any darn names you please, and I'll bear 'em like a lamb?"

His voice rose. Obviously his temper was already beyond control. He was, in fact, lashing it on to fury. Maud knew the process well.

It was enough for her, and she waited for no more. She stepped quietly to the bell.

She was nearer to it than he, and she did not for a moment imagine that he would dare to molest her. But she had not realised the maddened condition to which he had worked himself.

Even when he suddenly and violently strode forward, she did not draw back or dream that he would touch her.

Only as his hand caught her outstretched arm did the knowledge that he was as utterly beyond control as a wild beast burst upon her. She uttered a desperate cry, and began a sharp, instinctive struggle to escape.

It was a very brief struggle, so taken by surprise and utterly unprepared was she. One moment she was fighting wildly for freedom; the next he had her at his mercy.

"Oh, you may scream!" he gibed. "No one will hear you! Now, do you know what I am going to do to you?"

"Let me go!" she panted, crimson and breathless.

He locked her two wrists together in one iron hand. His strength was utterly irresistible. She was as a pigmy in the grip of a giant.

"I'll let you go when I've done with you," he

said, gloating openly over her quivering helplessness. "But first you will have your lesson. I'm going to give you the beating of your life!"

With the words he suddenly wrenched her round and forced her, almost flung her, face downwards over the sofa-head.

"You've been spoiling for this for a long time," he said, "and, being your step-father, I'll see that you get it. Never had a good spanking before in all your life, I daresay? Well, we'll see how you like this one!"

And he pulled off one of his carpet slippers and proceeded to flog her with it, as if she had been a boy.

What she went through during that awful chastisement, Maud never forgot. She fought at first like a mad creature, till she was suddenly aware of the light wrap she wore ripping in all directions, and from that moment she resisted no more, lying passive while he wreaked upon her all the pent-up malice of the past few weeks.

It was a brutal punishment, administered with the savage intention of breaking down the stark silence with which she sought to meet it.

Even when he succeeded at last, even when the girl's strength went from her, and as he held her she collapsed into a wild burst of hysterical crying and broken, unnerved entreaties, he did not stop.

Now was his grand opportunity for vengeance, and he might never get another. He did not spare her until he had inflicted the utmost of which he was capable.

Then at last roughly he set her free.

"That's right! Blub away!" he jeered. "I've taken all the stiffening out of you at last, and a damn good job too. P'raps you'll keep a civil tongue in your head for the future, and give me no more of your dratted impudence. There's nothing like a sound drubbing to bring a woman to her senses. But I don't advise you to qualify for another."

He put on his slipper, breathing somewhat heavily after his exertions, then stood up and wiped his forehead. His fury had exhausted itself. His mood had become one of semi-malicious elation.

He looked at the girl, still crouched over the sofa-head, sobbing and convulsed, utterly broken, utterly conquered.

"Come!" he said. "Don't let us have any more nonsense! You won't give me any more of your airs after this, and we shall be all the better friends for it. Stand up and say you're sorry!"

She gasped and gasped again, but no words could she utter. The hateful callousness of the man could not so much as rouse her scorn. Her pride was in the dust.

He took her by the arm and pulled her roughly up, making her stand before him, though she was scarcely capable of standing.

"Come!" he began again, and broke off with a brutal laugh, staring at her.

A flame of fierce humiliation went through her, burning her from head to foot as she realised that her nightdress had been rent open across her bosom. She caught it together in her trembling fingers, shrinking in an anguish of shame from the new devil that looked at her out of his bloodshot eyes.

"Well, my fine madam," he laughed again, "we seem to have pitched the proprieties overboard quite completely this time. All your own fault, you know. Serves you jolly well right. You aren't going to say you're sorry, eh? Well, well, I'd give you another spanking if I felt equal to it, but I don't. So I'll have the kiss of peace instead."

He caught her to him with the words, gripped her tightly round the body, tilted her head back, and for one unspeakable moment the heavy moustache was crushed suffocatingly upon her panting lips.

In that moment the strength of madness entered into Maud, such strength as was later wholly beyond her own comprehension. With frenzied force she resisted him, fighting as if for her very life, and so suddenly, so unexpectedly, that in sheer astonishment his grip relaxed.

It was her one chance of escape, and she seized it. With a single furious wrench she tore herself from him, not caring how she did it, found herself free, and fled, fled like a mad thing, panting, dishevelled, frantic, from the room.

His laugh of half-tipsy derision followed her, and all the devils of hatred, malice, and bitter cauterising shame went with her as she fled.

*   *   *

It was a rainy, squally morning and Jake was returning from the stables after an early ride.

On the breakfast-table was a letter bearing a purple crest of a fox's head and under it the motto *Sans Vertu*. He eyed it as he ate, and presently took it up. It bore a Swiss stamp.

He opened it and read:

Dear Bolton,

I meant to winter in Cairo, and heaven alone knows why I am here. It is fiendishly cold, and blowing great guns. Some of the female portion of the community are quite passably attractive, but I always preferred one goddess to a crowd, and she is not to be found here.

Unless it freezes within the next forty-eight hours, I shall come back to beastly old England and look for her. So if I should turn up at Burchester within the next few days, please accept this (the only) intimation and have the stud ready for inspection.

Yours sincerely,
Saltash.

Jake's face wore a curious expression as he folded the letter and returned it to the envelope. He continued his breakfast and helped himself to coffee.

The cup, however, was still untasted beside him when his housekeeper, Mrs Lovelace, entered the room.

"Miss Brian has called, sir. Wishes to see you for a moment. Shall I show her in?"

Jake's chair scraped back and he was on his feet in a single movement.

"Of course! Where is she?"

In the passage he almost ran into his visitor.

"Miss Brian! Is that you? Come right in! Goodness! You're wet. Come along to the fire!"

Maud, still panting from her recent struggle with the elements, found herself in an easy chair, holding numbed fingers to the blaze.

He knelt beside her, unbuttoning her streaming waterproof. She saw the glint of the firelight on his chestnut hair.

"Thank you," she said, with an effort. "You are very . . . kind."

He looked at her with those lynx-like eyes of his.

"Say, you're perished!" he said, in his soft, easy drawl.

She smiled quiveringly at the concern in his face. She had expected a precipitate enquiry about Bunny, but it was evident that he had thoughts only for her at that moment. And she was very badly in need of human kindness and consideration.

She sat huddled over the fire, all the queenliness gone out of her, tried to speak to him twice and failed; finally, she shook her head and sat in silence.

He got up and reached across the table for the coffee he had just poured out.

"Drink a little!" he said, holding it to her. "You need it."

She made a small gesture of impotence. Somehow the warmth and comfort of the room had upset her. She still smiled, but it was a puckered, difficult smile, and her eyes were full of tears. She could not take the cup. Her throat worked painfully. Again she shook her head.

Jake stood beside her for a moment or two, looking down at her; then, with swift decision, he set down the coffee, stepped to the door, and quietly turned the key.

He came back to her with the steady purpose of a man quite sure of himself, knelt again by her side, and put his arm about her.

"You lean on me!" he said softly. "Don't be afraid!"

She gave him a quick look. The tears were running down her face. She covered it suddenly with both hands and sobbed.

He drew her to him so gently that she was hardly aware of the action till her head came to rest on his shoulder. His free hand, strong and purposeful, took possession of one of hers and sturdily held it.

"It's all right," he murmured to her soothingly. "It's all right."

She wept for a while without restraint, her nerves completely shattered, her pride laid low. And while she wept, Jake held her, strongly, sustainingly, his red-brown eyes staring unblinkingly full into the heart of the fire.

At the end of a long interval she grew a little calmer, made as if she would withdraw herself. But very quietly he stopped her.

"No, not while you're feeling so rotten. Let me take off your hat! I can do it without you moving."

She was not in a condition to forbid him, and he removed it with considerable dexterity, while she still hid her quivering face against him with an instinctive confidence that paid a dumb tribute to the man's complete mastery of himself.

"I'm dreadfully sorry . . . to have behaved like this," she whispered at last.

"You needn't be sorry for that," said Jake. "No one will know except me. And I don't count."

"I think you do," she faltered, and made a more-decided effort to free herself.

"What's that skunk Sheppard been doing to you?" he asked.

She shrank at the straight question. "How . . . how did you know . . . ?"

He lifted his hand and pushed back her sleeve without speaking. There was something dreadful about him as he regarded the bruises on her white skin.

A quick fear went through her.

"Jake," she said sharply, "that . . . is no affair of yours. You are not to . . . interfere."

His eyes came up to hers, and the hardness went from him on the instant.

"I reckon you're going to make some use of me."

She trembled a little and turned her face away. She was disconcerted, frightened, and uncertain as to his attitude as well as her own.

Jake waited a few seconds; then, with the utmost gentleness, he laid his hand again upon hers.

"Are you afraid to say it?" he said.

"To say . . . what?"

Her hands moved agitatedly beneath his till, strangely, unexpectedly, they turned and clasped it with convulsive strength.

"Yes, I am afraid," she said, with a sob.

"But I asked you to marry me weeks ago," said Jake.

Her head was bowed. She sought to avoid his look.

"I know you did."

"And you are going to marry me," he said, in a tone that was scarcely a question.

She turned desperately and faced him.

"I must have . . . a clear understanding with you first."

"I—see," said Jake.

He met her eyes with the utmost directness, and before his look hers wavered and fell.

"Please!" she whispered. "You must agree to that."

He did not speak for a moment, but his fingers wound themselves closely about her own.

"I don't want you to be scared," he said finally. "But that's a mighty big thing you've asked of me."

Maud's face was burning.

"I know it isn't for me to make . . . conditions."

"I guess its up to me to accept or refuse," he said, and a gleam of humour crossed his face. "But suppose I refuse, what are you going to do then? Will you marry me all the same?"

She shook her head instantly.

"I don't know what I shall do, Jake. I . . . I must go back and think."

She mustered her strength and made as if she would rise, but he checked her.

"Wait!" he said. "I haven't refused—yet. Lean back and rest a bit! I've got to do some thinking, too."

She obeyed him because it seemed that he must be obeyed. He got to his feet.

"Poor girl!" he said gently. "It hasn't been easy for you, has it? Reckon you've just been driven to me for refuge. I'm the nearest port, that's all."

"The only port," Maud answered, with a shiver.

"All right," he said. "It's a safe one. But . . ."

He left the sentence unfinished and turned to the window.

She lay back with closed eyes, counting the hard

throbs of her heart while she waited. He was very quiet, standing behind her, with his face to the storm-driven clouds.

She longed to know what was passing in his mind, but she could not break the silence. She whispered to her racing heart that the moment he moved she would rise and go.

She was worn out, physically and mentally, was almost too weary for thought.

He moved at length rather suddenly, wheeled round before she was aware, and came back to the fire.

"Don't get up!" he said. "You look ready to drop, and you may just as well hear what I have to say sitting. It won't make a mite of difference."

She raised her eyes to his in unconscious appeal.

"I am afraid I have made a mistake."

She saw his smile for a moment.

"No, you haven't made a mistake. You're safe with me. But I wonder if you have the faintest idea now why I want you for my wife."

The simple directness of his speech touched her as she did not want to be touched. She sat silent, her hands clasped tightly together.

"You haven't," he said. "And p'raps this isn't the time to tell you. You've come to me for refuge, as I hoped you would, and I shan't abuse your confidence. But I had a reason."

He paused, but still she said nothing. Only she could not meet his eyes any longer. She looked away into the fire, waiting for him to continue.

"Say, now," he said, after a moment, "if I make

a bargain with you, you won't accuse me of taking advantage of your position?"

"I wish you . . . to forget . . . that I ever said that."

"All right. It is forgotten," said Jake. "I'll go ahead. We haven't mentioned Bunny, though I take it he is a fairly big factor in the case. That is to say, if it hadn't been for Bunny, you would never have taken this step."

Maud's eyes went swiftly up to his.

"But of course I shouldn't! I thought you understood that."

"I quite understand," said Jake. "I assure you I'm not taking anything for granted. But now supposing the impossible happened, supposing Bunny was cured, yes, it's only the hundredth chance, I know, still, just for a moment, suppose it!

"Bunny cured, able to look after himself like other lads! You would be married to me. What then?"

"What then?" She repeated the words, still with an effort meeting his look.

"You would stick to me?"

The hot colour flooded her face and neck.

"Of course, that goes without saying."

He bent slowly towards her.

"Maud, if we ever live alone together, it must be as man and wife."

His voice was low, too, but she heard in it a deep note that seemed to pierce through and through her. His eyes drew and held her own. She wanted to avoid them but could not. They burned like the red, inner heart of a furnace.

The blood receded from her face. She felt it go.

"We . . . need never live alone," she said faintly.

He held out a quiet hand to her.

"P'raps not. But I should like your promise to that, all the same. I have sworn already to be good to you, remember."

She laid her hand in his. She could not do otherwise. He held it and waited.

"Very well," she said at last, her voice almost a whisper. "I . . . agree."

He let her go, and straightened himself.

"It's a deal, then. And now for more-immediate details. You've decided to marry me, and I gather you don't mind how soon."

He picked up a clay pipe from the mantelpiece and knocked out some ash against the fireplace.

Maud watched him with a curious species of fascination. There was something in the man's serenity of mien that puzzled her, something that did not go with those fiery, possessive eyes.

He looked at her with a smile that was half-quizzical, half-kindly, and her heart began to beat more freely.

"We must somehow get away from the Anchor today," she said. "I have a little money. Perhaps if you would help me to move Bunny, we could go into lodgings again until . . ."

"I have a little money, too," said Jake. "And I will certainly help you. But first, do you object to telling me what has been happening at the Anchor?"

She coloured again vividly, painfully, but he was fully engrossed with the filling of his pipe and did not notice her embarrassment.

"To begin with," she said, with difficulty, "he . . . Mr Sheppard . . . has turned us out of the room downstairs. He carried Bunny off himself to an attic under the roof, and hurt him horribly. I was driven nearly mad at the time."

She broke off, shuddering at the remembrance.

Jake frowned.

She went on with increasing difficulty. "That happened yesterday. I hoped you would come round in the afternoon or evening, but you didn't."

"I couldn't get away," he interrupted. "Yes? And then?"

"Then . . . in the evening . . . that is, late at night," Maud stumbled like a nervous child, "I went down to fetch something. And he . . . he came in after me, half-tipsy; and . . . and . . . he . . ." She halted suddenly. "I can't go on!" she said, with quivering lips.

Jake laid aside his pipe and stooped over her.

"Did he beat you, or did he make love to you? Which?"

There was a sound in his voice like the growl of an angry beast. She could not look him in the face.

"Tell me!" he said, and laid an imperative hand on her shoulder. "You need never tell anyone else."

"I don't see why I should tell you," she said reluctantly.

"You must tell me," said Jake, with decision.

And after brief hesitation, miserably, with face averted, she yielded and told him. After all, why should he not know? Her pride was crushed forever. She could sink no lower.

She leaned slowly back in her chair, till she rested against the hand he had laid upon her.

"Do you know," she said tremulously, after a moment, "I think it has actually done me good to tell you? You are very kind to me, Jake."

"That may be," he said enigmatically. "And again it may not. Thanks, anyway, for telling me."

He picked up the horsewhip that he had flung down on entering, and began with his square, steady fingers to remove the lash.

"You are right. You can't spend another night at the Anchor. If you will allow me, I will find some comfortable rooms where you and Bunny can stay till we can get married. I will go up tomorrow and get a special licence. The marriage might be arranged for Sunday, if that will suit you."

"Next Sunday?" Maud started round and looked at him with startled eyes.

He nodded.

"In church. After the eight o'clock service, if there is one. Your mother must give you away. Afterwards, we will come on here with the boy."

He glanced round at her.

"He shall have this room for the daytime and the one over it to sleep in. I'm sorry there are not two ground-floor rooms for him; but I know how to carry him in comfort. Of course, if necessary, this room could be used as a bedroom as well."

He threw down the worn lash and went to a drawer for a new one. Maud still watched him in silence.

"Does that meet with your approval?" he asked at length.

"I think you are . . . more than good," she said, a tremor of feeling in her voice.

He kept his eyes lowered over his task.

"I am not hustling you too much?"

"I am asking myself if I ought to let you do it," she said. "It doesn't seem very fair to you."

"It happens to be the thing I want," said Jake, his fingers still busy. "And I reckon you won't disappoint me!"

"It isn't going to spoil your life?"

Jake stood upright with a jerk. She met the extraordinary brightness of his eyes with an odd mixture of boldness and reluctance.

"Don't you know it's your friendship I'm after?" he said, with a touch of aggressiveness. "Why, I've been after it ever since that night I found you down in the dark alone on the edge of the parade."

She drew back a little. He saw her gesture, and her quick, protesting blush.

A fitful gleam of sunshine suddenly pierced the clouds behind him and shone on his bent head. His hair gleamed like burnished copper. The tawny glint of it made her think of an animal, a beast of prey, alert, merciless, primeval.

She put on her hat.

"I must be getting back to Bunny."

"I am coming with you."

She looked at him sharply.

"You will walk?"

"Yes, I shall walk."

She pointed with nervous abruptness to the whip he held.

"Then you won't want that."

Jake smiled, and tested the whip without speaking.

Maud waited a moment; then steadily she spoke.

"You realised, of course, that when I told you about Mr Sheppard's behaviour of last night, it was in strict confidence?"

Jake squared his broad shoulders.

"All right, it's safe with me. There shan't be any scandal."

Maud was very white, but quite resolute.

"Jake," she said, "you are not to do it."

He raised his brows.

"You are not to do it!" she said again, with vehemence. "I mean it! I mean it! The quarrel is not yours. You are not to make it so." She paused, and suddenly caught her breath. "Oh, don't look at me like that! You make me . . . afraid!"

Jake turned and tossed the whip down on the window-seat.

"You've nothing to be afraid of," he said rather curtly.

She made her way out into the fleeting sunlight and racing wind with a strong sense of relief.

Jake followed her, and she stretched a nervous hand towards him.

"Jake, if you meet my step-father, you will not . . . not . . ."

"Most unfortunately, I can't," said Jake. He held her hand for a moment, and let it go. "I won't do anything indiscreet, I promise you. There is too much at stake. Now you get back to Bunny as quick as you can! I shan't be long."

She shivered suddenly and violently as she walked. The relentless force of the man had in it an element that was terrible. What had she done? What had she done?

She encountered her mother as she mounted the hotel stairs.

"Oh, my dear, here you are at last!" was her greeting. "I have been so worried about you. Come into my room!"

But Maud resisted her.

"I must go to Bunny. He has been alone for so long."

"No, dear, no! Bunny's all right for the present. I've been to see. He doesn't want anything. He told me so. Come into my room, just for a moment, dear child! We can't talk in the passage."

As Mrs Sheppard was plainly bent upon talking, Maud concluded she had something to say, and followed her.

"Shut the door, my darling! That's right. How white you look this morning. Dearie, I am more sorry than I can say for what happened last night. Giles told me about it. But he says he is quite willing now to let bygones be bygones. So you won't bear malice, darling; will you?

"Of course, I know he ought not to have done it," she said with a slightly uneasy glance at her daughter's rigid face. "I told him so. But he assured me he only did it for your good, dear. And he seems to think that you were rather rude to him earlier in the day.

"He is old-fashioned, you know. He thinks a whipping clears the air, so to speak. It's better, anyhow, than saving up grievance after grievance, isn't it, dear? You'll start afresh now, and be much better friends. At least, it won't be his fault if you're not. He is quite ready to treat you as his own daughter."

She paused for breath.

Maud was standing stiff and cold against the door.

"Is that what you called me in here to say?" she asked.

Mrs Sheppard still looked uneasy, though she tried to laugh it off.

"Not quite all, dear. But I really should go and make friends with him if I were you. He isn't a bit angry with you any more. In fact, he has been joking about it, says his arm is so stiff this morning he can hardly use it. You couldn't possibly keep it up if you heard him."

"I shall not hear him," said Maud.

White and proud, she faced her mother, and the latter's half-forced merriment died away.

"Child, don't look so tragic! What is it? Come, he didn't hurt you so badly, surely! Can't you forgive and forget?"

"No," said Maud. "I shall never do either. I am going away with Bunny today. And I hope . . . with all my heart . . . that I shall never see his face again."

"Going away?" Mrs Sheppard opened startled eyes. "But, Maud . . ."

"I am going to marry Jake Bolton," Maud said, her voice very deep and quiet. "He will take me and Bunny too."

"Oh, my dear. That man!" Her mother gazed at her in consternation. "He . . . he is infinitely rougher than Giles."

"I know he is rough. But he cares for Bunny. That matters most," said Maud. "In fact, I believe he likes Bunny best."

"My dear, it's you he wants, not Bunny," said Mrs Sheppard, with a rare flash of insight. "I saw that at the very beginning of things, at our wedding-party. He looked at you as if he could devour you."

Maud put out a quick hand of protest.

"Mother, please! That doesn't prove he cares about me, any more than I care for him. It . . . it's just the way with men of his sort. He . . . he has been very kind, and he is genuinely fond of Bunny, and . . . and . . . in fact, it's the only thing to be done. I can't . . . possibly . . . stay here any longer."

Her lip quivered unexpectedly. She turned to go. But her mother intercepted her quickly, endearingly.

"Maud darling, wait a minute! I haven't finished. You took my breath away. But listen a moment! This sacrifice won't be necessary, I am sure, I am sure. You couldn't marry that horsey creature. You would never bear life with him.

"You are not adaptable enough nor experienced enough. You could never endure it. It would be infinitely worse than poor Giles and his tantrums. No, but listen, dear! If you really feel you must go, I think a way of escape is going to be offered to you and poor little Bunny too.

"I have had a letter from your Uncle Edward, and he is coming expressly to see you both."

"Mother!" Maud almost tore herself free, gazing

at her with that look in her eyes that was to haunt Mrs Sheppard for many days. "Oh, why, why, why didn't you tell me before? When did the letter come?"

"It was last night, darling. You were such a long way off, right at the top of the house, and I was too tired to go after you. I meant to tell you first thing, dear; but when I went to look for you after breakfast, you had gone. I am very sorry, but really it wasn't my fault.

"Still, you won't want to marry that common person now, for I am sure your uncle means to make provision for you. He can well afford it. He is very wealthy."

But Maud resolutely put her mother's clinging arms away from her.

"Jake is not common," she said in a voice that sounded flat and tired. "And I have promised to marry him. Nothing can make any difference to that now."

"My dear! What nonsense! I will get Giles to talk to him. How can you dream of such a thing, you, who might have married Lord Saltash, and may yet! There is no knowing. Maud, dearest, you must be reasonable. You must indeed.

"This Jake Bolton may be a very excellent man, a very worthy man, but as a husband for you he would be utterly unsuitable."

"I have given him my promise," Maud replied. "And you had better not let Mr Sheppard interfere. It would be wise of him to keep out of Jake's way, in fact. Jake knows exactly why I am prepared to marry him."

"My dear! How could you?"

"I wanted a man to protect me," Maud said very bitterly, "from the vindictive savagery of a brute!"

"Maud! How can you talk so? And I am sure Jake Bolton is much more of a brute than poor Giles. Why, look at the man! Look at his mouth, his eyes! They absolutely stamp him.

"Oh, dear, you're very headstrong and difficult. I begin to think Giles has some excuse after all. Perhaps your uncle will be able to manage you. You are quite beyond me."

"When does he arrive?" Maud asked.

"This evening. He has asked us to reserve a room for him."

"We shall be gone by that time. Jake is finding us rooms somewhere in the town."

Mrs Sheppard held up her hands.

"Jake finding rooms! Maud! how . . . scandalous! How do you know that he is to be trusted?"

Maud made a brief gesture as of one who submits to the inevitable.

"I trust him," she said, with that in her voice that stilled all further protest.

And with the words she passed with finality out of her mother's room and went away upstairs without a backwards glance.

*   *   *

A way of escape! A way of escape! How often during the hours of that endless day were those words in Maud's mind. They pursued her, they mocked her, whichever way she turned.

To Jake she merely very briefly imparted the

news of her uncle's expected arrival, and he received it without comment.

He spent a great part of the day with them, working to get them comfortably settled in their new quarters before dusk.

When he left, Maud followed him to the outer door. The evening air smote chill and salt upon her, and she shivered involuntarily. Jake stopped to light a cigarette.

"I shan't be coming round tomorrow," he remarked. "I shall be too busy. But I'll look in on Saturday, and tell you what I've fixed up. Will Sunday morning do all right if I can fix it?"

He looked at her, and she saw that his eyes were kindly. She held out her hand with a desperate little smile.

"Yes, I meant it."

His hand closed strongly, sustainingly upon hers.

"Guess there's nothing to be scared of," he said. "I'll take care of you."

She felt a sudden lump rise in her throat.

"You are so kind!" she said, with a catch in her voice.

"Oh, bunkum!" said Jake, in a tone of almost indignant remonstrance. He bent and kissed her hand.

She freed herself with a little gasp.

*   *   *

Some time later she started up in surprise to see her landlady usher in a little, spare, grey-whiskered man who walked with a strut, and cleared his throat as he came with a noise like the growling of a dog.

"My name's Warren," he said. "You, I take it, are Maud Brian. If so, I'm your Uncle Edward."

"How do you do? Yes, I am Maud Brian. Come and sit down!"

He uttered a grunting growl and sat down with a jerk.

"I've come straight from your mother to talk to you. She's a fool, always was. I hope you're not another."

"Thank you," said Maud sedately.

"I've come the length of England to see you, but I haven't any time to waste. I'm going back to-morrow. That letter of yours, I meant to answer it, but business pressed, and it had to stand over.

"Then I decided to come and see what sort of young woman you were before I did anything further. I couldn't stand a replica of your mother in my house. But, thank goodness, you're not much like her.

"She tells me you're thinking of making a marriage of convenience to get away from your step-father. Now that's a very serious step for a young woman to contemplate. It seems to me I've turned up in the nick of time."

"It was very kind of you to come," she said. "But, as regards my marriage, my mind is quite made up. He . . . the man I am going to marry . . . understands everything. I have been quite open with him. He has been most kind, most generous. I could not think of drawing back now."

"Pshaw!" said Mr Warren. He sat forward in his chair, his hands gripping the knob of his umbrella, and surveyed her with growing disapproval. "You're prepared to sell yourself to a man you don't love in return for a home, eh?"

She winced sharply, and in a moment her tired young face was flooded with colour.

"Certainly not!" she said, her voice very low. "Most certainly not!"

"Looks uncommonly like it," he maintained.

"It is not so!" she said, with low-toned vehemence. "I have told you . . . he . . . understands."

"And is prepared to give all and receive nothing for his pains?" pursued the old man relentlessly. "If so, he's a very remarkable young man; and let me tell you, for your comfort, it's an attitude he won't keep up for long, not, that is, unless he's a blithering idiot. Is he an idiot?"

Maud almost laughed.

"No, that he is not! But really you are wasting your time. If you had come this time yesterday, I would have listened to you. Tonight it is impossible."

"Why impossible?"

"Because I have promised."

"Tut-tut! He must release you."

She looked at him with her clear, straight eyes.

"I will not ask for my release. In fact, I . . . don't want it now."

"Don't want it! Then, young woman, you're in love with him. I've come on a fool's errand, and I'll wish you good-night!"

He was on his feet with the words. Maud rose too. She laid a hand of half-timid restraint upon his arm.

"I am not . . . in love with him, Uncle Edward," she said, her voice not wholly steady. "Such a thing would be impossible. But at the same time

. . . though I can't give him everything . . . he shall not repent his bargain. We are going to be . . . friends."

"Pshaw!" said Uncle Edward again.

"And then there is Bunny to be thought of," she said.

"Bunny? Who is Bunny? Oh, your brother, is it? And he's a hopeless cripple, I understand? Is it for his sake that you've hatched this mad scheme?"

"In a great measure. You see, he and . . . and Jake Bolton are very fond of each other."

"Pshaw!" the old man exclaimed. "So this Jake Bolton is to have the boy, with you thrown in as a make-weight, is that it? And you think you're all going to be happy together, do you? Never heard such a tomfool scheme in my life. Where does this Jake Bolton hang out? I'll go and have a talk to him."

"Oh, please don't!" Maud begged. "He'll think I sent you. And really . . . really there is nothing to discuss."

"We'll see about that," he rejoined grimly. "Seems to me it's high time somebody came along and interfered. Now look here, I'm going to get you out of this mess. You shan't marry a man you don't love just because there was no other way out.

"There is another way out, and you're to take it. You're to come and live with me, do you hear? You and your precious Bunny too! And when I die, I'll leave you both provided for. See? Come, I can't say fairer than that.

"My home is a dingy one," he continued, "but

you may be able to make it more cheerful. I shan't
interfere with either of you. Come now, you're going to be a sensible girl. I'm sorry I didn't turn up
before.

"But the knot isn't tied, so I'm not too late.
We must explain the situation to the young man.
Unless he's an absolute bounder, he'll be amen-
able to reason."

But Maud shook her head.

"I can't do it, Uncle Edward. I know you mean
to be kind. I am very grateful. But . . . I can't."

"That's nonsense," he said with decision. "Plainly the man is beneath you. You say you don't love
him, and never could."

"I am not . . . altogether . . . sure that he is beneath me," she said rather wistfully.

"But you don't love him?" her uncle insisted,
scanning her piercingly.

She bent her head with an instinctive desire to
avoid his eyes.

"No."

It was at this point that the door opened again to
admit the landlady, with a note on a salver.

"Mr Bolton's compliments," she said. "And will
you be good enough to send back an answer?"

Maud took the note with a glance at her uncle.

"Open it!" he said. "Don't mind me!" And he
stumped irately to the bay-window and pulled aside
the blind.

Maud opened the note. Her hands were not very
steady. The envelope contained a half-sheet of
notepaper with a few words scrawled thereupon,
and a short length of string.

Sorry to trouble you, but will you tie a knot in the enclosed to show me the size of your wedding-finger?

Yours,
Jake.

She looked up from the note as her uncle came tramping back. "Is it the young man himself?" he demanded.

"It's Mr Bolton, sir," said the landlady.

"Then show him in!" ordered the old man autocratically. "Show him in, and we'll get it over! No time like the present."

A swift remonstrance rose to Maud's lips, but she did not utter it. The landlady looked at her for confirmation of the order, but she did not utter a single word.

"Get along!" commanded Uncle Edward. "Or I'll fetch him in myself."

"I didn't mean to disturb you again," Jake said as he entered, "but I'd forgotten this little detail and I've got to catch an early train."

He turned with no sign of surprise and regarded Maud's visitor. "Good-evening, sir!"

Mr Warren gave him a brief nod. Maud still stood mute, Jake's note with the piece of string dangling therefrom in her hand.

He went quietly to her.

"Let me fix that for you."

She let him take her hand. It lay cold and quivering in his. He wound the string round her third finger and knotted it. Then he slipped it off, and took the hand closely and warmly into his own.

"I hope you haven't come to forbid the banns,"

he said, calmly returning the grim scrutiny that the
old man had levelled at him from the moment of
his entrance.

Uncle Edward uttered a sound indicative of intense disgust.

"I? Oh, I've no authority," he said. "I disapprove, if that's what you mean. Any decent person
would disapprove of the sort of alliance you two
are determined to make. But I don't expect my
opinion to be deferred to. If you choose to marry
a woman who doesn't care two straws about you,
it's your affair, not mine."

Jake turned in his deliberate fashion to Maud.
His face wore a smile that baffled her, as he said:

"It's my opinion that we should get on better
alone together, though it's for you to decide."

She looked at him rather piteously, and as if in answer to that look Jake slipped a steady arm about her.

"What about the head of the family?" he said,
speaking softly, almost as if to a child. "Reckon
he'll be wanting you. Won't you go to him?"

He went with her into the passage, and they stood
for a moment together under the flickering lamp.

"Bunny in bed?" he asked.

"Yes," she said.

He was still faintly smiling.

"You go to bed, too, and I'll settle this old fire-
brand."

"Don't . . . quarrel with him, Jake!" she said
nervously.

"What should I quarrel about?" said Jake.
"Good-night, forlorn princess!"

His voice had a note in it that was almost motherly. She went from him with a distinct sense of comfort. His touch had been so strong and yet so gentle.

As for Jake, he turned back into the room with the utmost confidence and shut himself in with an air of decision.

"Now, sir," he said, "if you've any complaint to make, p'raps you'll be good enough to mention it to me right now, and I'll deal with the same. I'm not going to have my girl bullied any more."

His voice was quiet, even slightly drawling, but his eyes shone with something of a glare. He came straight to the old man, who still leaned on his umbrella, and stood before him.

The latter gazed at him ferociously, and for a space they remained thus, stubbornly fixing each other. Then abruptly the old man spoke.

"You're very masterful, young fellow-my-lad. I suppose you think yourself one of the lords of creation, good enough for anybody, eh?"

Jake's stern face relaxed slowly.

"I don't claim to be a prince of the blood, but I reckon I've got some points."

"And you reckon you're good enough to marry my niece?" snapped Uncle Edward.

Jake went on with the utmost composure:

"You offer her a home where she can continue to be a slave to her brother. She hasn't brought all her troubles to you and cried her heart out in your arms, has she? No, nor ever will, now!

"You've come too late, sir—too late by just twelve hours! You may keep your money and your home to yourself! The girl is mine!"

A deep note suddenly sounded in the man's voice, and Uncle Edward was abruptly made aware of a lion in his path. He backed at once. He had not the smallest desire for an encounter with the savage beast.

"Tut-tut!" he said. "You talk like a Red Indian. I wasn't proposing to deprive you of her; only to give the girl a free hand and you the chance of winning her. If you take her without, there'll be the devil to pay sooner or later; I can tell you that.

"But if you won't take the chance I offer, that's your affair entirely. I have no more to say."

"I am taking a different sort of chance," Jake said. "And I have a suspicion that it's less of a gamble than the one you suggest. In any case, I've put my money on it, and there it'll stay."

He looked Uncle Edward straight in the eyes a moment, and then broke into his suddenly, disarming smile.

"Can't you stop over the weekend now, and give her away?" he asked persuasively. "Her mother seems to shy at the notion."

"Her mother always was a fool," said Uncle Edward irascibly. "The biggest fool that ever lived. Oh, yes, I'll give the girl away. If you're so set on getting married at once, I'd better stop and see that it's done properly."

"Thank you," said Jake. "You are most considerate."

"Mark you, that doesn't mean that I approve," warned the old man. "It's a hare-brained scheme altogether, but I suppose I owe it to my family to see that it's done properly."

Chapter Four

It was dark and draughty in the church. Maud was shivering from head to foot. Her heart felt as if it were encased in ice.

She did not know how to keep her teeth from chattering. Her hands lay in her lap, numbed and nerveless. She wondered if she would ever manage to walk as far as the dimly lit altar, where Jake would be awaiting her.

"Here comes your precious bridegroom!" Uncle Edward said. "I suppose they're ready at last. We had better get moving."

Jake's sturdy figure was coming down the aisle. She watched it with eyes that were wide and fixed. He came straight to her, and bent over her.

"I'm real sorry you've been kept waiting," he said. "It's the Parson's doing. He forgot all about us. And there was no fire either. I had to force the door of the stoke-shed to light it."

He bent a little lower over her, and suddenly she felt his hand against the icy cold of her cheek. She started back from it.

"Jake, I can't come yet. I'm so cold."

Stiffly her pale lips whispered the words; her whole body seemed bound in a very rigour of cold.

And through it all she still thought she could hear phantom echoes of that other wedding that once had seemed so near.

"Where is your mother?" said Jake.

There was a hint of sternness in the question. Uncle Edward answered it.

"I'm expecting them every minute. I drove up first to fetch Maud. Lucy is a hopeless fool. She's never in time for anything."

Even as he spoke, there came the rush of wheels on the hard road outside and the hoot of a motor-horn.

The sound as it reached Maud seemed to galvanize her into sudden energy. She rose, white to the lips, but resolute.

"I am ready."

Jake gave her a straight, hard look, and turned without another word. He went back up the aisle, square, purposeful, steady, and took up his stand by the waiting clergyman.

Maud's hand pressed her uncle's arm with urgency.

"Let us go! Let us go!" she said. "I can see my mother . . . afterwards."

It was all horribly unreal. The only thing of which she was vividly and poignantly conscious was the cold.

She heard Jake's voice beside her, very calm and steady, and when her turn came she spoke with equal steadiness, for somehow she seemed to be imbued with his strength.

Jake's hand, warm and purposeful, holding her

own, sent a faint, faint glow through her; but it
did not reach her heart, and when she knelt it
came under her elbow and supported her; when
she rose it lifted her.

When the dreadful nightmare service was over
at last, his arm was round her, and by its aid alone
she stumbled stiffly to the vestry.

* * *

It was over! Maud sat before the open fireplace
in Jake's oak-panelled parlour, gazing into the red
heart of the fire with a stunned sense of finality, a
feeling that she had been overtaken and made
prisoner by Fate.

She was terribly tired. Every limb seemed
weighted as if with iron fetters. She longed with a
sick longing for sleep and oblivion. She ached for
solitude and repose.

Overhead she could hear Jake moving. He was
helping Bunny to prepare for the night, by Bunny's
own decree. Very soon he would come down again,
and she would have to rouse herself and make
conversation. She wondered wearily how she would
do it.

She started up in her chair, alert, nervous, to see
him enter and shut the door behind him.

"Don't disturb yourself!" he said.

He came and stood before the fire, and Maud,
sinking back into her chair, strove to calm the
unreasonable inner tumult that his entrance had
excited.

"Perhaps I ought to go to Bunny for a little. He
will feel neglected," she said after a while.

"He's not expecting you," said Jake. "I was going to speak to you about him. I've decided to sleep with him tonight."

"You?" She looked at him in quick surprise.

He was not looking at her, being too intent upon his task. The firelight shone red on his bent head.

"Yes, I. You can sleep in my room. I've had it got ready for you."

The calm decision with which he spoke nearly took her breath away.

"Oh, but . . . but . . ." she began.

He looked up, and she saw his frank, reassuring smile. It sent a curious thrill of relief through her. It was such a smile as would have gained the confidence of a child.

"That's all right," he said. "Don't you start making difficulties, because there aren't any at present. I've fixed it all. You're going to bed tonight without any cares, and you're going to sleep the clock round."

"I couldn't sleep . . . away from Bunny," she said, somewhat breathlessly.

"I reckon you'll have to try," he said. "And if it's any comfort to you to know it, Bunny is delighted with the idea."

She was for the moment painfully afraid of being mastered by this man, whose strength was still such an unknown quantity that she braced herself to test it as if she were challenging a giant.

Then without another word she drew herself up and walked out of the room.

She knew, even as she closed the door, that by strength she would never prevail against him. She might beat her will to atoms against his, but not by a hair's breath would she thus turn him from the course upon which he was set.

* * *

Maud awoke out of a deep sleep, aware of a furtive movement in the room. Someone, a man, was on his knees before the grate, stealthily coaxing the fire to burn. She had a glimpse of brown leggings and a rough tweed suit.

There were spurs on his heels that shone like silver. His red-brown head was on a level with the bars at which he was softly blowing.

As she moved, a flame shot up in response to his efforts and he turned, still kneeling, and looked at her.

"You've had a real good night for once," he said, in a voice of soft approval. "How do you feel yourself this morning?"

Maud, crimson-faced, searched for words and found none. It was one of the most difficult moments she had ever had to endure.

Jake glance at the fire, pushed the poker into it, and got to his feet. He came to her side.

"Don't be mad with me!" he pleaded humbly. "Someone had to light the fire, and Mrs Lovelace is busy."

He smiled as he said it, and when Jake smiled he was hard to resist. Maud suddenly found the difficulties of the situation swept away. With Jake in a docile mood, she found it comparatively easy to deal.

"Thank you," she said, after a moment. "How . . . how is Bunny?"

He smiled again with more assurance.

"He had a splendid night. I've got him up and dressed. He is downstairs, waiting for you to take him out. There's a breakfast-tray waiting for you. May I bring it up?"

He turned at once to the door, but paused as he reached it.

This piece of diplomacy obviously came to Jake as an inspiration. His smile broadened at the brightening of her face. Maud raised herself on her elbow and pushed the thick hair back from her forehead.

"Oh, please don't!" she said hurriedly. "I never breakfast in bed. Besides . . ."

"I'll put it outside the door then," said Jake, and was gone.

She heard him clatter down the uncarpeted stairs, whistling as if well pleased with himself, and as she reviewed his unceremonious behaviour, she decided to treat it with the simplicity with which he himself evidently regarded it.

She ate her breakfast with a growing sense of reassurance, dressed, and went downstairs. Bunny was in excellent spirits. He had enjoyed having Jake in attendance, and unhesitatingly he let her know it.

Out in the stable-yard she came upon Sam Vickers sucking a straw while he cleaned a saddle. He greeted her with a smile and informed her that the boss was in one of the loose boxes round the corner.

Maud followed his directions. A bony red setter came up to her and poked a friendly nose into her hand. She bent to fondle him, and as she did so she heard Jake speaking in a building close to her.

She turned towards the voice with the intention of joining him; but, so turning, she heard the words he uttered, and stood petrified.

For Jake, with the utmost calmness and deliberation, was speaking a language that made her blood run cold. His words came with a fluency and distinctness that made them all the more terrible.

If he had been stuttering with rage, she felt it would have horrified her less. She stood rooted to the spot, white-faced and powerless, while the kindly setter fawned about her knees.

She thought his voice would never stop. Someone had done wrong and was being cursed for it with appalling thoroughness. Such oaths as Jake uttered she had never before heard or dreamed of, and the scathing cruelty of his speech was like a stinging lash.

No remonstrance or protest of any sort was offered in return; but after what seemed to her an intolerable length of time there came the sound of heavy, shuffling feet, and a small sandy-haired stable-lad of about seventeen came blundering out into the yard.

His face was crimson and screwed up like the face of a crying baby. He sniffed emotionally as he went past her.

Maud remained where she was. She was sick with disgust. Her whole being, physical and mental, was in revolt. She wanted to turn and go, but something kept her there.

She stood like an outraged princess, clothed in

a dignity that was wholly unconscious, while despair, grim and relentless, forced a way to her quivering heart.

This, this was her husband. This coarse-mouthed brute, this monster of evil eloquence! This was the man to whom she had fled for protection, to whose chivalrous instincts she had entrusted herself! Oh, what had she done?

And then suddenly he came out upon her, striding forth, his riding-whip clenched in his hand, his brows drawn in a ruddy, threatening line.

He saw her, and in a moment, magically, his face changed. The cruel, lynx-like vindictiveness went out of it. He came to her smiling.

"Hullo, Maud!" he said.

Maud shrank so visibly that he could not fail to see; then she drew herself together, instinctively summoning her pride.

"I came to look for you," she told him, with icy aloofness. "Bunny is waiting to be moved."

"Right-o!" said Jake.

He moved towards the passage by which she had entered the yard, and she walked beside him, very pale, very erect, yet tingling with a disgust that almost amounted to loathing.

"It is really quite unnecessary to trouble you. I am fully capable of moving him myself," she said after a pause.

He turned his head towards her.

"Princess, what's wrong?"

She quivered afresh at his tone; it had the possessive quality that she so dreaded.

She did not answer, and he passed on with scarcely a pause.

"I know you can lift the boy; but it's very bad for you, and not over-good for him. Where's the point of it, anyway, when you've got me at hand to do it for you?"

"It is quite unnecessary to trouble you," she said again, "unnecessary and absurd."

"All right, my girl," he said unexpectedly. "Call it just one of my whims and humour it!"

She felt herself flush. His tone, though perfectly good-tempered, had been almost one of command. As they emerged from the stone passage into the outer yard she gave abrupt rein to her indignation.

"I really cannot submit to any interference in my care of Bunny. I told you so last night, and I meant it. He has always been my especial charge, and I cannot give him up."

Jake's eyes were upon her, vigilant, intent, dominant. He spoke in a drawl that sounded to her slightly derisive.

"I wonder, what will you do if Bunny is cured?"

She turned her face sharply from him. What would she do, indeed? But the thing was an impossibility. She put the thought away from her.

"I am not discussing that," she said, speaking with a grim effort at calmness that cost her all her strength. "It is the present with which I am dealing now. I believe you mean to be kind, but . . ."

"You don't say!" interjected Jake softly.

"But," she said again, with emphasis, "it is a

mistaken kindness. I am very grateful to you for your help, but really you must let me do my share."

An involuntary note of wistfulness in the last words softened the look in Jake's eyes. He even smiled a little as he said:

"Bunny being the only person in the world for whom you entertain the smallest spark of affection?"

She looked at him quickly.

"He is all that I have," she said, in a low tone of protest.

"That so?" said Jake deliberately. "Well, I'm sorry."

She felt the flush deepen to crimson in her face, and she quickened her steps as they neared the house, longing to put an end to an encounter that had brought her nothing but discomfiture.

At the door of his house he paused.

"Say, Maud," he said into her ear, "someday, when the boy is well and off your hands, I'd just enjoy to see you with a child of your own in your arms."

She started away from the whispered words, started and quivered like a wild thing trapped. For a single instant her eyes met his in open, passionate revolt; then swiftly she passed him by.

*   *   *

Someone was whistling in the stable-yard It was Christmas Day, and from the church halfway down the hill there came the gay peal of bells.

There was no one about beside the solitary rider, who was heading his horse straight for the white gate that led to Jake Bolton's dwelling.

He was a young man, with a swarthy face of undeniable ugliness that yet possessed a monkey-ish fascination that was all its own. His eyes laughed out of it with a merry wickedness, odd eyes, one black, one grey, that gave a most fantastic expression to his whole countenance.

They were not trustworthy eyes, but they were full of humour.

Reaching the closed white gate, he stooped from the saddle, and with the end of his riding-switch lifted the latch. On the little finger of the hand he thus extended he wore a slender gold ring in which was set a single sapphire surrounded by diamonds.

He walked his horse up the footpath to the door, and on this he beat a rousing tattoo, still without dismounting.

The door opened in haste, and Mrs Lovelace appeared, curtseying in the entrance.

"A merry Christmas to you, Mrs Lovelace!" said his lordship, with that most engaging grin of his. He leaned towards her confidentially. "Take this for love of me, in honour of the occasion!"

He slipped a coin into her hand that caused her to curtsey again ecstatically and wish him every blessing she could call to mind on the spur of the moment. But he laughed easily and cut her short.

"Hear, hear! But I can't stop to listen. Where's Jake Bolton? Is he in?"

"Well, no, m'lord. I'm sorry to say Mr Bolton's gone to church."

"I've never known Jake go to church before. Is he courting, or what?" Lord Saltash said with a chuckle.

"Why, can it be as your lordship hasn't heard?"

"Heard! Heard what? Tell me quickly!" urged his lordship.

"About Mr Bolton's marriage, sir," explained Mrs Lovelace, looking suddenly prim.

"What!" ejaculated her listener. "You don't say Bolton's been caught?"

"The marriage took place last Sunday, my lord," said Mrs Lovelace, still looking prim, but plainly enjoying her role of informant.

Lord Saltash slapped his thigh with a yell of laughter.

"Poor old Jake! And who is the bride?"

"Mrs Bolton, my lord, is the step-daughter of Mr Sheppard of the Anchor Hotel," said Mrs Lovelace.

"What's she like? Pretty?"

Mrs Lovelace pursed her lips.

"She is a lady, my lord, own daughter to a baronet. And her brother, Sir Bernard Brian, is in the house at the present moment. He, poor young gentleman, has the misfortune to be a cripple."

"My good woman, do you know what you're talking about?" Saltash's mobile brows came suddenly low over his eyes in a heavy scowl that added years to his appearance.

Before she could answer, Lord Saltash dropped with a thud to the ground. He threw his horse's bridle over the gate-post and turned to enter.

"Just ring up one of the stable-lads, and tell him to walk Moscow up and down!" he ordered, his voice no longer bland but curt and imperious. "Show me in!"

He entered Jake's sunny parlour with absolute assurance, though the frown still drew his forehead.

"Lord Saltash!" announced Mrs Lovelace.

"Hully, Bunny!"

Bunny gave a quick cry of "Charlie!" and Mrs Lovelace withdrew with a greatly enhanced opinion of the importance of the Brian family.

"He might have been greeting his own brother," she said to herself as she trotted back to her kitchen.

There was certainly no cordiality lacking in Bunny's reception of the visitor. He clung to Lord Saltash's hand with shining eyes upraised.

"I say, what a bounder you are to have stayed away all this time! I thought you'd have come back long ago. Maud's married. I suppose you know?"

"Married to Jake Bolton?" There was a peculiar intonation in the question.

"Yes; and he's the best of good fellows. But I wanted her to wait for you all the same," said Bunny, with the candour of the confidant. "It was no good talking, though. She couldn't wait."

"How long has she been married?" Lord Saltash's tone was settling into studied indifference.

"Only a few days," Bunny told him. "Only since Sunday."

"Was it so urgent as that, then? She isn't generally in such a desperate hurry."

"You see, it was that brute of a Sheppard at the Anchor. Mother married him, you know. Thought she was going to do a good thing for us all. I think it has turned out all right so far as she is concerned. But he was a perfect beast to Maud and me."

"I never did think your mother was over-endowed with wisdom," he commented. "And how did you come to know Bolton? Is he a friend of Sheppard's?"

"No, I don't think Jake likes him. Jake's a good sort, isn't he?" said Bunny, almost pleadingly. "He's been jolly decent to us."

Lord Saltash was gazing before him through eyelids that were slightly contracted.

"I believe he is quite a good sort. And Maud? Is she in love with him?"

"Good gracious, no!" said Bunny.

Lord Saltash turned towards him sharply.

"You're very emphatic. Why?"

"Well, she isn't," Bunny asserted. "Jake knows she isn't. He is much more pally with me than he is with her."

Lord Saltash laughed.

"Does he know that I am, so to speak, a friend of the family?"

"Yes, I told him," said Bunny.

"What did you tell him?"

"Told him that if Maud married anyone she ought to marry you." Bunny's tone was blunt, his face somewhat red.

Lord Saltash laughed. The drawn look had wholly gone from his eyes. He worked his brows up and down with astonishing agility.

"That pleased him, I'll bet. And so he decided to get married the next day, did he, and damn the consequences?"

"Oh, no, it didn't come off then. We had a big row with the Sheppard beast first; and it was after that Maud went off and fixed it up with Jake on her own. It was a pity you weren't there, Charlie. She'd have married almost anyone to get away."

"Any scoundrel?" laughed Lord Saltash. "Well, old chap, do you know, between you and me, I'm not sure that she hasn't done better for herself than if she had waited for me."

"Jake's a sport. I like him," said Bunny.

"He's a gentleman," said Saltash unexpectedly.

"Not exactly," protested Bunny. "He doesn't profess to be that."

"My dear chap, a gentleman is born, not made. Jake's sound. It's more than most of us can say. I wouldn't part with him for a thousand pounds."

Lord Saltash turned from the window with a pleasant smile on his ugly face, and broke into a careless whistle.

Bunny watched him with a puzzled frown.

Lord Saltash opened the door, and glanced back to wave a careless *adieu,* then passed out whistling.

"Well, I'm jiggered!" said Bunny. "Anyone would think he didn't care a jot!"

Which was precisely the impression that Lord Saltash had intended to convey.

* * *

When church was over and Maud and Jake were walking back home, he drew a deep breath and remarked:

"That's the first time I've been in church, except for our wedding, for twenty years."

Maud looked at him in amazement.

"So long as that?"

"I used to go regularly till my mother died. Af-

ter that, I went to sea and got out of the way of
it."

As they turned in at the white gates, he said:

"I was wondering if your mother could be persuaded to come up to tea if I went and fetched
her with the dog-cart. We couldn't squeeze Sheppard into that if we tried."

She knew that he made the suggestion solely for
her pleasure, and a sudden warmth kindled within
her.

"You are good to me, Jake!" she said gratefully.

"Oh, rubbish!" said Jake. "Being good to you is
all one with being good to myself. I'll go then as
soon as dinner is over. Now, who in thunder . . ."

He stopped abruptly, gazing straight ahead.
Maud was looking ahead too. She saw a man's
figure moving towards them over the stones of the
yard; she heard the ring of spurs.

Suddenly she stood still, white to the lip, panting, unnerved.

It could have been only for a second, that pause
of hers; for at once she was aware of Jake's hand
pushed lightly through her arm, leading her forward.

"I guess I don't need to introduce Lord Saltash,"
he said. "You've met before."

Yes, they had met before, met and parted, and
the memory of it stabbed her to the heart. She
moved forward as it were mechanically, under
Jake's guidance. She had known that this ordeal
would have to be faced, but it had taken her unawares. She was unprepared.

But the moment she heard his voice, his laugh,

her agitation was gone. There was a subtle *camara-derie* in Lord Saltash's greeting that smoothed the way. She remembered with a pang that it had always been his custom to take the easiest course.

"So you've got married, have you?" he said, his eyebrows working with monkeyish rapidity.

He made her a sweeping cavalier's bow, and lightly kissed her hand.

She laughed without effort.

"How odd to meet you like this, Charlie! I thought you were still abroad."

It seemed to her suddenly that the old cruel barrier had been removed. Since they could never again be lovers, they were free now to be friends.

"Have we time to go round the stables? Or is your Christmas turkey clamouring to be eaten?" Lord Saltash asked.

Maud shot a swift look at Jake, who, after a momentary pause, said:

"I can go round with you now if you wish, my lord."

"That's very obliging of you, Bolton. But don't let me interfere with your domestic arrangements! I can come over again later."

It was then that Maud very quietly intervened.

"If you care to join us at dinner, I am sure we shall be very pleased, and you can go and see the stud afterwards."

"What! Really?" said Lord Saltash. "Of course, I shall be delighted."

Despite her efforts, she could not fail to note that Jake was more self-contained, more unresponsive, than she had ever before seen him, and for a time she felt her own manner to be strained and unnatural in consequence.

Lord Saltash plainly noticed nothing. Throughout that Christmas dinner he was just as gay, debonair, and audacious as he had been in the old days, complimenting her with his usual effrontery, provoking her to laughter with all his old quick wit.

She found it impossible not to respond, impossible not to expand in the warmth of his good comradeship. She seemed to be drawn into a mgaic circle of gaiety.

Bunny also was well within that charmed region. He was full of animation, eager, excited, and merry.

It was so good to have Charlie with them again, and to bury all the troubles of the past.

Only Jake's presence held her to the present, and when at the end of dinner he rose to carry out his suggestion with regard to fetching her mother, she felt, as soon as the door closed upon him, that the old life she knew and loved had wholly returned.

She, Bunny, and Saltash were just children together, and they settled down to enjoy themselves as such.

Lord Saltash's desire to see the stud was obviously not urgent. He stayed and made himself extremely charming.

"I've some business to talk over with Jake, so I may as well wait till he comes back," said Lord Saltash comfortably, as they gathered round the blazing fire and sat in luxurious enjoyment.

"You haven't got a piano here, have you?" he asked, after a pause.

"No."

In the old days they had sung duets together. She wondered if he remembered.

"You will have to use the one at the Castle. You mustn't let your talents run to seed. Come up any day, you and Bunny. The place will always be open to you, whether I am there or not."

"We should love to come. I have had no opportunities for playing for months, not since we left London."

"I should have thought your mother might have chosen a sounder man than Sheppard of the Anchor for a husband," Lord Saltash said.

"Isn't he sound?" asked Maud quickly.

"I could sell him up lock, stock, and barrel, tomorrow, if I wanted," Lord Saltash said with a laugh.

"Charlie! You don't mean that!"

He looked at her with a gleam of mischief in his queer eyes.

"Of course I do! The Anchor and all that is in it belongs to me. It's mortgaged for considerably more than its value, and I hold the mortgage. Did he never mention that detail?"

Maud sat speechless.

"It's all right, Queen Maud. He is quite safe as long as he behaves decently to you and yours. He's something of a brute-beast, I believe?"

He moved his hand in the firelight, and the sapphire shone in the midst of the diamonds, like a deep blue flame in the heart of a leaping fire. He drew a little nearer to her.

"You sent it back to me," he said, "and I have worn it, like a faithful widower, ever since."

"Don't wax sentimental, Charlie!" she pleaded.

They began to talk again upon ordinary topics, until finally Lord Saltash took his leave.

"I should have been back sooner," Jake remarked, when he returned, "but Lord Saltash met me, and I had to take him back to the Castle in the dog-cart."

"I thought perhaps you would dine with him," she said, in a voice that sounded very cold and aloof.

"Not I," said Jake. "Give me my own fireside."

After a while he said Bunny looked tired and must go to bed.

"I'm not going to bed!" cried Bunny, his voice high and defiant. "I'm not going for hours yet. Jake, Jake, leave me alone; do you hear? You're hurting me!"

"Afraid you've got to be hurt," said Jake.

He was slipping steady hands under the boy's writhing body. Maud had risen. She came swiftly forward. She touched Jake's shoulder, her face pale and agitated.

"Don't, please, Jake!" she entreated. "It does more harm than good."

He did not look at her or pay the smallest attention. Bunny was already in his arms, Bunny purple with rage, waving his arms in blind impotence.

"P'raps you'd open the door for me!" said Jake, in his slow voice.

She went to the door. Somehow, it was the only thing left to do. Jake followed her with his burden. As he did so, Bunny ceased to struggle, realising the mastery of the steady arms that bore him, and said in a voice of tense hostility:

"You beastly groom!"

Jake said nothing whatever. He carried him firmly, unfalteringly, from the room.

Maud closed the door softly behind him, and went back to her chair. She sat gazing into the fire with wide, troubled eyes.

She was beginning to realise that old associations, old friends, could be nothing but a disturbing element in her life. She was beginning to wish that Charlie had not come back into it.

She was tired, so tired, so sick at heart.

As for Bunny, he had grown out of hand, and would never be the same to her again. She was sure of it. Nothing could ever be the same again in this new world that she had entered.

Jake came in, and she turned her head, masking her embarrassment with a resolute effort.

"Come and sit down! I am so sorry this has happened."

He pulled forward a chair and dropped into it.

"The little chap is overtired. He'll be better left to himself for a bit."

He spoke in a quiet, temperate voice. She realised with relief that he had not taken Bunny's bitter outburst seriously.

"He is always difficult to manage when he gets caught by one of these moods," she said. "And he is apt to say wild things."

Jake made no comment.

"I think," Maud said, "that if Dr Capper will

examine Bunny and . . . and perhaps operate on him, it had better be done . . . as soon as possible."

"That so?" said Jake.

She knew that he turned his head to look at her, and a hot sense of discomfiture surged through her.

"Of course . . . of course," I want him to have . . . every chance. I am not so selfish as that. But . . . but . . . the anxiety will be very hard to bear. I dread it more than I can possibly say."

He did not immediately respond, though she knew that he continued to watch her with those lynx-like, brilliant eyes.

"Say, now," he said, "when you married me, I made myself a vow that you shouldn't be burdened any more beyond your strength. This anxiety you speak of, will it be harder to bear than to see Bunny suffering and not be able to help?"

She shook her head. Her eyes were full of tears.

"Guess you're overwrought," he said gently. "Why don't you lie down on the sofa? P'raps you'd get a sleep."

"No, thank you. I am quite all right. Of course, Bunny's welfare comes before everything and always will with me. I think I will run up to him and see that he has all he wants."

"No, my dear, no! You stay where you are!" said Jake. "I've got him in hand. Don't you go making more trouble!"

She glanced at him with quick uneasiness.

"But is he happy? Is he comfortable? I never leave him for long when he is like this. Once he dragged himself right out of bed and onto the floor. He was worse for weeks after."

"He won't do that tonight," said Jake.

"He may. How can you tell? He can be quite violent sometimes."

"He won't be tonight," said Jake, with unmistakable conviction.

"What have you been doing to him?" she said with quick suspicion.

He put a restraining hand upon her, for she seemed on the verge of rising.

"Now, don't you meddle! The boy will be all right; only leave him alone! He won't come to any mischief, because he can't. I've tied him down.

"No, he ain't uncomfortable," he added as she uttered a sharp cry of protest. "I saw to that before I put out the light and left him to come to his senses. He won't hurt, I tell you. You leave him alone!"

"How could you?" she panted. "How dare you?"

He rose with her, still holding her.

"Now be reasonable! I'm real fond of the little chap, and I'm trying to make a man of him. He knows that, all right. It's discipline he wants, and discipline he's going to have. Don't interfere! You'll do more harm than good."

"Let me go!" breathed Maud.

She was white to the lips as she said it, white and desperate. Her eyes burned like two stars. But Jake held her still.

"Say, now!" he drawled. "Aren't you a bit unreasonable? I've taken a lot of trouble to bring him into line. And, as I tell you, I haven't hurt any part of him, except his pride, and that'll soon mend. Maud, now don't act the fool! Don't, I say, don't!"

She had made a sharp effort to wrest her arm free; but he frustrated it, taking her two wrists very gently but very decidedly into his square hold.

"Let me go!" she cried again, her pale lips trembling. "How . . . how dare you hold me against my will? Jake, you . . . forget yourself!"

He was looking at her with a hint of humour in his red-brown eyes. They were shining too, shining with a hot intensity, as if the leaping flames of the fire were reflected there.

But at her words he let her go very abruptly, and turned from her.

"All right," he said. "Have it your own way! I reckon he's your brother more than mine, and I know you have his welfare at heart. If you think it to his interest to go and undo him, I shan't interfere either way. Do whatever seems good to you!"

She stood irresolute, facing him.

"Well? Aren't you going?" he said after a moment.

Still she stood, feeling the strain to be past, yet not daring to relax her guard.

"Sit down!" Jake said, after a moment. "Leave the child alone for a bit! I'll go up to him myself before long."

She sat down again in the low chair before the hearth.

"I know he will have a bad night."

"It won't be any the worse for this," said Jake, with confidence. "And now, look here, I want to ask you something, just in a friendly way."

Maud's hands clasped each other hard. There was no repose in her attitude.

"What is it?"

"I don't want to give any offence," he said. "But it seems to me that Lord Saltash is on a footing of intimacy with you and Bunny that rather points to your not knowing the sort of person he really is."

Maud's eyes grew suddenly darker. She looked him full in the face.

"I know him too well to discuss him with any ... outsider."

"That so?" said Jake, slightly drawling. "Well, that certainly makes matters rather more complicated. I know him too, awfully well, so well that I shall have to request you to keep the young man at a respectful distance; for he certainly won't stay there if you don't."

Maud sat tensely still. Several moments of utter silence passed away. Then, almost under her breath, she spoke.

"Are you absurd enough to be jealous?"

Jake's eyes watched her unwaveringly through the smoke.

"Would it be very absurd of me?"

"Utterly." She spoke the one word with a free disdain.

He bent his head slightly.

"Since you say so—it goes. At the same time, it might be well for you to remember that Lord Saltash invariably hunts for himself. He is not a man that any woman can safely trust. He has his points maybe, but—he is not sound."

Very steadily he delivered his verdict, and Maud received it in unbroken silence. More or less she knew it to be true, and yet very bitterly did she resent its utterance.

It was as if he had exposed to her the worthlessness of a possession which for old time's sake she treasured, though conscious that in itself it was without value. For she had never idealised Charlie Burchester.

Even in the old days of close intimacy she had always seen the feet of clay, though in her fond woman's way she had sought to overlook them.

It was intolerable to have them pointed out to her by one whom she still curiously regarded as a comparative stranger.

Jake rose quietly.

"I'll go up and settle the youngster now. And you have made up your mind on the other subject? I am to write to Capper?"

She did not answer for a moment; her eyes were fixed upon the fire.

He paused beside her, and again there came to her that sense of warmth, of bodily force, that seemed to reach her from the very centre of the man's being, rushing out to her, enveloping her.

She made a slight involuntary movement of withdrawal.

"I have said so."

"Then so be it!" he said, and walked away to the door.

*   *   *

"Is that you, Jake?"

Outraged pride and sullen submission combined in the utterance of the question. The room was in complete darkness.

"Yes, it's me," said Jake.

He went forward into the darkness, feeling out before him.

"Why don't you strike a match?" said Bunny.

Jake found the bed and stood beside it.

"Going to behave yourself, my son?"

There was silence from the bed, a dogged, uncompromising silence.

Jake stooped. Feeling over the boy's body, he began to undo his bonds.

"Say, Bunny, I reckoned you were a bigger man than this," he said.

Bunny remained silent, stiff and unyielding.

Jake completed his task and stood up.

"If you're wanting to tell me to go to blazes, you may as well say it as not."

"I'm not," growled Bunny. "But you've no right to treat me like a dog. I'm not used to it."

"A damn good hiding is what you're most in need of," said Jake, in his imperturbable voice. "You'd learn a lot that way. There's too much pride in your family, my son, and it ain't always the proper sort of pride, either. It's likely to lead you into difficulties."

He paused a moment.

"Say, Bunny, climb down a bit; climb down! I can't get within a mile of you on that high horse of yours."

There was a hint of coaxing in words and action, to which Bunny, taken by surprise, made instant, almost involuntary response.

Jake sat down on the bed, holding him, rocking him a little, soothing him in the darkness that seemed to banish all barriers and link them in a brotherhood more close than either had anticipated before that moment.

Bunny's surrender was complete and unconditional. He clung fast to Jake with whispered words of penitence.

"I'm always like that when I feel bad. I've had that filthy neuralgia in my back ever since tea. It makes me want to bite and kick. I didn't mean to be a beast to you, Jake. I take back all I said. You'll forget it, say you'll forget it!"

"I have forgotten it," Jake assured him. "Don't you fret now!"

They were both silent.

"My friend Capper, you've heard me talk of him," Jake said after a while, "he's coming over from the States, and maybe he'll be able to put you right. We'll give him the chance, eh, Bunny? We'll get him anyway to come along and look at you."

Bunny's frail body had begun to tremble. He held very fast to Jake's arm.

"Guess it's a big proposition," said Jake, "but you've got the courage for anything. I'm going to send him a letter right away. Maud views the matter as we do. She says, the sooner the better."

"What ever made her say that?" said Bunny curiously.

"She was thinking of you," said Jake. "She thinks more of you than of anyone else in the world. Reckon you owe her a mighty lot, Bunny. Ever thought of that?"

"Reckon she'd be rather lost without me," said Bunny perversely.

"Not for long," said Jake.

"She would," persisted Bunny. "If I were to get well, she'd be glad for my sake, but she'd be utterly miserable for her own."

"She won't be miserable when she has children of her own to look after," Jake said. "That's what she wants and what I want too. They'll make all the difference in the world to her."

Bunny was momentarily surprised. This was a possibility that had not occurred to him.

"Oh, that's the idea, is it?"

"What's the matter with it?" said Jake.

"I don't know," said Bunny. "Somehow I don't seem to realise that she actually is married to you."

"She doesn't realise it either," said Jake, rather shortly.

"That's because you don't make love to her," said Bunny wisely. "Why, you don't even kiss her, do you?"

"I haven't." Jake's voice was an odd compound of humour and dissatisfaction.

"Why on earth don't you?" said Bunny.

"You'd better ask her," said Jake, somewhat grimly.

"Aren't you friends?" There was quick sympathy in the boy's voice. "I know Maud is a bit difficult to get on with."

"Say, young fellow! Will you tell me something?" he said.

"Of course! If I can," said Bunny.

"Just this," said Jake, and his voice sunk to a whisper. "Have you any real reason, any good reason, for believing that Maud still cares for Lord Saltash? Honestly, now!"

"She'd soon forget him if you started making love to her," Bunny assured him. "Why don't you, Jake? Why don't you?"

"Ah! Why don't I?" Jake uttered again his dry, somewhat scoffing laugh. "P'raps I'm waiting for someone else to make the running."

He stooped, and laid Bunny gently down on the pillows.

"I'll light your lamp now and leave you. Maud will be up with your supper directly."

But Bunny clung to his arm.

"You'll come back, Jake? You, you'll sleep with me?"

"Oh, yes, I'll sleep with you, if Maud will let me. But it's a sore point, I warn you."

"Of course she'll let you. She can't help herself. She knows I'm ten times more comfortable with you to look after me. It's jolly decent of you, Jake." Bunny hugged the arm a little closer. "Sure you've forgiven me for being such a beast?"

"Don't think any more about it! We're all beasts sometimes, though we don't all take the trouble to be sorry afterwards."

Jake stooped abruptly and kissed his forehead, a token received by Bunny with a satisfaction as great as his surprise.

"Be decent to Maud, little chap. Remember, nearly the whole of her life has been one big sacrifice to you!"

"Oh, I know she's a brick," Bunny said quickly. "I'm awfully fond of her, of course. You, I suppose you're fond of her too, Jake?"

He put the question with slight hesitation, not wholly certain as to whether Jake would welcome it, yet oddly desirous of a reply.

"My God!" he said, and in his voice was a deep throb as of a force that rose unfettered from the very heart of the man. "I—worship her!"

In the awed silence that followed the words, his arms fell. He stood a second or two as one in a dream, striving to grip afresh the realities of life. Then, quite calmly, he turned aside and crossed the room to light the lamp.

Bunny, watching him, marvelled that the kindling flame revealed only the resolute face and steady eyes of the man he knew. For it seemed to him that another man had spoken in the darkness.

Chapter Five

Jake and Lord Saltash were returning from a successful day at the Graydown meeting. As they were drawing near the outskirts of Burchester Park, Lord Saltash said:

"I want you to come up to lunch on Sunday, you and Maud and the boy."

He spoke jerkily, almost curtly. Jake turned his head.

"Have you put the proposition before—my wife?" he asked.

"I asked her to come," said Saltash carelessly. "But I didn't mention any particular day. Why? Have you any reason to suppose she would refuse?"

He laughed as he said it, but there was a challenging note in his laugh.

"It is kind of your lordship to think of it," he said. "I can't, of course, answer for my wife; but I shall be very pleased to accept."

Saltash made a curious sound, half of ridicule, half of exasperation.

"If she doesn't come, I shall know whose doing it is."

Jake was silent.

Impatiently Saltash turned towards him, and said aggressively:

"Look here, Bolton, it's no manner of use your raising any objection to the intimacy between us. It began long before you came on the scene, and it's going to continue. Understand?"

"Look where you're going!" said Jake. "Or else jam on the brake!"

He uttered the words with a sharpness so unexpected that Saltash started. As a consequence, the car swerved and instantly skidded in the mud, jerking the wheel from his hold.

In a moment they were halfway up a steep bank at the side of the road, and a moment after, with a crash of splintering glass, they were over, flung headlong into the roadway.

"Damn!" said Jake.

"Damnation," cried Lord Saltash with violence. "It was your fault! Why the devil did you startle me?"

He sprang up with the agility of a monkey, unscathed and furious.

Jake remained seated in the mud. He was panting a little, but his speech when it came was unhurried.

"What the blazes did you want to drive at that preposterous speed for, you all-fired fool?" he said.

"What?" Saltash stamped in the mud to relieve his feelings. "Do you dare to say it was my fault?"

"I say you're an all-fired fool," Jake replied.

He proceeded to get up with an effort so obvious that Saltash's attention was caught.

"Hullo! You're hurt, are you? Where?"

"I reckon that's what I've got to find out," said Jake. "Maybe it's no worse than a broken head. What about you?"

"Oh, I'm all right," Saltash declared impatiently. "I say, are you really hurt, man? Curse this dark! Wait while I strike a match!"

"Curse everything!" said Jake whole-heartedly. "I wonder if there's a lamp not smashed."

Saltash struck a match and regarded him by its flare.

"Great Scott!" he ejaculated in dismay.

For the illumination had revealed to him that which he had certainly not expected to see; one side of Jake's face streaming with blood.

Jake strove ineffectually to staunch the flow with a handkerchief.

"I don't know where the mischief is exactly. Somewhere above the temple, I fancy. Don't alarm yourself, my lord! I always bleed a lot!"

"I say, this is a bad business!" Lord Saltash said, as the match went out. "Are you feeling bad?"

"Oh, not in the least," said Jake dryly. "Sorry to give you so much trouble."

"My dear fellow, I'm sorrier than you are," declared Saltash impulsively. "I've driven for ten years and never had a smash before. Here, strike another match and let me see what I can do!"

It was no easy matter to bandage adequately under such conditions, but Saltash was not without a certain rudimentary skill.

He went to work with business-like promptitude, and had succeeded in securing a handkerchief round Jake's head with a firmness calculated at least to check the flow of blood when the sound of wheels warned them of the approach of some vehicle.

It proved to be the dog-cart of a farmer known to them both, who was himself returning from the races.

Saltash was relieved to bundle Jake into the cart and see him depart for home. He remained with the overturned car till help should arrive from the stables.

Jake also was not sorry to find himself jogging homeward, unpleasant though he found the jogging to be. He was nearer to collapse than he would have allowed.

He sat with his head in his hands, struggling desperately against a deadly sense of weakness that threatened at every instant to overcome him.

His companion was full of solicitude.

"What ever will your missus say?" he said, as they drew near the stables.

Jake roused himself.

"Don't drive in! Put me down at the gates! I must make myself respectable before I go in."

"Lor' bless you, man, if she's a woman of sense she'd sooner know the worst at once," declared the old farmer. "Don't ever try to hide anything from your wife! It don't pay. I've been married three times, so I ought to know."

But Jake adhered firmly to his intention of descending at the gates, resolutely declining all further help.

There was no one in the stable-yard when Jake entered it. He staggered forward over the stones like a drunken man, his cap pulled forward over his face, feeling vaguely out before him with his hands.

His brain was reeling and he did not know how he covered the ground or maintained his balance.

With an immense effort he pulled himself together and made his way to the door. Here the thought of Maud made him pause. She must not see him like this.

Then, reflecting that she would almost certainly be safe upstairs with Bunny, who had not left his room that day, he fumbled with the door, opened it, and entered.

All was quiet within, with the quiet of a well-ordered household. The passage was dimly lit. Slowly he made his halting way along it, reached the stairs, and stopped at the foot, leaning on the banisters while he summoned his strength.

At last heavily, like a man in a trance, he began to mount.

The stairs seemed endless. Once or twice he stumbled. At the top he slipped and came down upon his knees.

"Oh, damn!" he ejaculated, with weary vehemence.

At the same moment Bunny's door opened, and he heard the light tread of a woman's feet close to him.

She was coming towards him, moving swiftly, when suddenly something seemed to strike her. She stopped dead, recoiling as from a thing unclean.

"Jake!" she said.

He heard the frozen horror in her voice and thrust out a groping hand.

"It's all right. Don't be scared! I didn't mean you to see me—like this."

She drew back from him sharply, speaking no word, gazing at him in the dim light with eyes of wide abhorrence.

"It's—all right," he said again, and with a labouring effort managed to blunder to his feet.

She drew back still further. He saw her slim white figure standing before him, erect and rigid against the wall. He caught the blazing scorn of her blue eyes.

"Say, Maud," he said, in confused apology, "you're looking kind of vexed. It wasn't any fault of mine. It was—it was that fool Saltash." He spoke the name with difficulty. His tongue felt dry and powerless. "Guess I want a drink."

She spoke then, briefly and witheringly.

"You had better go to bed and stay there till you feel better. There is plenty of water in your room if you want it."

Her words were icy. He felt as if she had flung the water of which she spoke full in his face. And then suddenly the truth flashed upon him, and he uttered a laugh.

"Columbus!" he said. "I believe you think I'm tipsy!"

She did not attempt to contradict him.

"You had better go to bed," she reiterated.

He put up a trembling hand, but it was only to draw the cap down further still over his face.

"I reckon I'd better," he said, and staggered past her to his room.

The door closed behind him, and Maud, white and quivering, turned from the scene.

"O God!" she whispered passionately. "What have I done? What have I done?"

It was late that night when Mrs Lovelace called Maud out of Bunny's room with a white, scared face to tell her that Lord Saltash was below, asking for her.

"He wanted Mr Bolton first," she said, "but I told him as I didn't know if he was back, and then he said something about a slight motor accident and seemed surprised like that Mr Bolton hadn't come home."

"It's all right. He is home," Maud said. "There is no need to be anxious about him."

She hesitated a moment.

"Tell Lord Saltash so!" she said. "I think I won't come down now. He will understand."

Nevertheless, after she had dismissed the old woman, something prompted her to go and listen at Jake's door. She was convinced in her own mind that there had been no accident. Charlie had seen her husband's condition and was anxious to know if he had returned home safely.

That was the explanation, doubtless, and she felt she could not face him.

She listened intently, but she heard no sound. Jake was sleeping, no doubt, sleeping heavily. An overwhelming disgust came upon her. She turned away, shuddering.

*   *   *

Life was horrible, life was repulsive. Whichever way she turned some evil monster crouched across her path. Coming from the kitchen with Bunny's breakfast-tray the next morning, she almost ran into Jake. He had evidently just entered the house, and was hanging up his cap on the rack that stood in the darkest corner of the passage.

"Good-morning!" he said.

Her face was burning. So great was her agitation for the moment that she thought she must drop the tray she held. Jake evidently thought so too, for he reached out and steadily took it from her.

"I'll take up this," he said. "I shall be down directly."

In the parlour the fire burned brightly. She went and stood before it, striving desperately for composure. She would have given all she had to escape the coming interview.

She heard Jake descending the stairs, and braced herself with a throbbing heart to meet him. But she was trembling in every limb. She did not turn to greet him as he entered, but kept her face resolutely averted.

He came in, closed the door with evident purpose, and drew near to her. She shrank at his coming. A quick, involuntary shudder went through her. She stiffened herself instinctively.

He spoke in a soft, half-wheedling note of remonstrance.

"It isn't reasonable to condemn a man unheard, Maud."

Her breath came short. She would not look at him. With a quivering effort she spoke.

"I don't see any point in discussing the obvious. I am bound to believe the evidence of my own eyes."

"Without doubt," conceded Jake. "And they testified to my being drunk last night?"

"You can't . . . with truth . . . assert that you were sober," she said.

Jake did not make the assertion. He stood considering.

"Do you object so strongly to the sight of me that you can't bear to look at me?"

His tone was faintly humorous. She resented it on the instant, hotly, almost fiercely. It was so exactly the attitude that she had anticipated.

"I do object . . . yes," she said, her voice low and vehement. "I can't think how you can have the effrontery to speak to me until I give you leave."

"That so?" he said.

There was insolence in his tone this time. She turned and faced him. Then she saw a large cross of strapping-plaster across his temple. She looked at it a moment before defiantly she met his eyes.

"I suppose you are going to make that your excuse," she said.

"I was," said Jake imperturbably.

She bit her lip. His utter lack of shame made her pitiless.

"If I hadn't met you on the stairs last night, I might believe you."

"You're real kind," he rejoined. "As a matter of

fact I didn't cut my head open tumbling upstairs, but I reckon that detail won't interest you. You'll think what you want to think, whatever I say. And p'raps, as you say, there's not much point in discussing the obvious. Shall we have breakfast?"

His eyes shone with a mocking gleam into hers. She was sure he was laughing inwardly, though his mouth was grim.

"I shall breakfast upstairs," she said coldly.

"Oh, I think not," he said suavely. "It won't hurt you any to sit at table with me. I am a very ordinary sinner, I assure you."

Something in his tone made her flinch. The colour went out of her face. She turned without a word to the table.

They sat down, and he helped her to food, she knew not what. There followed a silence that she felt to be terrible, a silence through which it came to her that for the first time in her experience Jake was angry. She looked at him no longer, but she felt as if his eyes were upon her unceasingly.

"What about coffee?" he said suddenly.

She gave a great start. The coffee-urn was in front of her. She proceeded to pour out for him, the cup clattering in the saucer she held.

He did not move to take it; she rose, as if compelled, and carried it to him. As she set it down, his hand suddenly descended upon hers. He looked up into her face, faintly smiling.

"Maud, don't be such a fool!" he said. "Can't you see you're making a mistake?"

She froze in his grasp.

"Don't touch me, please! You . . . I . . . see

things from a different standpoint. It may seem a small matter to you, but to me . . . to me . . ."

She stopped.

"Let me go!" she said, with a nervous effort to free herself.

But he held her still.

"Do you think you're wise to treat me like this? You've got to put up with me, remember. Wouldn't it be to your interest to give me the benefit of the doubt?"

"There is no doubt," she said, speaking quickly, breathlessly. "You haven't tried to deny it. As to . . . to . . . putting up with you, I have a little self-respect. . . ."

"Call it pride!" interjected Jake softly.

She looked at him with eyes of burning revolt.

"Very well. Call it pride! And understand that if this shameful thing ever occurs again, neither Bunny nor I can stay with you any longer!"

His hand closed like a steel spring upon her wrist.

"So you think you'll make a fool of me! You just try it! You'll find it an interesting experiment, if a bit costly."

"Are you . . . coward enough . . . to threaten me?" she said through panting lips.

"Reckon you've done all the threatening this journey," Jake rejoined, with a smile that made her shiver. "It wasn't exactly a wise move on your part, but p'raps you'll think better of it presently."

He let her go with the words.

When he had finished breakfast he bent over her chair.

"You aren't going to keep it up, are you, Maud? That's not like you. I'll tell you all that happened last night if you'll listen."

She made a slight gesture of distaste. Her face was white, and cold as marble.

"I would rather not hear, thank you. I would rather you went away."

He turned away with the words; she heard him go with relief.

*　　*　　*

"Why wouldn't you see me last night?" said Saltash.

He sat on the corner of the table as he watched Maud arrange a great bunch of violets in a bowl. He had ridden over to present them to her.

"It was late," she said. "And I was attending to Bunny."

"Bunny!" He echoed the name with half-mocking surprise. "Does he still engross the whole of your energies? I thought you would have been more occupied with Jake."

"I only saw him for a few moments," she said.

"What! Didn't he come to you to tie up his broken head?" said Saltash. "I nearly killed him, you know. But it was his own fault."

"I am aware of that," Maud said coldly.

"What!" ejaculated Saltash again, "Did he have the impertinence to tell you so?"

She raised her eyes momentarily; they shone almost black.

"He told me . . . nothing," she said, her voice deep with a concentrated bitterness that made him stare. "He was not in a condition to do so."

Saltash continued to stare.

"He was talkative enough when he left me."

Her eyes gazed full into his.

"Why should you try to deceive me? Really, you needn't take the trouble."

Comprehension dawned on his face. He laughed a little in an amused fashion, as if to himself.

"What! Wasn't the rascal sober when he got back?"

"You know he was not," she said.

"I know he tumbled out of the car and cracked his head," said Saltash. "I daresay he'd been celebrating the Mascot's victory. They all do, you know. But, my dear girl, what of it? Don't look so tragic! You'll get used to it."

"Don't!" Maud said suddenly in a voice that shook. "You make me sick."

She bent her face swiftly to the violets, and there was a silence.

"Please remember that this is quite unofficial!" he said suddenly. "I don't want a row with Jake!"

"You needn't be afraid," she said, putting the bowl of violets steadily from her. "No more will be said on the subject by either of us."

"I'm not afraid." Saltash was looking at her hard, with a certain curiosity. "But with my best friend tied to him for life, it wouldn't, naturally, be to my interest to quarrel with him."

She flashed him a sudden glance.

"I think you had better not call me that, Charlie."

He laughed carelessly.

"I'll call you my dearest enemy if you like. It would be almost as near the mark."

She was silent.

He bent suddenly towards her, the laugh gone from his face.

"Maud, you're not wanting to throw me over?"

She shook her head very slightly.

"I can't be on really intimate terms with you any more. You must see it's impossible."

"No, I don't," he said. "Why is it impossible?"

She did not answer.

"Come," he said. "That's unreasonable. What have I done to forfeit your friendship?"

She leaned slowly back in her chair, and met his eyes.

"I am quite willing to be friends. But . . . now that I am married . . . you mustn't try to flirt with me. I detest married women's flirtations."

"My precious prude, you don't even know the meaning of the word," he said with a wry grimace. "Did you ever flirt with anyone in all your pure, sweet life? The bare idea is ludicrous."

Maud's eyes held his with severity.

"No, I never flirted with you, Charlie. But I gave you privileges which I can never give again, which you must never again expect of me. Is that quite clear?"

He stooped towards her, his hands upon her shoulders, his dark face deeply glowing.

"Oh, Maud the Sincere! Dare you look me in the face and tell me that in marrying you have not done violence to your soul?"

She looked him in the face with absolute steadiness.

"I have nothing whatever to tell you."

"There is no need," he said. "I can read you like a book. I know that if I had been at hand when your mother brought you down here you would have been ready enough to marry even me."

He stopped, and over his ugly, comic face there came a strangely tragic look.

"You could have dictated your own terms, too. I'm not too hard to please."

"Charlie, hush!" Sharply she broke in upon him. "That is a forbidden subject. I told you definitely long ago that I could never marry you. You know as well as I do that it wouldn't have answered.

"You would have tired very quickly of my prim ways . . . just as you did tire in the old days when you fancied you cared for me. I couldn't have satisfied you. I am not the kind of woman you crave for."

"No?" He laughed whimsically. "Yet, you know, you are unjust to me—always were. By the way, are you coming up to lunch at the Castle on Sunday?"

"I?" She raised her brows momentarily. "No, I don't think so."

"What! You won't? Jake's coming."

"No, Charlie," she said firmly. "Bunny has had one of his bad attacks. He won't be well enough for any excitement, and of course I couldn't dream of leaving him."

"How you do worship that boy!" said Saltash, with a touch of impatience.

Maud was silent.

"Look here!" he said abruptly. "Why don't you

have a proper opinion for Bunny? I'll lend you the wherewithal. I'm quite well off just now."

She looked up then, with eyes of frank gratitude.

"Charlie, that's more than kind of you! But as a matter of fact . . . Jake has the matter in hand. He knows an American surgeon, a Dr Capper, who is coming to England soon. And he is going to get him to come and examine Bunny. He . . . it is really very good of Jake."

She spoke haltingly, with flushed cheeks. Saltash was watching her with critical eyes.

"Oh, so the worthy Jake has the matter in hand, has he?" he said, as she paused. "Wise man! I suppose it is no part of his plans to be hampered with a helpless brother-in-law all his days."

"Charlie! That is ungenerous!" she broke in upon him swiftly.

"My dear girl, it is the obvious." He laughed. "Were I in Jake's position, my first thought would be to relieve you of the all-engrossing care of Bunny. You don't suppose he married you just to make a home for Bunny, do you?"

Maud moved from him to the window and stood before it very still, with a queenly pose of bearing that was wholly unconscious and inapproachably aloof.

He watched her for a space, an odd, dancing gleam in his strange eyes. At length, as she made no movement, he spoke again, not wholly lightly.

"See here, Maud! As a proof of my goodness of heart where you are concerned, I am going to make you an offer. The doctor will probably want to perform an operation on Bunny, and it couldn't possibly take place here. So if it comes to that, will you let it be done at the Castle?

"There's room for an army of nurses there. The whole place is at your disposal, and Bunny's. And I'll undertake not to get in the way. Come, be friends with me! You know I am as harmless as a dove in your sweet company."

He stood up with the words, came impulsively to her, took her hand and, bending with a careless grace, kissed it.

She started at his touch, seemed as it were to emerge from an evil dream. She met his laughing eyes, and smiled as though in spite of herself.

"You are going to be friends with me," said Saltash, with pleased conviction.

She left her hand in his.

"If you don't suggest . . . impossible things."

He laughed carelessly, satisfied that he had scored a point.

"Nonsense! Why should I? Is life so hard?"

"I think it is," she said sadly.

"It's only your point of view," he said. "Don't take things too seriously! And above all, stick to your friends!"

She looked at him very earnestly.

"Will you be a true friend to me, Charlie?"

He bent, pressing her hand to his heart.

"None so true as I!"

She caught back a sigh.

"I want a friend . . . terribly."

She drew her hand slowly from him.

"But don't make love to me! Not even in jest!

Let me trust you! Let me lean on you! Don't . . . don't trifle with me! I can't bear it!"

Her voice trembled suddenly. Her eyes filled with tears.

Saltash made a quick gesture as if something had hurt him.

"I am not always trifling when I jest. That is the mistake you always made."

Maud was silent, struggling for self-command. Yet after a moment she gave him her hand again in mute response to his protest.

He took it, held it a moment or two, then let it go.

"And you will consider my suggestion with regard to Bunny?" he said.

"Yes, I will consider it," she replied with an effort.

"Good!" he said. "Talk it over with Jake! If he doesn't view it reasonably, send him to me! But I think he will, you know. I think he will."

He turned as if to go, but paused, and after a moment turned back. With an air half-imperious, half-whimsical, he held out upon the palm of his hand the sapphire and diamond ring which till that moment he had worn.

"As a token of the friendship between us," he said, "will you take this back? No, don't shake your head! It means nothing. But I wish you to have it, and, if ever the need should arise, the need of a friend, remember, send it to me."

She looked at him with serious eyes.

"Charlie, I would rather not."

"It isn't sentiment," he said, with a quick lift of the brows. "It is a token, just a token whereby you may test my friendship. Here, take it! He is coming!"

He almost thrust it upon her, and wheeled round. She did not want to take it but the ring was already in her hand. Her fingers closed upon it almost mechanically as Jake opened the door, and as they did so she was conscious of a great flood of colour that rose and covered her face and neck.

She turned her back to the light, as one ashamed.

Jake came in slowly, as if weary.

Saltash greeted him with airy nonchalance.

"Hullo, Bolton! I came round to enquire for you. How's the broken crown?"

Jake's eyes regarded him, bright, unswervingly direct.

"I reckon that was real kind of your lordship. I had it stitched this morning. I am sorry I omitted to send help along last night."

"Oh, that's all right," Saltash laughed. "I hardly expected it of you. As a matter of fact, the car didn't turn over as you supposed. I soon righted her. You were a bit damaged, eh?"

Jake's eyes were still upon him. There was something formidable in their straight survey.

"So the car didn't turn over."

"No. If you'd hung on a bit tighter, you wouldn't have been pitched out. Old Harris brought you home safe, did he? No further mishaps by the way?"

"None," said Jake.

He advanced into the room, and stopped by the table. His riding-whip was in his hand.

"I came home too dazed to give an intelligible account of myself," he said, speaking very deliberately, wholly without emotion. "My wife imagined that I was not sober. Will your lordship be good enough to convince her that she was mistaken?"

"I?" said Saltash.

"You, my lord." Jake stood at the table, square and determined. "I was in your company. You can testify, if you will, that up to the time of the accident I was in a perfectly normal condition. Will you tell her so?"

Saltash was facing him across the table. There was a queer look on his swarthy face, a grimace half-comic, half-dismayed.

As Jake ended his curt appeal he shrugged and spoke.

"You are putting me in a very embarrassing position."

"I am sorry," said Jake steadily. "But you are the only witness that I can call."

"And why should she accept my testimony?" said Saltash. "Evidence given, so to speak, at the sword's point, my good Bolton, is seldom worth having. Moreover, if she had seen my crazy driving last night she might have been disposed to doubt whether my own condition were above suspicion."

"I see," said Jake slowly. "In that case, there is nothing more to be said."

Saltash made him a slight bow that was not without a touch of hauteur.

"I quite agree with you. It is an unprofitable subject. With Mrs Bolton's permission I will take my leave."

He turned to her, took and pressed her hand, sent a sudden droll smile into her grave face, and walked to the door.

Jake held it open for him, but very abruptly Saltash clapped a hand on his shoulder.

"Come along, man! I'm going round the stables. I'm sorry you've got a sore head, but I'm off to town this afternoon, so it's now or never. By the way, we shall have to postpone the luncheon-party till a more convenient season. I've no doubt it's all the same to you."

He had his way. Jake went with him, and Maud drew a breath of deep relief. She felt that another private interview with her husband just then would have been unendurable.

She sat down and leaned upon the table, feeling weak and unnerved.

Not till several minutes had passed did she awake to the fact that she was holding Saltash's ring, that old, dear gift of his, tightly clasped within her quivering hands.

Chapter Six

Maud had heard nothing of Lord Saltash since his departure, so one afternoon she decided to avail herself of his permission to use the piano at the Castle.

She had an intense love of music and a natural gift for it which she had never been able to develop very freely.

Jake had wholly ceased to take any interest in her doings. He treated her as the most casual acquaintance. When he greeted her, he never so much as touched her hand.

He was everything to Bunny, he was nothing to her; and every day it seemed to her that he drew a little further away from her.

She had tried to make overtures more than once, but he never seemed to understand. He would look at her in his straight, impenetrable way, and change the subject. He had never tried to be kind to her since the day that she had refused to hear his explanation.

A great bitterness was growing up within her. She felt as if he had deprived her of all she cared for, and given her nothing in return.

It was the bitterness of spirit that drove her to

Burchester Castle and, added to it, an intense and feverish desire to escape, if only for an hour, from the atmosphere of her daily existence.

She felt as if it were crushing out her individuality, and she longed desperately to be herself, her best and happiest self, if only for an hour.

She entered the Castle with a curious sensation of unreality, and found herself in an immense stone hall, carpeted with rich Persian rugs, and splendidly warmed by a great fire that roared in an open fireplace.

"The grand piano, madam, is over by the west window," the butler told her.

Maud went forward into the room. The first impression she received was one of great loftiness. The whole of one side was lighted by south windows that looked out over terraced gardens to the pine woods of the park.

At the end was a turret in the western angle of the wall, and here stood the piano, full in the glow of the sinking sun. There were two fireplaces in the room, and in the one nearest to the piano a red fire was burning.

A low couch stood before it, and a great tiger-skin, the only rug in the whole vast place, was spread on the hearth. The whole effect was spacious and Eastern, curiously attractive to the senses and yet curiously elusive.

The piano was thrown invitingly open. A French song was on the rack. It had the appearance of having been placed there but a moment before.

A sudden doubt assailed her, a sensation as of

having walked unwittingly into a trap. Some force had drawn her here, some magnetism had surely been at work.

The impulse came to her then to leave, yet she resisted it. Later, it seemed to her that she had lacked the motive power to do anything but move straight to the piano and drop into the music-stool.

She began to play, at first very softly, then with gathering tone as she felt the instrument respond to her touch.

At length all sense of strangeness left her, and she began to sing a little French ditty that once had been one of her favourites.

She stopped suddenly with the conviction that a man's voice had joined hers. Yet, if this had been so, the accompanying voice ceased as abruptly as her own. She found herself sitting in absolute silence, with every pulse racing, every nerve strained to listen.

No sound came to her. The great room was as still as death. The fire burned red and silent. There was not so much as the ticking of a clock to be heard. And yet it seemed to her that eyes watched her from some vantage-point unseen. She had a firm conviction that she was not alone.

She controlled the curious excitement that possessed her and slowly set her fingers once more on the keys. She played the old refrain again, singing it very softly, listening intently while she sang.

This time she was sure, quite sure, that a man's voice hummed the air. She went on to the end, and suffered her hands to fall.

"Charlie!" she said, without turning.

There came a slight sound behind her, the click as of a spring catch. She looked round, and saw him standing against the high panelling of the wall.

"What a childish game to play!" she said, with lips that slightly trembled.

"We are all children," observed Saltash. ""We may think ourselves mighty clever, but the fact remains. Greetings, my Queen Rose. I am enchanted to see you."

"But why did you pretend you weren't at home?" she said, in a voice of protest.

"But I wasn't," he said. "I motored down on purpose to receive you. Are you so disappointed?"

She shook her head, but she still looked at him somewhat dubiously.

"You know, Charlie, I like people to behave quite straightforwardly, and to tell the truth."

"Heavens above!" laughed Saltash. "Why so grievously moral? Well, look here, let me be quite, quite honest, and admit that it was wholly by chance that I came down here tonight! Now you are going to play and sing to me while I smoke and admire."

He turned from her and threw himself upon a low settee in the window embrasure. The scent of his cigarette came to her, aromatic, Eastern, fragrant of many subtleties. She breathed it as one who inhales the magic of the gods.

"Now play!" he commanded, his strange, restless eyes upon her. "Play as the spirit moved you! Never mind me! I am of no account."

She had done it often before in the old days. It was not difficult to do it now, with the spell of his personality upon her. Her own spirit responded instinctively to the call of his.

Saltash lay without moving, as if half-asleep. He also seemed as one under a charm.

Time passed, and the red sun with it. The early dark began to fall, the shining visions to wane. She came out of her trance at last with a deep sigh, and suffered her hands to fall.

Instantly Saltash sat up.

"Bravo. Your touch is like velvet to the senses. You have scarcely sung to me at all. But no matter! You have closed the gates now, and we can't go back. But wasn't it good? Come, be honest and say so!"

She lifted her eyes to his with something of her dream still lingering there.

"It was . . . very good."

"And you'll come again?" he insinuated.

The dream began to fade. With her right hand she picked out a nervous little air on the piano, saying no word.

He leaned towards her.

"Maud, surely you'll come again!"

"Charlie," she said, her fingers still softly pressing the keys. "I can't come here when you are here. I like to come . . . oh, yes, I like to come. But I mustn't."

"Why not?" said Saltash. "Afraid of the cowpuncher?"

She shrank, and struck a sudden discordant chord.

"I am not afraid of anyone, but I must think of appearances, I owe it to myself. I should like to come sometimes and play. But . . . with you here . . . I can't."

"All right," he said abruptly. "I'll go."

Her eyes flashed up to his. She took her hand from the piano and gave it to him.

"You are going to be a true friend to me, Charlie."

"My friendship is to take a somewhat negative form, it seems to me; but perhaps it will stand the strain. Have you heard anything yet about the American doctor?"

She shook her head.

"I must be going. I promised Bunny I would be back to tea."

"I'll walk back with you," Saltash said.

She shook her head.

"No, I would rather go alone."

"Why don't you tackle the situation boldly and ask me to tea?" he said.

She was walking down the long room, and he sauntered beside her, smoking a cigarette, careless and debonair.

"I think it wiser not, Charlie."

"As you will." He laughed. "But remember, life is short. We may as well enjoy ourselves while it lasts."

He threw open the door, and they found the great hall below them ablaze with electric light.

"I suppose I may accompany you downstairs," he observed.

He went with her to the door, but he did not offer a second time to accompany her further. On the threshold she gave him her hand in farewell.

"You will come again?"

She met his strange, unstable eyes for a moment and fancied that they pleaded with her.

"Not to see you, Charlie," she said, and was conscious in a vaguely troubled way that the words cost her an effort.

"No, not to see me," he said lightly. "Of course not. Just for your own enjoyment. You will enjoy that piano, you know. And you can have it all to yourself."

She smiled, in spite of herself, even against her will.

"Very well. I will come again someday. And thank you very much."

"Oh, don't do that!" he protested. "It spoils everything."

She released her hand, and turned from him, still smiling.

"Good-bye."

"Farewell, Queen of the Roses!"

She passed through the wide stone porch and out into the dark of the winter evening.

It was very dark along the avenue of pine trees, darker than she had anticipated. She almost wished that she had allowed Saltash to accompany her. She went as quickly as she dared in the gloom, conscious that it was growing late.

She began to quicken her steps somewhat recklessly, but the road curved more abruptly than she realised, and she presently ran into the grassy bank, nearly falling into the outstretched arms of a fir tree.

She recovered herself sharply with a gasp of dismay, and paused to try to discern more clearly the winding of the way. It was at this point that there came to her the sound of advancing footsteps.

Someone was approaching with a slow, purposeful stride that suddenly sent the blood to her heart in a quick wave of something that was almost apprehension. She stood quite still and waited.

Nearer and nearer came the leisurely tread. Instinct, blind and unreasoning, prompted her to draw back into the shielding recesses of the tree with a desperate desire to escape notice.

It was a footfall that she had come to know, and, why she could not have said, she did not want to meet Jake at that moment. With a very curious dread at her heart she stood and waited.

He came to within a couple of yards of her, and stopped.

"You can come out," he remarked dryly. "I've come along to fetch you."

His voice was perfectly quiet and natural, but there was that in the words that fired within her a burning indignation. She came forward and faced him in the gloom.

"Why should you take that trouble?" she said.

She saw his eyes glitter in the darkness, and knew that they were upon her with a lynx-like intensity.

"I reckon I have the right. You've no objection, I presume?"

Her cheeks burned hotly in the darkness. She knew that he had her at a disadvantage.

"I am fully capable of taking care of myself,"

she said, beginning to walk on down the dim avenue.

He fell into his easy stride beside her.

"Is that why Lord Saltash left you to walk home alone?"

She clenched her hands in the darkness.

"What do you mean?"

"I think I am right in concluding that you have spent the afternoon with him," Jake said, in his measured tones.

Maud stood suddenly still. She was quivering from head to foot.

"You are . . . quite right," she said, in a voice that she strove in vain to steady. "I think I have told you before, Lord Saltash and I are old friends."

"Yes, I am aware of that."

He reached out his hand and took her by the arm, leading her calmly forward.

She went with him because she could not do otherwise, but she would have given all she had at that moment to wrench herself free. There was no escape for her, however; she was forced to endure his touch, forced to go forward with him along a road that she could not see.

He led her in silence, calmly, unfalteringly, with the utmost confidence. She was sure that those lynx-like eyes of his could see in the dark.

But his silence speedily became intolerable. It seemed to her to bristle with condemnation. It goaded her against her will into speech.

"Lord Saltash has given me his permission to use the piano at the Castle. I did not know when I went that he had returned."

"I could have told you that," commented Jake.

Again her resentment rose to a flame, burning fiercely. Yet his words held no insult. With all her strength she strove for calmness.

"I did not know of it. In any case, I do not see that it was a matter of very vital importance An hour at the piano is a great treat to me, and I shall probably go again."

"For an hour?" said Jake.

This time the peculiar intonation of his voice was unmistakable, not to be ignored. She flung him instant defiance.

"For as long as I choose. My time is my own."

He was silent a moment, but she was conscious of the tightening of his hand.

"All right," he said. "But remember, my claim to it comes before Lord Saltash's. Someday it may happen that I shall put in my claim. I never have been content to be passed at the winning post."

Her heart quivered at the deliberate purpose with which he spoke. She walked on, saying no word.

They were nearing the gates, and the glare from the two great lamps shone towards them, lighting the way. She braced herself, and made a resolute attempt to free her arm from his hold.

"Easy! Easy!" said Jake. "We haven't got there yet. It's dark beyond those lights."

She abandoned her effort, feeling that she had no choice. They walked on together silently.

They reached and passed through the gates. The road stretched before them steep and winding.

"We'll cut across the fields," said Jake.

He led her to a stile almost concealed in the

hedge, and here his hold upon her relaxed. He vaulted the rail, and waited for her.

He did not offer to assist her though the step was high. She mounted in nervous haste to avoid his touch.

But for the darkness she would have found no difficulty in springing down, but, as it was, she misjudged the distance, slipped, and fell.

She threw out her hands with a cry, and the next moment she was caught in Jake's arms. He held her fast, so fast that for a few palpitating seconds she felt the hard beating of his heart against her own.

Then, in response to her desperate efforts for freedom, he let her go, without excuse, without apology, in a deep-breathing silence that somehow appalled her. They walked side by side along the field-path, saying no word.

There was a gate at the further end that led into the training-field below the little orchard. As they reached this, Jake paused very deliberately and spoke.

"I reckon I've got to prepare you for a visitor."

"A visitor!" She stopped in swift dread of she knew not what.

"A friend of mine," drawled Jake, with an odd touch of aggressiveness. "You're not precisely dead nuts on my friends as a rule, I know. But I guess this one may prove an exception. Dr Capper turned up this afternoon. I left him having tea with Bunny."

"Dr Capper!" Maud gasped the name, scarcely conscious of speaking at all.

"Dr Capper from the States," said Jake, unmoved. "He chanced to be just leaving for this country when my letter reached him, so he thought he'd answer it in person and look us up first. He and Bunny are pals already. He's a regular magician."

"But . . . but . . . you never expected him so soon!" faltered Maud. "Surely . . . he won't want to . . . to . . . examine Bunny yet?"

"Not before tomorrow, maybe," said Jake. "We can't expect to keep him very long, you know. He's a busy man. I've heard that people in this country simply tumble over each other to consult him."

"Jake," she said, "this thing has come very suddenly. But Lord Saltash said if . . . if there is to be anything of the nature of an operation, he has offered to place any part of the Castle at our disposal. It is a very generous offer, and it . . . it would be an excellent thing for Bunny."

"Then you have decided to accept it?" said Jake.

His tone was perfectly quiet and matter-of-fact, but it amazed her. She had expected a determined opposition. Disconcerted, she paused before replying.

"I don't think it is especially generous," Jake said. "But it might be a good thing for Bunny. If you like, I will go up tonight and see Saltash about it."

He opened the gate for her with the words, and she passed through with feelings too mixed to bear any analysis.

As they walked through the last field, she tried

to banish her embarrassment and recover her normal composure of mien. But strive as she would, she could not wholly reassure herself.

Nor could she forget the fast holding of his arms and the strong, deep throbbing of his heart against her own. That moment had been a revelation to her upon which she dared not dwell.

They reached the house, and as Jake opened the door they heard the sound of Bunny's cracked laugh. Maud entered in front of Jake, hesitating, uncertain.

Instantly a man's voice greeted her, a quiet, casual voice, with an unmistakable New York accent.

"Ah, I guess this is the lady of the house. I am very pleased to make your acquaintance, madam. Mr Bolton will have told you who I am."

"It was so kind of you to come," she said, with a quivering smile.

He smiled in answer, a sudden, transforming smile that warmed her heart.

"I guess I followed my own inclination. Say, now, you're cold, and Bunny and I have been keeping up a good fire for you. Sit down and make your husband do the waiting!"

His manner was so kind and withal so courteous that Maud's embarrassment passed like a cloud. She came to the fire, pulling off her gloves and stretching her fingers to the glare.

Bunny accosted her with eager eyes.

"Maud, he's going to overhaul me and see if he can do anything for me. Maud, can't he do it to-night? I won't sleep a wink if he doesn't."

Her heart sank inexplicably. She leaned upon the mantelpiece, looking towards Capper with more appeal than she knew.

He pushed up a chair for her.

"I suspect there is no harm in my looking at the lad; but we won't take any further action at present. I've a lot to get through in this old country, and I'd just like to know right now if this is a case for me or not."

"It is so good of you even to think of helping us," she said, rather unsteadily. "Please make your examination whenever it suits you best! But Bunny is not a good sleeper. You will remember that, won't you?"

Capper picked up the cup of tea that Jake had prepared and handed it to her.

"I should like to make my examination tonight, if you have no objection. I am ready to get to work," he said, "and I don't want an audience. If I want anything I'll let you know. But I've a very decided notion that my patient and I will get on best alone."

Jake raised his eyes suddenly.

"That so, Doctor? Then I guess I'll carry the youngster up right now."

Capper looked at him with a smile.

Maud drank her tea in utter silence, feeling as if it would choke her.

The silence became prolonged; until at last Maud said:

"I am very grateful to you."

"I hope someday you may have cause to be," he rejoined.

Jake went to Bunny's side. She saw the boy raise his arms as he bent, and clasp his neck.

In that moment it seemed to Maud that the beloved burden had been taken finally from her, and she was left to wander alone in a desert that was very dark and bare.

*   *   *

"May I come in?" said Capper.

Maud started. She had been sitting huddled over the fire for what seemed like countless ages, listening with straining nerves to every sound overhead, and sometimes shrinking and trembling at what she heard.

At the sound of Capper's voice she turned an ashen face and rose to receive him, trying to force her quivering lips to practical speech. But she could only articulate:

"I heard him cry out several times. Does he want me?"

"Not yet," said Capper. He laid a very steady hand upon her shoulder. "Leave him alone for a little! He'll pull himself together best alone. He's got the spunk all right."

She stood still under his hand, piteously awaiting the information for which she could not bring herself to ask. He was looking at her keenly, she knew; but she could not face his look.

"I want a straight talk with you," the great doctor said.

"Do you think you can cure him, Doctor?"

Capper laughed, too, with a species of grim exultation.

"Is that what troubles you? If that's all, I guess

I can soon set your mind at rest. I can cure him absolutely, within three months. But I shall want your co-operation. Can I count on that?"

His hand pressed upon her with something of insistence. His yellow face looked searchingly, with an odd elation, into hers. She met his look reluctantly, and became dominated by it.

"Of course you can count upon it," she said.

He nodded, pulling restlessly at his beard with his free hand.

"To what extent, I wonder?"

He stood silent a moment, his hand still upon her shoulder.

"Mrs Bolton, do you know your young brother has got a curious notion into his head that you don't want him to be made sound?"

"But that is a mistake!" she said quickly.

"Is it a mistake?" said Capper. "No, don't answer! Why should you? But it's curious that I should have sensed the same.

"Did you know that your husband, Jake, saved my life at sea? But you'll never get him to speak of that episode; but it was about the finest piece of work I've ever come across. He was utterly unknown to me and I to him. Yet he never thought of passing me by, but hung on to me.

"I've never quite lost sight of him since that night. When I make a friend like that, I can't afford to lose him again. But I've never had a chance of doing him a service till now.

"He's considerably more civilised than he was in those days. But I have a notion that there's a touch of the wild spirit still in his composition.

That's why I'm afraid you may not realise that he's gold all through."

He smiled.

"By way of light relief, I guess you know the fascinating story of the princess and the frog. She had to take the beast as he was, and even give him her pillow o'nights. But only when she struck at last and threw him against the wall did she find out that she'd caught a prince after all.

"I guess the man who wrote that story was a student of human nature. It's a comic story, anyway."

Maud was laughing. Somehow, inexplicably, the man had eased her burden.

"Thank you for telling me, Doctor," she said. "You are very kind."

"It's mighty fine of you to take that view," said Capper. "I shall do my best to deserve it."

* * *

It was on a frosty morning in February that Maud sat in one of the great guest-chambers of Burchester Castle, waiting for news of Bunny.

Jake walked into the room, and stooping over her took her hand before she had time to draw back.

"It's all right," he said, and she heard a note of reassurance in his voice. "The little chap's come through it fine. There's nothing to be anxious about. Capper says so; and whatever Capper says, goes."

"Guess that's so," said Capper from the doorway. "You shall see him presently, not yet, not for another hour, and then only for a few seconds.

He's got to be kept as quiet as an infant. But I've done just what I figured to do. In another six weeks he ought to be learning to walk."

"Bunny . . . walking!"

Maud spoke the words as one dazed. The whole of her world seemed suddenly to have changed. It was as if she actually breathed a new atmosphere. She caught her breath, feeling half-afraid.

"Is it . . . is it true?" she said.

"Seems like a miracle, does it?" Capper laughed. "Never met with a miracle before? Yet there's quite a lot of 'em to be seen in this curious old world. Maybe you'll come across some more, now that you've started."

He came quietly to her, bent, and took her free hand into his. She felt his thin, sensitive fingers press her pulse.

"Please tell me more about Bunny! I want to hear everything."

"My dear lady, you know practically all there is to know," he answered. "Bunny is going to be one of my proudest successes. But there's just one thing to be arranged. I want to have him under my own eye for a time.

"I will give him a month here, and then I want to fetch him up to London and keep him in a Home there, belonging to my colleague, Sir Kersley Whitton, until I am able to discharge him as cured. Will you agree to that?"

His eyes, shrewd and kindly, looked down into hers. His hand still held her wrist. She felt the magic of his personality, and found it hard to resist.

"Take him away from me!" she said rather piteously. "Must you take him away?"

Jake had withdrawn a little, as if he did not wish to take part in the conversation. Capper sat down beside her.

"Mrs Bolton," he said. "I guess that young brother of yours is just one of the biggest factors of your existence. It'll be a very critical time, and I want to have him under my own eye.

"I also want to have complete control of him. I'm not hinting that your influence isn't good. I know it is. But for all that, he'll do better with comparative strangers. I want to lift him entirely out of the old ruts.

"It'll make all the difference in the world to him, or I shouldn't be urging it so strongly. Say now, you promised me your co-operation, you are not going to refuse?"

She could not refuse. She realised it with a leaden heart. Yet she made one quivering attempt to pierce through the ever-narrowing circle.

"But the cost!" she said.

"It won't cost you a single cent," said Capper. "It's just for my private satisfaction that it will be done."

Her last hope faded. She made a little gesture of helplessness.

"He is in your hands, Doctor. I . . . I am much more grateful to you than I seem."

Capper's hand pressed hers.

"You will never regret this sacrifice as long as you live. I'm even ready to prophesy that you'll one day reap a very considerable benefit from it."

But Maud's only answer was a dreary little shake of the head.

*   *   *

Slowly the dreary winter days gave place to spring. At Burchester Castle, Bunny, lying perpetually flat on his back by the doctor's unalterable decree, alternated between fits of bitter complaining and fits of black despair.

Jake came and went, but he was never with him at night. The nurse slept in his room and Maud in the one adjoining. Jake went back to his home to sleep.

He and Maud saw but little of each other. They met daily, but she avoided all intimacy with him so strenuously that only the most ordinary commonplaces ever passed between them.

She saw much more of Saltash, though he was often away. His comings and goings were never known beforehand, and he never intruded himself upon her.

Only when she went in the afternoons or evenings to the music-room and, propping the door wide, played and sometimes sang to Bunny, he had a fashion of dropping, as it seemed, from nowhere, and lying outstretched upon the settee near her while he smoked his endless cigarettes.

How he entered she never discovered; he was always there before she knew, and he never came in by the door. When she asked him, he would only jest.

"Someday I will show you my secret chamber, *ma belle Reine*. But not yet, not yet."

No intimate conversation took place at these

times. They were seldom really alone, being always within call of Bunny's imperious voice.

It was on a warm afternoon towards the middle of the month that Maud was sitting at the piano, trying to soothe Bunny with the music he loved, during the absence of the nurse, when the sound of a footfall in the room made her turn.

Saltash had been away for a few days, but she was half-expecting him. He never remained away for long.

"Why, Charlie . . ." she began, with a quick smile of welcome, and broke off sharply. It was Capper.

Her face must have displayed something more than surprise, she reflected later, for his first words, albeit he smiled whimsically as he uttered them, were words of apology.

"So sorry, Mrs Bolton! I shouldn't have taken you off your guard like this, only I had a notion that, being somewhat overdue, you might be more or less prepared to see me."

She left the piano and went with outstretched hand to meet him. Her heart was beating wildly, uncontrollably. She felt suddenly cold, as if she had stepped into a stone vault.

Capper bent a little over her hand; she saw his eyes flash over her.

"I don't find the frog in attendance," he remarked. "Has he been shunted for a spell?"

She felt her colour come again.

"Don't you want to hear about Bunny?"

"I know my own business so well, madam," he smiled at her, "that I know all I need to know about

Bunny. The boy is just mad to be allowed to try his strength, and between you and me he'll have about the biggest disappointment of his life when he does. It won't do him any harm, though, so don't worry!"

She smiled faintly.

"What are you going to do when Bunny is gone?" he asked.

"You are really going to take him away?" she said, and her face paled.

"Tomorrow," said Capper.

She removed her hands with a gesture that was piteous; she said nothing whatever.

"Maybe you'll take up housekeeping," he said practically. "If I dare to venture upon the suggestion, you would make a charming hostess."

She did not answer, and he glanced at her.

"Mrs Bolton, I guess you'll think me several kinds of a nuisance; but your husband has offered me his hospitality for tonight. And I—well, I have accepted it provisionally, that is, on the condition that he can supply me with a hostess."

She looked at him in blank dismay.

"But I sleep here! I . . . I must be always at hand, in case Bunny should want me."

"Isn't the nurse in attendance?" asked Capper, with a touch of sharpness.

"Oh, of course," she answered. "But . . . but . . ."

"And how often in the night does she generally call you?"

Maud was silent.

Capper's hand patted her shoulder again, paternally, admonishingly.

"Guess he could spare you for tonight. Pack your grip and come home! Jake will be pleased to see you, sure."

"It isn't home to me," she said with a shiver.

"What?" said Capper. "Not your husband's house?"

The hot colour rushed up over her face. She turned away from him.

A few minutes later she stood alone in the music-room, gazing forth from the western window with eyes that seemed to search the horizon for help. She turned swiftly when she heard a step behind her.

"Charlie!"

He came to her, a smile on his swarthy face, a gleam of wickedness in his eyes. He took the hands that almost involuntarily she stretched to him.

"You summoned me!"

Something in his look warned her of danger. His clasp was electric in its tenseness.

She stood a moment before replying:

"I didn't so much as know you were in the house."

She left her hands in his. An odd recklessness was upon her, the recklessness born of despair.

He laughed into her eyes.

"Yet you summoned me, most tragic Queen of the Roses. You weren't so much as thinking of me, perhaps? Yet subconsciously your spirit cried to mine, and behold—I am here."

He had drawn her close to him, holding her hands against his breast, so that the quick, ardent beat of his heart came to her, sending a curious, half-reluctant thrill through her own.

"No, I wasn't thinking of you, Charlie," she said. "I was thinking of myself, hating the life before me . . . hating everything!"

"Why don't you think of me, for a change?" he said.

She turned her face swiftly aside. Her lips were suddenly quivering.

"No one . . . not even you . . . can help me now."

"You are wrong," he answered instantly. "I can help you. It's just what I'm here for."

"As a friend, Charlie?" she said, as she glanced at him again.

He bent his dark head over her hands.

"Yes, a friend."

"But . . ." She had begun to tremble; the old dread was upon her, the old instinctive recoil, the old ache of distrust. She set her hands against him, holding him from her. "How can you help me?"

"I can't keep you out of the furnace altogether," he said. "But I can save you from living in bondage to a man you loathe. You will have to trust me, to a certain extent. Do you trust me?"

"I don't know." Her voice was low, quivering with an agitation she could not repress. "Tell me what you are thinking of. Tell me how . . . how . . ."

"I will tell you," he said, "when you have made up your mind as to my trustworthiness."

"Oh, don't play with me, Charlie!" she besought him. "Don't you see I'm cornered . . . desperate? Of course I will trust you."

"Well, my dear girl, the case is simple enough. You are ready to trust me because you must. Disappear with me for a week or so, we'll run away and hide, and all charitable-minded folks will jump to the obvious conclusion. The result will be an undefended divorce suit, and I shall pay the damages."

His smile became a grimace.

"That is your road to freedom, *ma belle Reine.*"

He bent over her hands, holding them pressed to his lips.

Maud stood mute. The audacity of the suggestion seemed to deprive her of the power of speech. None but Charlie could ever have evolved such a plan. None but Charlie, who loved her!

The sudden realisation of his love went through her like a sword thrust in her heart. She actually gasped with the pain of it.

"Oh, Charlie," she said, in a broken, passionate whisper, "if I were only free!"

He raised his head on the instant.

"But you can be free. I am offering you freedom. A little courage, a little confidence! Can't you face it with me? Are you afraid?"

She shook her head.

"No, Charlie. It isn't that. But . . . but . . . my promise!"

"Oh, what of that?" he said impetuously. "A promise made under compulsion is no bond at all. You can't keep it and yet be true to yourself."

His hands were drawing her closer. His dark

face, aglow with the ardour of his quest, was close to hers.

"You want to be free," he urged. "And, my darling, I want you free, I want you free!"

His voice throbbed into silence. He was drawing her, drawing her. In another moment he would have had her in his arms; but she held back from him with quivering, desperate strength.

"No, Charlie! No!" she said gaspingly.

He released her hands at once, and abruptly, with a species of royal indifference curiously characteristic of him. He saw no defeat in failure. He regarded it only as victory postponed!

*   *   *

"I have called him the Hundredth Chance," said Jake. "But I guess he is going to be a winner."

He was stooping over a tiny black foal that stood with trembling legs pressed against its mother's flank. She was looking round at the master with questioning eyes. Even he was only allowed in the loose-box on sufferance.

"You're very hopeful," said Capper.

He stood leaning on the half-door, looking in upon Jake's latest treasure.

Maud was standing with him, but slightly apart, fondling the red setter, Chops.

Jake had received her without comment when she had arrived with Capper half an hour before. She fancied his manner was somewhat guarded, but he treated her as if he had expected her and her coming had caused him no surprise.

When supper was finished she took refuge upstairs in the room that had been Bunny's, standing there in darkness, striving with herself, fighting desperately for composure.

The thought of Charlie arose within her; Charlie, careless, debonair, gay of soul. He had offered her his protection. Should she go to him, even now? Could she? Dared she?

The temptation drew her, drew her. She knew Charlie so well. She was sure he would be chivalrous. She was sure she could count upon him. But his protection, what was it worth?

Now that she had seen Jake, had felt the primitive force of the man anew, her heart misgave her. She was possessed by the appalling conviction that in the matter of lawlessness Jake could outdo Charlie many times over, if once roused.

No trammels of civilisation would hold him. He would go straight for his prey, and no power on earth would turn him aside, or make him relinquish his hold till he had wreaked his vengeance.

A long time passed, until there came a step upon the stair, a steady, quiet step. A hand pushed open the door.

"Maud, are you here?" Jake said.

She tried to answer him, but could not. She knew that the moment she spoke, she would betray herself.

He came forward into the room. She saw his square figure against the light outside the door.

"Capper has gone back," he said. "He wouldn't stay any longer."

That startled her to a tragic activity. She sprang up in wild dismay.

"Dr Capper . . . gone! I . . . I thought he was spending the night!"

"I wanted him to," said Jake. "He wouldn't. He said I was to wish you good-night and thank you for your hospitality."

Maude stood still, her hands at her throat. For the moment she was too electrified for speech. Then anger, bitter, furious resentment, came to her aid.

"So you brought me here by . . . a trick!" she said, her voice pitched very low, but full of a quivering abhorrence that must have reached him where he stood.

"I don't know what you mean," said Jake.

His voice was curt and cool; he spoke without the smallest evidence of indignation or constraint.

"I never asked you to come, nor did I ask Capper to bring you. I presume you are a free agent so far as that goes. But since you are here, there is not much point in running away again. It's here that you belong."

The finality of his speech came upon her with stunning force.

She stood and waited tensely while he struck a match and lighted one of the candles upon the mantelpiece. All the blood in her body seemed to be throbbing at her throat. She had not been alone with him for weeks. She had never been alone with him as she was tonight.

Jake turned from the lighted candle and pointed to a low chair by the bed.

"Sit down," he said. "There's something I've got to say to you."

She looked at him with hunted eyes. She thought his face was very grim, but the dim flickering light threw strange shadows upon it, baffling her.

He came to her as she still remained upon her feet, took her between his hands, and held her so, facing him.

"Say now," he said, and a hint of half-coaxing kindliness softened the measured resolution of his speech, "where's the sense of fighting when you know you can't win? You're not a very good loser. But I reckon it's just a woman's way. I won't be hard on you on that account."

She drew back from him swiftly, with the old, instinctive shrinking from the man's overwhelming force of personality.

"Oh, need we talk about that now?" she said hurriedly. "I . . . there is still Bunny to think of. It is his last night, and . . . and . . ."

She broke off with a sound half-choked that was almost a cry. For Jake's hands were holding her, drawing her, compelling her. She realised that in another moment she would be in his arms. She set her quivering hands against his shoulders, pushing him from her with all her strength.

He set her free then, with a gesture half-contemptuous.

"So it's to be the same old fool game to the bitter end, is it?" he asked.

She heard in his voice a new note as of anger barely held in check.

"Well, I reckon it's up to you to make good sooner or later. It was not my intention to hold you down to that bargain of ours; but if you must have it, you shall. I want to know when you propose to make good."

She shrank away from him in quivering disgust.

"Oh, never, never."

The words rushed out almost against her will, and the moment they were uttered she wished them back. For Jake's eyes leapt into sudden furious flame, such flame as seemed to scorch her from head to foot.

He did not speak at once, but stood looking at her, while the awful seconds crept away.

"It's rather—rash of you to put it that way," he said, and there was a faintly humorous sound in his voice, as though he restrained a laugh. "So you're not a woman of your word, after all? That's queer, damned queer. I could have sworn you were."

She wrung her hands hard together in a desperate effort at self-control.

"Oh, Jake," she said piteously, "it isn't my fault that we're not made of the same stuff, indeed! You . . . you wouldn't ask the impossible of me?"

"P'raps not," said Jake, and now he spoke in the drawl that she knew well as a cloak to unwavering determination. "But has it never occurred to you that I might leave asking and take?"

She recoiled further from him. The man's deadly assurance appalled her. She had no weapon to oppose against it. And his eyes were as a red-hot furnace into which she dared not look.

She was so frightened that she waited, her head bent, wishing she could die.

Then she heard him say violently:

"God knows I do not want you like that!"

The door slammed and she was alone.

Chapter Seven

The wheels of the dog-cart clattered back over the stone paving, and a wild whoop of welcome echoed through the yard. A small, boyish figure leapt impetuously to the ground to be caught and fast held in Maud's straining arms.

"Hullo, Maud!" cried Bunny.

He hugged and kissed her. They had not seen each other for three months.

Maud's greeting was quite inaudible; she could only hold him passionately close, feeling the abounding activity of his light young frame, and realising with a great throb of rejoicing that the miracle had been wrought indeed. Bunny had been made whole.

"I say, isn't it fine?" the boy cried eagerly. "I've been doing gymnastics and physical exercises. I can swim, too, and Dr Capper says I may learn to ride. Jake's going to teach me, aren't you, Jake? Isn't it wonderful, Maud?"

She held him a little from her, gazing at him fondly before she gathered him close again. He was very slight and thin, but he was taller than she had thought possible.

The deep hollows about his eyes were far less

marked than before, though his whole face bore that indelible stamp of suffering which had always made him appear older than his years.

He gave her another hearty hug.

"I'm as fit as a fiddle. But I still have to do four hours flat on the floor every day. I told Jake I wasn't going to do it any more, but he swears he'll tie me down to the table-legs if I don't."

He left his sister abruptly to attach himself to Jake, whose threats of violence were plainly a huge attraction.

Jake thrust an arm about the narrow shoulders.

"We've got to make a man of you somehow, my son," he said. "And Capper is very emphatic about keeping up the treatment for another six weeks."

"Yes, and after that I'm going to school," said Bunny, with the assurance of a man who holds the ruling of his own destiny. "There's Fairharbour College up on the hill, Jake. That'll do for me. And I'll be a weekly boarder, and you'll take me to races on Saturdays."

"Not at your time of life, young feller," said Jake. "No, when you go to school you'll stay there. You've got to make up for lost time. P'raps in the holidays we'll see. But I make no rash promises. What about tea?"

They went to the meal prepared in the sunny parlour with its doors thrown open to the garden.

"The Burchester Cup will be run in a fortnight," Jake remarked.

"Oh, Jake, do let me see that!" urged Bunny, with shining eyes. "Is the Mascot going to run again?"

"No, not the Mascot this time, the Albatross. You remember him? Reckon he ought to carry it off if his jockey is good enough." Jake spoke with something of a frown.

"The Albatross! Wasn't he the chap you were forcing into the water that day you first spoke to us? What's up, Jake? Isn't he any good?"

"I wanted Vickers to ride him," Jake said. "He's been training. But he has just broken his thumb, confound him. That leaves it to Dick Stevens, and I don't feel just sure of him. He may pull it off; but he's not like Sam Vickers. The animals haven't the same faith in him, any more than I have."

He got up from the table as he spoke.

Bunny gulped down his tea and sprang up too.

"I'm coming round the stables with you," he said. "I won't be in the way."

Jake turned.

"Not tonight, my son. You've got another two hours' floor-drill before you. You go and do it!"

Bunny's face fell.

"Damn your eyes, Jake! Not tonight!"

Jake's hand shot forth and grasped his shoulder.

"Who taught you to say that?" he demanded.

"I don't know. Lots of fellows say it. Charlie often does."

"I do myself," said Jake grimly. "But you're not to. I mean it."

He patted Bunny's shoulder and left the room.

Maud put her arms round Bunny.

"I've missed you horribly, dear."

"I thought you would," said Bunny with complacence. "I missed you too at first. When they gave me that beastly massage, I used to howl for you."

"Was it so terribly bad?" she murmured, holding him closer.

"It was unspeakable," said Bunny. "I shouldn't have stuck to it if you'd been there. As it was, well, I couldn't help myself."

He twined his arm in hers, and they went upstairs side by side.

A little later they separated, and Maud went to her own room. Down in the training-field below the orchard, a solitary horseman was riding a young, untamed animal that fought savagely against his mastery, striving by every conceivable artifice to unseat him.

She paused at the casement window and watched the struggle, marked the man's clean assurance, his inflexible strength of purpose, his ruthless self-assertion.

And, as she watched, that evil thing that she nourished in her heart opened its first poisonous flowers and bloomed in rank profusion.

She hoped with a sickening intensity that the animal would win the day, and that Jake Bolton would be killed.

*   *   *

Maud took Bunny to see his mother, and she sat outside waiting for him, as she would not permit herself to enter the Anchor.

On their drive home she asked few questions about his visit, and Bunny did not seem inclined to volunteer anything till, as they reined in to a walk at the steep hill by the church, he turned abruptly and said:

"Did you know that Charlie owns the Anchor?"

"Yes, I know he does. He holds the mortgage."

Bunny's face wore a troubled frown. "Well, it seems that the place isn't answering and they can't go on paying interest. In fact, they are badly in arrears already, and he, or his agent, is tightening the reins and threatening to sell them up.

"Mother is pretty desperate about it. She says it means ruin, and no one can prevent it but Charlie. She wants you to get hold of him; says he will do anything for you, though I don't know how she knows that. In fact, she went on as if it was a matter of life and death."

Bunny looked at her with worried eyes. Evidently Mrs Sheppard had succeeded in impressing him with the urgency of the situation.

"How much money do they want to tide them over?" Maud asked.

"Rather a lot," said Bunny unsteadily. "Four hundred pounds, at least, she said. I suppose it would be no good to write to Uncle Edward? He wouldn't do it for Mother, I know, but he might for you."

"I couldn't ask him," Maud said. "I might if it were for you or myself. But not for Mother. I am sure he wouldn't do it."

"It's a beastly mess," said Bunny gloomily. "You'll have to get round Charlie, there's no other way."

"I must think," said Maud.

When they arrived back Maud found a letter

waiting for her. It was from Saltash, written in French, and contained the announcement of his approaching return.

Somehow the very thought of him at the Castle had been intolerable after what had passed between them on the day of her return to her husband. But they had corresponded ever since.

She had not wanted to see him, but now that he wrote to announce his return she found that she was glad. The first meeting with him might be a little difficult, but Charlie always knew how to deal with difficulties. They would be friends again, just friends.

She slipped the letter away with a smile. He always allowed himself a little more latitude when he wrote in French. It was but natural. It meant nothing, she knew. How could anyone take him really seriously?

The thought of Bunny's education was beginning to weigh upon her. She wanted to talk about it to Jake, but somehow she did not know how to broach the subject. She wondered if she should write to Uncle Edward, but hesitated to do so. Letters were never satisfactory.

She was pondering this matter as she undressed that night when a sudden thought struck her, a thought that darted through her like a flash, leaving a shining trail of possibilities behind. Why should they not accept the old man's invitation and go to him for a little while?

He would be glad to see them, she was sure; and she would be glad, oh, unspeakably glad, to get away for a time. Face to face with him, she might even plead for her mother. She would infinitely rather be under an obligation to him than to Charlie.

The idea drew her more and more. She wondered why it had not occurred to her before. In the end, finding it still early, she sat down at the table and began to scribble a hasty note.

She determined that she would not tell Jake until Uncle Edward's reply reached her. She felt convinced that it would contain the invitation she was soliciting.

Feverishly she penned her appeal. Would he invite them to spend a few days? Bunny was well, or nearly so; she herself was feeling the heat, and would like a change.

She had scarcely finished addressing the envelope when she heard Jake's step on the stairs. Startled, she caught up letter and writing-case and pushed them into a drawer.

He seldom retired late, but she had not expected him so early as this. Swiftly she turned, shut the door, blew out her lamp, and slipped into bed.

But he did not pass on to his own room. He stopped at the door of hers, paused a second, then quietly opened it. She heard the creak of his gaiters as he entered. He had a candle in one hand; he put up the other to shield it from the draught, and the door blew gently to behind him.

Maud leaned against her pillow and watched him. Her heart was beating very fast. She wondered if he had heard her hasty movements of the past few moments.

He came to her side and set down his candle.

"I saw your light go out, so I guessed you weren't asleep," he said.

Maud's eyes, blue-black and sombre, looked up to his.

"What do you want?"

"I wanted just to speak to you," he said, "and I thought if I waited to undress, maybe you'd be asleep."

With the words he sat down rather heavily in the chair by her side, and there fell a silence, a dragging, difficult silence. Maud's heart was beating very fast.

His stillness began to act upon her nerves. She turned towards him restlessly.

"What is it?"

He stretched out a strong hand and took one of hers.

"It's you," he said, and in his voice was a note of anxiety, which partly reassured her. "You've not been yourself lately. Guess there's something the matter."

"There is nothing the matter," she said hastily.

He held her hand closely.

"You've no call to be afraid of me," he said gently. "Maybe I've been rough and rude at times. I've never meant it, my princess. I can't live up to you always; but I try, God knows I try!"

A sudden tremor sounded in his voice; he became abruptly silent.

Maud's hand was hard-clenched in his. She did not look at him; but the beating of her heart rose up between them, a hard, insistent drumming that she was powerless to control.

After a brief space he spoke again, his voice quite steady and controlled.

"Reckon you're not happy. Reckon you're not well, either. I've been thinking maybe you'd like to go away for a spell, you and the boy. If so, I'm willing to manage it. It'll be a bit of a rest for you."

He paused. The clenched hand he held had made a sharp, convulsive movement as if at a sudden twinge of pain. Maud lay breathing rapidly, her eyes fixed upon the flame of the candle.

He waited a few moments.

"What do you think of the proposition?" he asked.

She turned her head slowly towards him.

"Bunny and I alone?"

"That's the idea," said Jake.

Her eyes met his resolutely, with a certain challenging directness.

"As a matter of fact, I had thought myself that we might go to Uncle Edward for a little."

He showed no surprise.

"You would like that?"

"Yes." She spoke with instant decision.

"Then go!" said Jake.

* * *

"He's going to be a winner, is he?" asked Saltash.

"That depends how he's ridden, my lord," said Jake dryly. "He's a hot favourite."

"Pity you can't ride him yourself," observed Saltash, watching the Albatross with a critical eye as he cantered down the field. "Who is in the saddle? Not Vickers?"

"No. Vickers is incapacitated. I have put Stevens

up. He seems keen for the chance, though I'm not so keen to give it him."

"He ought to pull it off," said Saltash.

"He ought, my lord."

Saltash turned.

"Come along and show me the latest offspring! What was it you called him? The Hundredth Chance? A curious name to choose!"

Jake's grim face relaxed to a smile.

"Oh, he's in the paddock along with his mother. He promises to be the most valuable animal in the stables. He'll carry everything before him when the time comes."

"Is that why you've given him such a hopeful name?" asked Saltash.

"Even so, my lord. He carries my luck with him wherever he goes."

"You're a queer fish, Bolton," observed Saltash, turning to leave the field.

As they reached the house Saltash suddenly looked up.

"I believe someone is calling you, Bolton. You'd better go. Never mind me!"

Jake raised a hand to his cap and turned away.

Instantly Saltash straightened himself. He uttered a low, clear whistle, and almost immediately Maud, clad in white, came to the window. He sprang up the steps in a single bound and caught her hands into his own.

"I had your letter," he said. "Quick! When can you meet me?"

Maud was gasping a little. Her face was deeply flushed.

"Charlie! You are so sudden! I only want . . . a few minutes alone with you."

"When?" he said, and held her hands.

His eyes were gazing into hers freely, ardently; but he was laughing as he always laughed, ready to turn his ardour into a joke at a moment's notice.

She hesitated.

"Quick!" he said. "They are coming, and I must go. Come down to the orchard gate after dinner to-night! No one will know, Queen Rose. That is settled, then. I shall be at the gate alone."

He laughed under his breath, and the next instant was gone.

* * *

The dew was thick on the orchard grass as Maud ran down under the trees. An orange moon was rising behind them and the shadows lay deep and mysterious across her path.

She was trembling as she went, yet as she neared the trysting-place, she was sure he would be waiting for her.

They saw each other simultaneously, and in a moment he had sprung to meet her with the ardour she knew so well. Her hands were in his almost in the same instant. He held them closely.

"At last!" he said.

"Yes, but I can't stay," she said rather breathlessly. "I want to speak to you . . . only to speak to you . . . about my mother."

"Good heavens!" said Saltash. His hold relaxed for a second, then tightened again. "My dear girl, how absurdly prosaic of you to come to me on such a night as this and talk about anybody or anything on earth besides ourselves! I won't allow it, and that's a fact."

"But it just that I have come for, Charlie; and nothing else. And I can't stay either. You must let me say what I have to say quickly, and then go."

He drew her gently through the gate and led her to the summer-house close by, which overlooked the town. The moonlight filtered in upon them through a lattice-work of leaves.

"Don't tremble, *ma belle Reine!*" he said. "You shall go whenever you will. But need we waste to-night? I will call upon you formally in the morning if you desire it, and talk about anything you wish."

"I am so troubled," she whispered. "I want your help."

"It is yours forever," he made answer. "You have but to command."

"That is a promise?" she urged.

"My solemn promise," said Saltash. "Now, shall we forget?"

His voice was full of a tenderness that stirred her to the depths. A piteous sob caught her throat; she put up a swift, silencing hand.

"Oh, if I only could!"

"You can," said Saltash. He moved also, slid a gentle arm about her. "Close your eyes, dear heart, and forget all your troubles! I can charm them all away."

She shook her head. Her eyes were full of tears.

"I am caught in the whirlpools, Charlie. I shall never get away. All the romance is gone out of my life . . . forever."

"I can bring it back," he said.

Her tears overflowed. She could not hold them back.

"I wish I were dead!" she said.

His arms were about her. He drew her to his breast.

"Come to me, Queen of my heart! I have been cheated of my right long enough. You have belonged to me always, and you know it.

"You have called me back to you. You are mine. Turn your face to me, sweetheart! There is no love in all the world like ours. How can we resist it? It is greater than we ourselves."

But she kept her face covered, hidden low against the throbbing of his heart.

His words went into silence, a silence that was stark and cold, the very shadow of Despair. It bound them both for a while; then shudderingly she spoke.

"It is no good, Charlie. I can't do it. . . . The whirlpools caught me . . . drew me down. I am married. I can't come now. I am bound . . . hand and foot . . . in outer darkness."

"I can deliver you," he said.

"No one can deliver me. Say good-bye to me, Charlie," she whispered, "and . . . go!"

He caught her to him. He looked closely into her quivering face.

"You love me still?" he whispered, with passionate insistence. "Tell me you love me still!"

She seemed to hesitate, as if reluctant or irresolute. She seemed about to draw back. And then something magnetic in his face or his touch must have moved her; or was it the weird enchantment of the night?

She gave him her lips without a word, and so he had his answer. . . .

There came the click of the orchard gate, the sound of a quiet voice, and Maud at once sprang up and ran back into the house.

Half an hour later she stood in her bedroom, waiting. The window was wide open, and the night air blew in cold and pure, with a scent of dew-drenched roses and the salt of the sea behind.

If she could have chosen death in that moment, instead of this numb waiting for an ordeal which she felt would be beyond her strength, she believed she would not have hesitated.

Suddenly she heard his step at last, and turned, bracing herself.

She faced him stiffly in utter silence. One glimpse she had of his face, and only one; for she could not look again. The red-brown eyes were alight with a fire that seemed to consume her even from afar. She stood and numbly waited.

He came straight to her.

"So, you have decided to make a fool of me, have you?"

His voice was very low, but it had in it the sound as of an angry animal. There was something of the animal in his pose, also, something from which her whole being shrank a-frighted.

Yet she was not without courage. She forced herself to a certain calmness.

"Will you tell me what you mean?"

He made a slight gesture that seemed to cry aloud of a savagery scarcely restrained.

"I guess you can do that. What do I mean? Tell me!"

She drew back from him with an instinctive movement of recoil, but on the instant, as though she had stepped into a trap, his hands came out and caught her by the wrists. He held her firmly before him.

"Tell me!" he reiterated.

But she took refuge in silence. She had no words.

He held her so for many seconds, and she knew that during those seconds his eyes remained immovably fixed upon her. She made no attempt to resist him. She knew beyond all question that resistance would be worse than useless.

But she refused with mute determination to meet his eyes. Crush her, conquer her, as he would, he should not force his way past every barrier unopposed. Her submission was physical, but not mental. She had always held back from him her soul.

He spoke at length, and still in his voice she heard that terrible, deep menace, as of a savage force that gathered and gathered under the thinning surface of his civilisation.

"I reckon you think I'm easier to fool than I am. Old friends must have their privileges. And if they include a little genteel love-making, where's the harm? Who is to raise any objection?

"Not the husband who has been too big an oaf ever to make love to you in his life! He should be the last person to interfere, I reckon."

She shivered in his hold, but she spoke no word.

Had they not always been utterly at variance with each other? How could she hope to make him see anything but evil now that his brutal passions were aroused?

How could she ever attempt to convince him that he alone was responsible for the fact that temptation had become even possible to her?

And so she stood in silence, while the dreadful force of the man mounted and mounted, menacing her.

He waited for several seconds for some response from her; then at last, as she made none, he moved, drew her locked wrists behind her, forcing her slowly back till her face was turned up to his gaze.

She felt the scorching fire of the eyes she would not meet, and in a moment her whole body seemed to burn in a furnace of shame. The hot blood stung her from head to foot, pricking every vein. Crimson and quivering, she hung there in his hold, waiting.

"So you won't speak to me?" he said. "Won't even try to defend yourself? Well, maybe you're wise. Maybe explanations would do more harm than good. I know well enough how it is with you. You've got to the pitch of enduring me like a loathsome but incurable disease.

"You never reflected, did you, that in so doing you were making your own hell? You hate me, but you don't realise that the thing you hate is not me at all, but a brute of your own creation. And because of that, p'raps it's a natural consequence, you've come to prefer another man's love to mine."

His hold was tightening upon her; she felt herself being drawn to him, felt the warmth of his body like the glow of an open fire. And a sudden wild wave of rebellion goaded her into action.

She resisted him fiercely, passionately, striving with all her strength to free herself from that pitiless hold.

"You never offered me love," she panted, straining back from him even while he mastered her. "Love . . . love . . . is a very different thing!"

Her voice went into a gasp that was almost a cry. He was holding her crushed to him in a grip that nearly suffocated her. His eyes blazed down into hers, terrible in their intensity, cruelly, appallingly bright. The savage in him had leapt free of all shackles at last, and had her utterly at his mercy.

"Well?" he said, speaking with lips drawn back, showing his set teeth. "And is love, as defined by you and Saltash, something peculiarly holy?"

The taunt pierced her like a knife with a pain so unbearable that for the moment she was almost beside herself. For an instant she winced from that intolerable thrust; but only for an instant.

The next, with a furious wrench, she freed one hand and struck him, struck him across his grim, menacing mouth.

"How dare you say that?" she cried. "How dare you?"

She struck him afresh with each repetition, so stung to frenzy was she by that sneer. But when the sudden realisation that he stood to endure her blows without the smallest attempt to check or avoid them came upon her, the spirit went out of her.

She became passive again, trembling from head

to foot, so that but for his upholding arms she must have fallen.

"Let me go!" she whispered. "Let me go!"

He was still gazing at her, but his look had changed. His eyes still burned, but they no longer threatened. He held her awhile longer, and then very gradually he let her go.

She drew away from him, her bosom heaving, her lips panting, and leaned upon the dressing-table for support. She had withstood him indeed, but it had cost her every inch of her strength.

She did not know how she endured his silence. It seemed to pierce every nerve, while he still stood observing her, as it were appraising her.

Then at length very slowly he spoke.

"I take back what I said about Saltash. I see I was wrong."

He paused a moment. She had made a sharp gesture of surprise, but she spoke no word.

"I realise, now, that you do not know what love is. If you did, you wouldn't be so ashamed. Maybe you never will know. It isn't given to all of us, not that sort. But let me tell you this! Your friendship, or whatever you call it, with Saltash must end.

"There must be no more letters, no more secret meetings. Saltash is not a white man. I believe in your own heart you know it. Trust him, and he will let you down."

He spoke with sombre force. She heard him in utter silence, her head bent, still striving to call back her vanished strength.

He came a step nearer to her.

"Maybe you think you can hoodwink me, disobey me, and I shan't know. You haven't a very great opinion of my intellect, I guess. But, you may take it from me, I shall know. And if you try to deceive me, you will repent it.

"You wouldn't fancy life on a lone ranch with not a soul but me to speak to, and all the dishes to wash?"

A grim note that was not without a hint of humour crept into his voice.

"That's what it will mean, my girl, if you don't obey your husband now. I'm a man of my word, and I think you know it."

He was standing close to her. She felt the vitality of the man, encompassing her, enthralling her. Her brief resistance was over. The very heart of her felt too tired to beat.

He had not forcibly quelled her rebellion, yet in some fashion he had taken from her the power to rebel.

Suddenly he spoke again with an odd, restrained vehemence; she felt that he spoke in spite of himself.

"That's a prospect that doesn't attract you, I reckon. You've no use for me, never have had, save once. My love is just an insult to you. You even call it by another name. But I tell you this . . ."

His voice deepened with a strong vibration that affected her very strangely, gripping her close attention.

"Whatever it is, it's a driving force that I can't restrain. It may be an obsession, it may be a curse; but there is no getting away from it. It simply is and it has got to be. If any man ever dares to come between us, you had better mark what I say, I'll shoot him!"

He moved with the words, turned in his sturdy, purposeful fashion, and went to his room.

She did not watch him go, but she listened with straining ears for the closing of the door between them. It did not come to her. There was to be no relief from his presence that night. The door remained half-open.

She sat on, motionless, for a moment or two, listening in a numb, hopeless fashion to his quiet, methodical movements.

She got up sharply at length and began with quivering speed to undress, not daring to linger lest she should have to meet again the straight, unsparing scrutiny of those terrible bright eyes. Then trembling she crept into bed. And the darkness covered her soul.

*   *   *

Saltash did not come to her on the following day, and Maud was thankful. But the problem of her mother's difficulties had begun to vex her sorely.

Without communicating with him, she knew that it could not be solved. He had given his promise to help her, yet somehow she did not feel the task before her to be a very easy one.

She watched the post with nervous anxiety, but nothing came for her. She was relieved to have nothing to conceal, but her mother's anxieties weighed upon her. She hesitated to write to Charlie, but told herself she would have to do so if no word came from him.

It was all highly unsatisfactory, and behind her uneasiness there lurked a deep sense of self-reproach, self-distrust. She had suffered him to go too far, too far. It might be difficult to recover a normal footing.

It might be that he was even now planning some deep game, some master-stroke to follow up the advantage he had gained and win her for his own.

He would not succeed. He could not succeed. She would not so much as allow her thoughts to wander in that direction. She had been mad that night. There had been witchery in the very air.

But now she was awake to the crude realities of life, awake and sane and bitterly ashamed of her weakness.

He might plot and intrigue, but he could not overthrow her reason a second time. The madness had passed, and it would not return. But the necessity for seeing him remained, and it was an urgent one. She found it hard to wait in inactivity.

The whole day passed without a sign from him, and her patience began to wear thin. Surely, surely he could not fail to keep that solemn promise of his! Surely he could not have forgotten, or be waiting for her to make the first move!

She went for a walk in the evening on the down with Capper, who had arrived earlier on. She did not greatly want to go. She was a little afraid of his shrewd insight. But she found that she had no cause for fear.

He was full of kindly common-place topics, and he touched upon no intimate subject whatever. She

returned from the walk feeling soothed and re-
freshed.

They went through the training-field on the way
back, and here they came upon Jake, giving Bunny
his first riding-lesson. It was good to see the boy's
eagerness, his flushed face and shining eyes. He was
utterly fearless and even impatient of Jake's care.

They stood awhile and watched, then turned and
walked up through the garden.

"He is very happy," Maud said.

"Jake is an A-one companion for him, Mrs. Bolton," Capper smiled. "He is thrice lucky to be in the
care of a man like Jake."

"Yes, Jake is very kind," she agreed without enthusiasm.

"That's so. And he won't spoil him either. Also"
—Capper spoke with emphasis—"he'll never learn
anything that isn't clean and straight from Jake.
Guess he'll make a fine man someday."

"Thanks to you, Doctor!" Maud said.

"No, madam. Thanks to Jake! My part was a
very small one. I am just a mechanic; but Jake is
a driver of engines, a maker of men."

Maud said nothing, and he changed the subject.

They lingered in the garden till Jake and Bunny
joined them; then they separated, Bunny, contrary
to custom, attaching himself to Maud, and Jake taking possession of Capper.

Brother and sister ascended the steps into the
house and entered the parlour. Bunny was still
flushed and excited. Life was full of absorbing interest to him. He had actually been off the leading-

rein most of the time, yes, and he had cantered too.

Jake said he was to go and have a warm bath and then do his time on the floor. It was a great bore, but he supposed he'd have to. What was Maud looking so sick about? Wasn't she well?

This amiable enquiry was made just as Maud's eyes had fallen upon a letter lying on the table. She almost snatched it up, and then found with a mingling of relief and disappointment that it was not from Saltash.

The crabbed writing was wholly unfamiliar to her. She stood gazing at it while her sudden agitation subsided.

"Who's it from?" said Bunny, coming to peer over her shoulder. "Liverpool postmark. Why, that's from that queer old codger who was down here in the winter, I'll bet. What on earth does he want?"

"To be sure . . . Uncle Edward," Maud said.

She opened the letter with Bunny looking on. They read it together.

My Dear Grand-Niece,

I am pleased to acknowledge your letter of the 4th inst., and I write to inform you that I shall be delighted to receive you and your brother on whatever date it may suit you to come. I am glad to hear of the latter's excellent progress. I presume you are capable of keeping him in order. You will, of course, be prepared to find your own entertainment. Should your worthy husband care to join the party by any chance, I have room for all.

Your affectionate uncle,
Edward Warren.

"Holy Christopher!" ejaculated Bunny. "What on earth did you want to write to him for? I'm not going there, jiggered if I am! And to be tied to your apron-strings too, not much!"

"I thought you might like to go away with me for a little," she said.

He stared at her.

"What! Away from Jake? Not much!"

"You're not very flattering, Bunny."

"I can't think what's come over you! Jake's the best chap in the world, and yet you don't seem to get on with him. What the blazes is the matter with you, anyway?"

"I wish you wouldn't be so horribly imitative, Bunny. You never used to talk like that."

"I'll talk as I damned well please! It's no affair of yours. As to leaving Jake, I'm hanged if I will! You can jolly well go by yourself!"

"And for behaving like a beastly bounder, you'll apologise for it before you leave this room," a voice said.

Both started violently. Jake had come up the steps from the garden. He walked over to the mantelpiece, then turned.

"If we were alone, my son, I'd punch your head for you. Maud is quite right. You've no call to talk like a cowboy. Now apologise—quick!"

But Bunny stood sullenly silent.

Maud turned to the door.

"Pray don't trouble to make him do that! I am accustomed to cowboy manners."

The door closed upon her, and in the same instant Jake's hand closed upon Bunny's shoulder.

"Go after her!" he commanded. "Catch her up and say you're sorry!"

"I won't, Jake! I'm not sorry! And I won't go and stay with Uncle Edward. If you send me, I'll run away."

"I'll be mad with you in a minute, my son. Go after her, do you hear? Go after her and make it up before she starts crying!"

"She won't cry!" said Bunny incredulously. "She never does."

Jake swung him round to the door.

"Bunny, don't you be a skunk! If you don't go, there'll be trouble, bad trouble."

"But it was her fault!" protested Bunny, stung to remonstrance. "She set on to me first."

"I don't care whose fault it was," said Jake. "You're to go."

Bunny capitulated, and flung his arms round his brother-in-law's shoulders.

"All right, Jake. I'll go, old man. Don't look so confoundedly grim!"

Jake held him back with one hand on his rough, dark head.

"Be off with you, boy! I'll see you later, maybe when you're in bed. Go now!"

He smiled upon Bunny, for there were tears in the boy's eyes, patted him on the back, and turned to go as he had entered.

Ten seconds later Bunny was beating a rousing tattoo on his sister's door.

"Maud, let me in—quick—quick!"

He wriggled at the handle, for the door was locked, and, meeting with no response, beat again.

"Maud, I say, let me in! I've come to say I'm sorry. Don't be waxy, old girl! Open the door!"

There came a lagging footstep. The key turned. Bunny burst into the room headlong.

"You're not crying, are you? I knew you weren't. It's all right, isn't it? What makes you so touchy nowadays? You never used to be."

Her arms held him tightly in a mute embrace. She kissed him with a yearning tenderness.

"You know Jake is worried about you. Poor old boy! He's getting as lean as Chops. Have you noticed?"

She had not. They sat down together on an ottoman near the window, Bunny's arm protectingly round her.

"He sent me up after you in such a hurry because he was afraid you were going to cry," he went on. "He was furious with me for vexing you. Poor old Jake!"

A curious little pang of resentment went through her.

"You seem to think he is very much to be pitied," she said.

"I do," said Bunny instantly. "He looks so down in the mouth nowadays. I saw it directly I came home. He's got a sort of hurt look at the back of his eyes, as if he wasn't getting on with himself. I sometimes wish you'd be a bit kinder to him, Maud. I'm sure he mopes."

This was a point of view so new to Maud that she hardly knew how to regard it. Somehow it had never occurred to her that Jake could take her attitude to heart, Jake, who trampled down all rebellion with so merciless a heel.

She had always told herself that Jake had all he really wanted. That he was aware of any need of the spirit, she had never seriously believed.

"Guess I must be going," said Bunny. "I've got to have a bath. You might turn on the water for me like a brick, while I go and undress."

There was subtle tact in the suggestion. Bunny knew, none better, than to wait upon him was his sister's dearest privilege and he judged by her sad face that it was time to change her thoughts.

When he arrived in the bath-room a few minutes later, he found everything put ready for his comfort, and Maud waiting to turn off the water at his command.

"Thanks, old girl. You're jolly decent to me! I don't know how I managed to be such a beast. Guess my temper must have got warped in its youth. By the way, there's a letter for you from Charlie on my dressing-table. He told me to give it to you when we were alone. I suppose it's something to do with mother's affairs."

"Oh, perhaps," Maud said; and hoped he did not note her sudden start or the quick flushing of her face. "When did you see him?"

"He came up the garden way this evening, just before I went riding with Jake. You were out with Dr. Capper. He was in rather a decent mood," said Bunny. "He gave me half a sovereign. Not a bad sort, Charlie."

The letter from Charlie was not on his table, but

tossed carelessly on the bed with his clothes. She shivered at the thought that Jake, and not she, might have found it there.

Her hands were trembling as she tore open the flap. She was impatient, yet half-afraid. Her heart throbbed at the sight of the dashing scrawl, once so familiar and so dear.

"Ma belle Reine des roses,"—her heart throbbed a little faster. The old, sweet name, how it brought back to her those free happy days of her youth! How she marvelled now at the high girlish pride that had sent him away! How cruel had been the cost of that same pride!

She read on. It was a characteristic epistle, half-mocking, half-tender, throughout. Would she meet him again? But of course she would! Had she not said that he could serve her? But they would not risk another interruption.

He would manage to return early, and come to her by the garden way. They would thus be sure of at least half an hour together, before anyone else got back.

He seemed confident that she would not refuse, and she knew, even as she read, that she could not.

She must see him somehow. She must somehow get back to normal relations with him. She could not sacrifice his friendship to that one night's madness. Besides, there was her mother.

A trampling of hoofs in the yard below drew her to the window. She looked forth.

It was the Albatross being led out of his stable for the evening canter.

Dick Stevens held the bridle. He wore a heavy,

glowering look. She remembered, and the memory seemed to scorch her, that morning after her wedding-day when she had stood and listened in petrified horror to Jake pouring forth terrible invective upon the lad's head.

He was standing by now, watching with a frown, as if the boy's movements displeased him; and even as she looked, he went forward and took the bridle into his own hand.

Stevens stood aside sullenly, while he readjusted the bit with set lips. The Albatross nozzled against him, and after a few moments Jake's hand went to his pockets and brought forth a piece of sugar.

Then, while the animal munched it, he turned round upon the sulky stable-boy and spoke.

"If any harm comes to him through any damned carelessness of yours, I warn you, and I'm a man of my word, I'll leather you to a jelly, if it costs me fifty pounds."

His words were quiet, but absolutely distinct. His right hand was hard gripped on his riding-whip.

Stevens slunk back a step, not speaking, his face crimson and defiant.

Maud, at the upper window, clasped her hands suddenly and very tightly upon the letter they held. Yes, Jake was a man of his word. And what if he kept that other promise he had made to her? Life alone on a ranch with Jake!

Her whole being rose in revolt at the thought. She turned away with a shudder.

Chapter Eight

The day fixed for the race for the Burchester Cup was inclined to be showery.

Maud did not go, and spent most of the afternoon in pacing to and fro, for she could not rest. If only she could send a message to Charlie not to come. But it was impossible.

Back and forth, back and forth, she wandered, conscious sometimes of a dreadful, physical sinking, but for the most part too torn with anxiety to be aware of anything else.

Much later, when it was obvious that Charlie was not coming, she heard some commotion in the stable-yard.

She rushed to the front door. Bunny was on the step. But she brushed past him without so much as seeing him, tearing forth bare-headed, ashen-faced, into the rain.

For there in the murky twilight, terrible as a lion newly roused, stood Jake, gripping by the collar a struggling, writhing figure, while he administered to it as sound a horse-whipping as his great strength could accomplish.

His right arm moved slowly, with a deliberate regularity unspeakably horrible to behold. She had a glimpse, only a glimpse, of his face, and the savage cruelty of it was such that it seemed no longer human.

Of his victim she saw very little, but of his identity not the smallest doubt existed in her mind.

And as the sound of those awful blows reached her, the last shred of her endurance was torn away. She shrieked and shrieked again as she ran.

Those shrieks reached Jake as the cry of its mate in distress might reach an animal intent upon its prey. He flung the prey from him on the instant and wheeled.

He met her a full ten yards from the spot, just as her feet slipped on the wet stones of the yard.

He caught her, she almost fell against him, and held her hard in his arms.

She was sobbing terribly, utterly unstrung and hysterical.

She struggled for speech, but the wild sounds that left her lips were wholly unintelligible. She struggled to free herself, but her strength was gone.

In the end, her knees suddenly gave way under her. She collapsed with a gasping cry. And Jake, stooping, raised her, and bore her, senseless, in out of the drenching rain.

*   *   *

"You've only yourself to thank," said Capper. "You might have known what to expect if you'd had an ounce of sense."

"Guess I always was an all-fired fool," said Jake.

The great doctor looked down at him from his post on the hearth, and his eyes softened a little.

For Jake's dejection was very thorough. He sat as it were in dust and ashes.

"Not always, my son," he said. "Well, it's done. She may get over it, but she won't love you any the better for it. It'll be up to you to make a fresh start presently."

Jake was silent. He sat with bent head and lowered eyes.

Capper contemplated him awhile, till at length a faint glint of humour began to shine in his green eyes. He moved, and laid a long, wiry hand upon Jake's shoulder.

"Don't take it too hard, man!" he said. "Let it be a lesson to you, that's all! And the next time you want to whip a stable-boy, do it on the quiet, and there'll be no misunderstandings! Guess you'll have to sing small for a bit, but it's not a hanging matter. She'll forgive you by and by."

"I doubt it!" Jake's voice was deadly calm. His eyes shone like a still, hot fire. "I thought I could win her, though the odds were dead against me. I staked all on the chance, the hundredth chance, and it's gone.

"I've lost. There's no sense in pretending otherwise. I can't hold her any longer, unless it's by brute force; and I reckon there's more lost than gained that way.

"And yet I know, I know"—his voice suddenly took a deeper note—"that where I've failed no other man has ever yet succeeded. No one else had ever got to the heart of her. That I know."

He spoke with grim force, as though challenging

incredulity on Capper's part, but Capper made no attempt to contradict him. He even nodded, as if he held the same opinion.

"Then I guess it's up to you to find the way," he said. "There's a better way for all of us than brute force, my son. There is a power that all the violence in the world can't beat. It's greater than all the devils. And you'll win out, you'll win out, on the strength of it."

He paused. Jake's eyes had kindled a little. He set his hands on the arms of his chair as though about to rise.

"You speak as one who knows."

"I do know." Capper's voice was very emphatic. "It's not an easy world to live in. It's a mighty difficult one. But we've been given a compass to steer by, a Divine compass, Jake my lad. Guess it's our own faults in the main if we fail to get there!"

He waited. The light was gradually growing in Jake's eyes. He had a speculative, half-doubtful look.

"Show her what Love, real Love, is worth!" Capper went on. "She's a woman. She'll soon understand."

Jake got to his feet with the quiet, purposeful movement of a man who has work before him. He gripped Capper's hand for a moment, and looked him straight in the face.

"I reckon you're right, sir," he said, speaking rather heavily. "I've made a damned muddle of the whole show. I'll make her trust me again."

He turned towards the door.

"Where are you off to?" Capper asked.

Jake made a gesture as of one who contemplates an unpleasant task.

"I must go up to the Castle. I said I would. I've got to tell Lord Saltash why the Albatross failed this afternoon. I ought to have scratched sooner than run the chance of having him pulled. I never trusted Stevens, never. I'll see him drawn and quartered before he ever rides another horse of mine!"

"But you've no evidence?" suggested Capper.

"I've the evidence of my own eyes," said Jake bluntly. "And there'll be further evidence presently, I'm convinced."

Up in the room above, Maud lay, white and still, her dark hair all about her, her eyes closed, an aloofness that was almost like the shadow of Death wrapping her round.

Mrs Wright, whom she had made friends with when she first married Jake, had arrived earlier and sat by her side, very alert and watchful. It was growing late, but she said she would stay for the night.

Maud tossed restlessly, and on waking she clung to Mrs Wright's plump soothing hand.

"If Jake comes in, he . . . he will want to send you away. Don't let him, please! I can't be alone with Jake . . . tonight."

She was becoming agitated, but Mrs Wright gently hushed her.

"You shan't be, dear. Jake wants me to be with you tonight. He is very unhappy about you, is poor Jake. Goodness knows you needn't be afraid of him."

"Oh, how can I help it after what he did to Charlie? Did you see? Did you see? Is Charlie very badly hurt?"

"Charlie?" questioned Mrs Wright.

"Lord Saltash. Didn't you see what . . . what Jake did to him? Oh, it was terrible . . . terrible!"

A great shudder shook her at the remembrance of what she had seen.

"My dear!" Mrs Wright leaned to her, smoothing her pillow. "Why, what a mistake to be sure! And to think you've upset yourself like this all for nothing! Dear, dear, dear, to be sure.

"That wasn't Lord Saltash. Whatever made you think it was? It was just one of them pesky stable-boys he was giving a jacketing to; and richly he deserved it, I'll be bound."

"Oh, Mrs Wright!" Maud's voice was suddenly eager. "Are you sure?"

Her dark eyes, wide and beseeching, were raised in earnest, questioning to her old friend's kindly face. She clung to the sustaining hand.

"My dear, of course I'm sure. I came along behind you. I saw it all. It was that young dog Dick Stevens. I know him well, never did like him; and I'm sure he deserved all he got, probably more. Now, you mustn't worry yourself any longer."

"You're sure Charlie is safe?" Maud said quiveringly. "He, he was coming . . . don't tell Jake! . . . to see me today. But he didn't come. And I thought . . . I thought . . ."

She broke off in sudden terror.

"My dear, you mustn't upset yourself like this. It's very wrong. Jake would know that there could be no reason why Lord Saltash should not drop in and see you."

"Oh, you don't know Jake!" moaned Maud. "He is so terrible . . . so terrible. He would shoot Charlie . . . if he knew!"

"My dear!" Mrs Wright was genuinely shocked. "You're talking wildly. You can't know what you're saying."

Maud had sunk back upon her pillows, white-lipped, exhausted.

"There is a reason," she whispered. "There is a reason! I love Charlie. I have loved him for years. And Jake . . . Jake would kill him if he knew. He does know . . . a little. That's why . . . why I am so . . . afraid. Oh, I wish . . . I wish I were . . . dead!"

She ceased to speak, and a dreadful pallor crept up over her face. Mrs Wright, anxiously watching, saw that Maud was slipping into unconsciousness, and across the bed she issued a sharp command.

"Quick, Jake! Fetch the doctor!"

Mrs Wright reached for a fan. The heat was intense. The darkness hung before the window like a pall. And the good woman trembled a little in spite of herself.

*   *   *

"So you've come to see your old uncle at last! Dear me, you've been a precious long time about it. Tut-tut, child, what a clothes-peg to be sure! Sit down! Sit down. You don't look fit to stand."

Old Uncle Edward pulled out a chair from his dining-room table and almost thrust his visitor into it. Then he turned, seized a decanter, and poured some wine into a large, old-fashioned glass goblet.

"You drink this! You're looking half-dead. What have they been doing to you? Starving you?"

He stood looking at her, sternly critical.

"So you've been ill, have you? I can see you have. Poor girl. Well, we must see what we can do to get you strong again. And you haven't brought your young brother along? How is he? Quite cured?"

"Yes, quite cured." Maud put out a hesitating hand and somewhat shyly slipped it into her uncle's. "He would have come too, but the school will soon be opening; and it seemed a pity not to let him go at the beginning of the term."

Uncle Edward grunted as if not wholly pleased. But his old knotted fingers closed very kindly about her own.

"So your good husband is going to pay for his schooling, is he? That's very generous of him, very generous indeed. He's a man of property, is he— your Jake?"

A quick flush rose in Maud's upturned face; she averted it swiftly.

"I don't know. He seems to be able to do anything he likes. He . . . he is very kind to Bunny."

Uncle Edward grunted again, and sat watching her. He did not ask her how her mother was faring, and she did not feel that the moment for speaking of her affairs had arrived.

She wished she knew where Charlie was; but she could not risk sending a letter to the Castle. There seemed to be nothing more she could do. She had begun to tell him of her trouble. He knew she needed help.

Yet whenever her thoughts turned towards him, the memory of Jake's words awoke within her, tormented her.

"Trust him, and he will let you down."

Why had he spoken so certainly? What did he know of Saltash and his ways? Was it possible, could it be, that he knew a side of Charlie's whimsical nature that had never been presented to her? Or was she so blind that she had failed to perceive it?

It was true that in the old days he had failed her, had wavered in his allegiance. But he had come back.

She was his fate. How often he had said it! And so he would return. She was sure he would return. And when he came, what then?

*   *   *

Life at Uncle Edward's was, as he had predicted, a very quiet affair indeed, but Maud slipped into it very easily, with a sense of comfort at her heart. It had a healing effect upon her.

At Uncle Edward's suggestion, she wrote once a week to Jake. It was not easy to write, but when her uncle remarked that the young man would probably come tearing hell-for-leather across England to find out what was the matter if she didn't, she thought it the wiser course to follow.

Her letters were very brief, very formal, and the letters she received in reply were equally so. She was sure that they were penned in that cheerless little den of his that faced north and overlooked the stable-yard.

Not far from her uncle's house, at the corner of

a busy street, there stood an old grey church. The doors were always open, and one day she decided to go in.

It was the first visit of many. The place was infinitely peaceful, full of silence and soft shadows. A red light burned before the altar, and there were always beautiful flowers upon it.

When Sunday came, she suggested to Uncle Edward that she should accompany him to Evensong. He was delighted with the proposal, and they sat near the door.

It was a beautiful service. The man who preached was young and spoke with the absolute simplicity of a man who speaks from his heart.

"Let your lights be burning," were the words he first uttered, and then he began to talk of Love— Love Divine, Unconquerable, Eternal—Love that stoops, but is never small—Love that soars, but is never out of reach.

"We do not know the power of Love," he said. "We only know that it is invincible and undying, the very Essence of God.

"We may not all of us be able to believe; but we can all have Love. Nothing counts in the same way. However blind we may be, we can keep that one lamp burning in the darkness, giving light to the outcast, and guiding the feet of the wanderers."

While he was speaking, the lights in the body of the church went down, and a red flame before the altar shone clear and unchanging in the gloom. Maud's eyes were drawn instantly to it.

She sat with bated breath, almost as one watching a miracle. And by some strange telepathy the man in the pulpit became aware of it also. He turned towards it.

"Look at that light!" he said. "It is kept burning perpetually, the symbol of undying worship, undying Love. Everyone may keep such a light as that burning always. The spark is ours for the kindling.

"It is not faith or hope that the soul needs above all things. It is Love, the power of Love, and the power to create Love.

"There are people whom everyone loves. They are the people who realise what Love means, who give and give, without measure, not counting the cost, rejoicing only in the power to give, till it all comes back to them a thousand-fold.

"It is then that the ploughman overtakes the reaper, for ploughman and reaper are one."

When Maud lay down that night, those words were still running in her mind.

She slept sooner than usual, but the echoes of that quiet voice still followed her down through the deeps of slumber, till she dreamed that she was back before that shining altar.

And a radiance that was not of the earth was all about her. She saw that it came from a red lamp above her, the symbol of undying Love.

As in a trance she waited, for the wonder of the thing held her spellbound. And while she waited she became aware of someone else in the holy place, someone who moved stealthily, as if half-afraid. And turning, by the light of that revealing glow, she saw her husband, with that look of silent misery in his eyes.

It pierced her then as it had not pierced her be-

fore. She was conscious of an almost fierce impulse
to comfort him. She went near to him, and gave
him both her hands.

Even as she did so, the look in his eyes changed.
She saw a deep, still fire come into them. It seemed
to be reflected from the red lamp above. He moved
forward into the glow.

Suddenly her own eyes were opened, and she
knew that he loved her . . . he loved her. . . .

Then she awoke with a palpitating heart, and
realised that it was a dream.

* * *

Not till she had been in her uncle's house for
close upon four weeks did Maud brace herself to
speak to him of her mother.

Her uncle heard her out, but so grimly that at
length, feeling that she was presenting the matter
quite inadequately, she gave him her mother's letter, which was an hysterical appeal to read.

He shook his head at first, but finally, as she
pressed it upon him, almost tearfully, he took and
read the letter. Then, while she anxiously watched
him, he tore it across and flung it back to her over
the table.

"Pshaw!" he said. "The woman's a hypocrite, a
confounded imposter. I know her. You don't. Leave
her alone and let her sink."

With that he stumped angrily from the room with
beetling brows and fiery eyes.

Maud sat very still after his departure. She had
known in her heart that it was hopeless to appeal
to him, but there was no doubt in her mind that
matters were desperate. She had not wanted to write

to Charlie, but it seemed now that she had no choice.

She sat over the letter for the greater part of the afternoon, and when it was finished at last she felt utterly dissatisfied with it. She had an urgent desire to tear it up. But she could not face the writing of another. With a weary sigh she closed and stamped the envelope.

It was then that there fell a step outside the drawing-room door, and Uncle Edward's discreet, elderly maid-servant peeped in.

Maud turned in her chair.

"What is it, Martha?"

Martha was about to explain, but a man's figure stood in the opening.

"Hullo!" said Charlie, with a smile of gay effrontery. "May I come in?"

Maud sat for a second or two as one in a trance, and stared at him. It was as if the afternoon's labour had suddenly taken concrete form.

He did not wait for her greeting, but came lightly forward with hands outstretched.

"Ah, Queen of the Roses," he said, "what a peculiarly unbecoming setting you have chosen for yourself! Why, what is that? A letter to me? How many times a day do you write them?"

With a lithe, elastic movement, he drew her to her feet, held her a moment, looking at her, then bent his smiling, swarthy face to hers.

She awoke then, came out of her trance, drew swiftly back from him.

"Oh, Charlie, is it . . . is it really you? You . . . how you startled me!"

He let her go, as always, at her desire, but with a faint monkeyish grimace of disapproval.

"You were always easily shocked. But on this occasion I assure you there is no need. I found myself in the neighbourhood, and thought it would be the correct thing to pay you a morning call."

"Sit down!" she said, mustering her dignity with an immense effort. "And I will tell you why I have been writing to you."

"Wouldn't it save trouble to show me the letter?" he suggested, with easy audacity. "Or have you decided, now that you have had a further opportunity of considering my personal charms, that you really can't?"

She flushed at the implied suggestion.

"You can read the letter if you like. It is on business."

She held it out to him, and he sank upon one knee to receive it.

"*Merci, ma belle Reine!* Do you wish me to read it in your august presence?"

"Please," she said.

He sat facing her, and read it.

She watched his mobile brows as his eyes travelled over the page. She saw amusement turn to humour and humour to merriment on his face. When he looked up at her at length he was laughing.

"You write as a serf appealing to a feudal lord," he said. "Did you mean to write like that?"

She shook her head at him gravely.

"It is not a laughing matter."

"What I am laughing at is," he rejoined, still

smiling, with a hint of derision. "By the way, have you heard from our worthy cow-puncher lately?"

She flinched sharply, before she was aware. Her whole body tingled with a sudden, burning blush.

And Saltash laughed again wickedly.

"I saw him yesterday. He was in a fiendish temper for some reason or other. Naturally I asked after you, when he was expecting you back. What do you think he said?"

"What?" Maud breathed the word through lips that panted. Her heart was beating violently, she knew not why.

Saltash's dark face seemed to exult over her agitation.

"He said, 'I guess I shall go, shortly, and fetch her back, my lord.' I wondered if you were aware of his amiable intention. There was the most deadly air of determination about him. I thought you might like to know."

Maud's face was no longer burning; she was white to the lips. But she turned from the subject with composure.

"How did you know where to find me?"

He laughed teasingly.

"You are curiously curious, Maud of the Roses. Don't you yet realise that I always know everything?"

She smiled faintly.

"Do you mind coming back to the subject of that letter? If Giles Sheppard goes under, my mother will go too."

Saltash raised his brows in amused interrogation.

"Oh, does that follow? I should abandon the sinking ship if I were Mrs Sheppard. She has nothing to gain by sticking to it."

Maud received the remark in silence. He leaned forward, his dark face still smiling.

"Do you know I love you for that?" he said. *"Chere Reine des fleurs,* Lady of the golden silences! Do you ever say what you really think?"

She shook her head.

"Charlie, I am learning . . . very slowly . . . a hard lesson. Don't . . . please . . . . make it any harder for me!"

"What?" he said. "You are really going back to him?"

She put up a hand to her face, almost as if she would hide it from him.

"I don't know, yet, what I shall do. But I do know that it would be wrong not to go back."

"Mais vraiment!" he protested. "Is life so simple as that? How do you arrive at that conclusion? Do you follow always the easy path of virtue?"

Maud's head was bent; she did not attempt to answer him.

He got up abruptly and came to her.

"Good-bye, Maud of the Roses!"

She started slightly.

"You are going?"

"Yes, I am going. I have received my discharge. My faithful service is at end, unless, or may I say until, that message comes to call me back."

He bent towards her.

"Even I cannot wait forever," he said. "Do you

know I stood by the orchard gate in the rain for two hours on the day of the races? You knew I was there, yet you never came."

She raised her head sharply, moved by something in his tone.

"But how could I? How could I?" she said. "Besides, Jake knew."

"Yes, Jake knew," he laughed. "He saw me that night of moonshine. He nearly challenged me. And then he changed his mind and passed on. I conclude it didn't suit him to quarrel with me. But what of that? He was bound to know someday."

She clasped her hands tightly together.

"If he knew all . . . he would shoot you," she said, with a sudden hard shudder.

But Saltash only laughed again, and touched a wisp of her hair.

"I don't think so, Queen of the Roses. I think he would have pity on my innocence. The point is that you choose bondage with him rather than freedom with me. And that being so, I can only bow to your ruling. Once more—good-bye."

She parted her hands with an effort, and gave him one of them.

"What about . . . my mother, Charlie?" she said.

He pressed her fingers lightly.

"I commend her to the kind care of her worthy son-in-law."

She raised her eyes to his almost incredulously.

"You are going to . . . to let them be ruined?"

He smiled at her, flashing his strange eyes.

"It wouldn't do for you to be under an obligation, a personal obligation to me, would it? Jake might object."

She rose quickly and stood facing him.

"Charlie, please don't jest!" she urged him, her voice low and very earnest.

"It rests with you," he said, "whether I jest my way to the devil or whether I live a godly, righteous, and sober life. If it is to be the latter, then I am quite prepared to fulfill my virtuous devoirs to my prospective mother-in-law.

"But if the former is to be my portion, well, I don't think even St Peter himself would have saddled himself with anyone else's. That is the position, *chere Reine*. Do you understand?"

Yes, she understood. There was nothing complex in the situation. She stood looking at him, her hand still in his.

"Then I cannot look upon you as a . . . friend?" she said at last, almost under her breath.

He smiled upon her, a sudden, baffling smile.

"But ask yourself that question, Maud of the Roses! You will find the answer there in your own heart, if you seek for it."

She quivered at the words, feeling the subtle attraction of the man even against her will.

"You have refused to help me."

He bent towards her, his dark face glowing.

"I offer you all I have," he said. "It is your own, to do with as you will. But you must take all or leave all."

His speech quickened to sudden vehemence.

"You love me! Why do you cling to your prison

when the door is standing wide? Now is your time to escape, if ever. I will take all your cares, all your burdens. You shall be free as air. Only now that the door is open, come!"

"Yes. I should shut the door another time if I were you," a gruff voice commented behind them. "It's a rash thing, young man, to leave the door open when you're talking confidences. What are you doing in this house?"

Both Maud and Saltash had faced round at the first sentence. Uncle Edward, his eyes very bright under the beetling brows, stumped up to them with the air of an old watchdog. He rasped his throat ferociously as he came.

"Who may you be?" he demanded.

"This is Lord Saltash," Maud said, in a low voice.

"Oh! Lord Saltash!" The old man turned back to him with a sound like a snarl. "Yes, I have heard of you before. You were corespondent in the Cressady divorce case a few years back."

Saltash laughed again with easy nonchalance.

"You have a good memory, sir. If it served you as it should, you will also recall the fact that the case was dismissed."

"I remember—all the facts," said Uncle Edward, with ominous deliberation. "And as it is not my custom to admit men of your stamp into my house, you will oblige me by quitting it without delay."

Saltash turned to Maud.

"I am sorry you have been caught in such bad company. Pray explain that I came uninvited!"

Uncle Edward followed him to the door, and

grimly watched his exit. Then still more grimly he came tramping back.

"And now to pick a bone with you, my niece!" he said.

She stood erect, facing him. Her face was very pale, but her eyes were quite unflinching. There was about her a majesty of demeanour that might have deterred a less determined man than Uncle Edward. But he stood upon his own ground and grappled with the situation quite undismayed. He was, moreover, very angry.

"You young hussy!" he said, bringing out his words with immense emphasis. "How dare you have your lover here? Thought you were safe, eh? Thought I shouldn't know? Oh, you're like the rest of 'em, crafty as an eel. What's the meaning of it, eh? What have you got to say for yourself?"

She did not attempt to answer him, and he stood looking down at her, grievously resentful, striving to select a weapon enough sharp to pierce her calm.

"I thought you were to be trusted," he said. "Goodness knows why. You didn't seem to have any leaven of your mother about you. But I see now I was wrong. You are just your mother over again. But if you think you are going to pursue an intrigue with that aristocratic blackguard in my house, you are mistaken.

"No doubt I'm very old-fashioned and strait-laced. But there it is. I object. I object strongly. The man's a liar and a thief and a scoundrel. Don't you know it, eh? Haven't you found him out yet?"

He stopped so pointedly for an answer that she

could not maintain her silence longer. She moved a little, turned her head slightly without raising her eyes, and spoke.

"I know him very well. But . . . forgive me, Uncle Edward, I can't discuss him with you. I . . . I am sorry you thought it necessary to insult him."

"Insult him!" Uncle Edward's anger boiled afresh. "Didn't I catch the hound making love to you? Here in my house, where I have lived decently and respectably for over fifty years! Didn't I actually hear him trying to tempt you from your husband and your duty? And you were calmly permitting it.

"Look here, young woman! I've been too kind to you. You've had too much liberty, too much indulgence, too much of your own way. You married in a hurry against my judgment. But, by Heaven, since you are married, you shall stick to your bargain!

"You take a pen now, do you hear?—and a sheet of paper, and write to your husband this minute, and ask him to come and join you here! I won't be surety for you any longer. Tell him to come tomorrow!"

But Maud only stiffened as she sat, making no movement to comply. She looked like a marble statue of Despair.

"Are you going to do as I tell you?" he said.

She glanced up at him momentarily.

"I think we will wait till tomorrow."

He stamped a furious foot.

"Will we, indeed, madam? Well, you may wait as long as you please; but I tell you this: if you don't write that letter instantly, I shall go straight to the post office round the corner and send your husband a telegram to summon him at once.

"He will be here by the morning, if I know him. And then I shall tell him exactly why I sent for him. So now you can take your choice. Which is it to be?"

He had moved her at last. Maud rose to her feet with a suddenness that was almost suggestive of pain.

"You would never do such a thing!" she said. "You could not be so . . . so wickedly cruel!"

He snapped his jaws like an angry terrier.

"Oh, that would be wicked, would it? You have some odd ideas of morals; that's all I can say. But wicked or cruel, it's what I mean to do. So take your choice, and be quick about it! For I shan't go back on what I've said."

"I can't decide anything just now," she said at last, and she knew that her voice trembled painfully. "Please, please let us wait a little! There is really no need to send for Jake. Lord Saltash has gone, and he will not come back."

"Don't tell me!" said Uncle Edward truculently. "Even if he doesn't, how am I to be sure that you won't take it into your head to go to him? No, my niece, I've heard too much. Why, he'd have had his arm round you in another second. If I'd waited another three seconds, he'd have been kissing you. And not for the first time, I'll be bound."

The hot colour rushed to Maud's face; she turned sharply aside.

"Ha! That touches you, does it?" snarled Uncle

Edward, with ferocious triumph. "I guessed as much. Now which is it to be? Are you going to write that letter?"

It was hopeless to carry the discussion further. A burning wave of anger went through her, anger that buoyed her up above despair, stimulating her to a fierce rebellion. She drew herself to her full height and faced him with supreme defiance.

"I will not write that letter!" she said. "I will not be forced into a false position. If you are tired of me, I will go. I will not stay to be insulted!"

She went to her room, outwardly calm, inwardly raging, and with hands that trembled she began to pack. Uncle Edward had made it impossible for her to stay.

No one came near her during those evening hours. The daylight waned, and she realised that it was nearing the dinner-hour. Then suddenly it came to her that she could not face her uncle again. She must make some excuse.

Her work was done; she rang the bell.

After a pause Martha came to her. There was a scared look on the woman's face. She seemed half-afraid to meet Maud's eyes.

"Did you ring, ma'am?" she enquired.

"Yes, Martha," she said. "I have packed everything up, and I am going away. I want you please to call a cab now, at once, to take me away before my uncle comes downstairs. I will write him a note while you are gone. Please, Martha, be as quick as you can!"

The sympathy in Martha's eyes became a sort of tragic friendliness.

"I knew as you wouldn't stay, ma'am, not after the way he hollered at you. I'll go at once, it won't take me five minutes. But I think he'll be sorry to lose you."

"I can't help that," Maud said. "It is quite impossible for me to stay. He will know why. But I will write him a note all the same."

And when Martha had gone, she sat down and scribbled two notes.

The first she addressed to her uncle:

Dear Uncle Edward,
    I do not think you will be greatly surprised at my leaving you. After what has passed, I could not stay. I am very sorry for what has happened, but I suppose it had to be. I wish I could thank you for all your kindness to me, but I know this is not the time. So I will only say good-bye.

Yours,
Maud.

The second note consisted of one sentence only: "I am going to my mother. *Maud.*" And when she had written it she picked up a tiny packet of tissue paper that lay beside her and dropped it into the envelope with the note.

She addressed the envelope to Lord Saltash, Burchester Castle, and later she sealed and registered it, stopping at a post office to send it on its way. She believed it would reach its destination almost as soon as he did.

And that packet, that tiny object wrapped in tissue paper, would convey its own message. No further words were needed.

She herself went for the night to a small hotel in a back street that was not far from her uncle's house. There would be a train in the early morning. She would not travel by night.

Her sleep was fitful and troubled, broken repeatedly by the persistent chime of a church clock. Towards the morning she slept and dreamed again that strangely haunting dream of the flower-decked altar and the red, shining lamp above.

For a space she held herself aloof from the dream, refusing to yield to it. But at length it seemed to her that someone came and took her hand, drawing her forward, and she had no choice.

Straight into the wondrous glow she went, and presently she knelt before those flowers of dazzling purity. The quiet hand still held hers in a calm and comforting grasp. She felt that she would have been frightened but for that sustaining hold.

And then suddenly she saw that the candles also were burning upon the altar, knew that she was kneeling there with Jake, and heard a voice above their heads, very low and clear, that seemed to be speaking to their hearts:

"Those whom God hath joined together, let no man put asunder. . . ."

And turning, she found Jake's eyes upon her, alight with adoration. . . .

She awoke with a gasping cry to a seething, passionate regret. Because in those first wild moments she knew with an awful certainty that her feet were set upon the downward path, and she could never turn back.

*   *   *

The entrance hall of the Anchor was empty when Maud entered, lit by one flaring gas-jet. The place looked bare and poverty-stricken, almost squalid. The rugs were gone from the floor, the pictures from the walls.

The door swung closed behind her, and she felt as if she stood inside a prison. The office window was shut, and no sound came from any quarter.

The utter solitude of the place began to possess her like an evil dream. She stood as one under a spell, afraid to move. And then, quite suddenly, she heard a step.

The impulse came to her then to flee, but she did not obey it. She stood stiffly, waiting. Even if it was Giles Sheppard himself, she would meet him before she went out into the dripping dark outside.

She heard the jingle of spurs upon the stones of the hall, caught one glance of a sun-burnt, dominant face and hair that shone like burnished copper in the light; and then she was tottering blindly backwards, groping, groping for the door by which she might escape.

He came to her before she could open it, and in a moment she became rigid, as one fascinated into passivity. He took her ice-cold hands and held them.

"Why, Maud! Maud!" he said, in the tone of one who would comfort a child.

A great shiver went through her at his touch; but she stood speechless. His face swam before her shrinking vision. She felt sick and faint.

"Snakes!" he said. "You're perished with cold. Why didn't you tell me you were coming? Come along into the office! There's no one there; and I'll soon have a fire for you. You lean on me. It'll be all right."

His arm went round her; he supported her strongly. The warmth of his body sent a faint glow through her. Almost without knowing it, she leaned upon him.

He took her into the deserted office, put her into a chair by the empty fireplace, lighted the gas, then knelt to kindle the fire. The wood was damp, and he coaxed it to burn, blowing at the unwilling flame, his head in the smoke.

"That's better," he said softly at length. "Now I'm going to give you something you'll hate, but I reckon you'll take it to please me."

He still knelt beside her, but there was no hint of authority, no possessiveness, in his bearing. Rather, there was about him something curious which was almost like humility.

She watched him dumbly as he pulled a small glass flask out of his pocket and withdrew the cork. He turned to her as he did it, and for an instant she met his eyes. The old, hot glow was wholly gone from him. She missed it with an odd sense of shock.

Only kindness shone out at her; only friendliness was in the clasp of the hand he laid on hers.

"You'll take it?" he said, in his voice of soft persuasion. "It's raw spirit; but it's not going to do you any harm. Just a drop, and then I'll feel easier about you!"

He was pressing it gently upon her; and she could not refuse. She took the flask from him and drank a burning drain.

"Has it gone?" said Jake.

She nodded silently, feeling the glow of the spirit spreading through her veins, and the deadly coldness of her heart giving place to it.

He smiled upon her, his pleasant, sudden smile. He bent again to the fire, blowing at it persistently, patiently, till it shot up into a blaze.

She watched him as one in a dream, a dream from which all nightmare horror had been magically banished. This . . . this was the old Jake to whom she had once turned in trouble, in whose arms she had sobbed out her misery and despair.

This was Jake the friend, into whose keeping she had given her life.

He straightened himself again, coughing a little. She caught again the gleam of the red-brown eyes, seeking hers.

"Better now?" he asked her.

She bent her head.

"Yes, I am all right now. You . . . you . . . I didn't expect to see you here."

"Guess it was a mutual surprise," said Jake. "What brought you, anyway?"

Her heart gave a sudden quick throb of dismay. Actually she had forgotten the desperate resolution that had urged her for so long. She turned her face quickly from him.

"I . . . came . . . to . . . to see my mother," she faltered.

He raised his brows momentarily.

"She wasn't expecting you."

"No." She felt her cheeks burning, and strove still further to avoid his look. "No. It . . . was a . . . surprise visit."

She was silent a moment.

Then an amazing thing happened. Jake's hand was suddenly laid upon her knee, pressing it reassuringly.

"Well," he said in his casual drawl, "I reckon you've come in the nick of time so far as your mother is concerned. Your amiable step-father has cleared out, bag and baggage, and left her to face the music.

"He pawned everything he could lay his dirty hands on first, and the place is empty except for the old ostler who is serving behind the bar till further orders."

"Oh, Jake!" Startled, Maud turned back to him. "And what is my mother doing?"

There was a faintly humorous twist about Jake's lips as he made reply.

"Your mother has gone to bed in hysterics. I came down this morning as soon as I got the news of Sheppard's departure, and tried to persuade her to come along to the stables; but she wouldn't hear of it."

He had not been home all day; he had received no message. The thought darted through Maud with a suddenness that nearly made her gasp with relief. He did not know of Uncle Edward's summons.

And then she remembered that it must be awaiting him, and her heart sank again.

"You're shivering still," said Jake gently.

"It's nothing," she answered. "It's nothing. You . . . you didn't get . . . a telegram from Uncle Edward . . . last night?"

"I?" said Jake. "No. What should he wire to me for?"

She hesitated a second, then feverishly faced the danger that menaced her.

"You . . . I expect you will find a message waiting for you. We . . . we had a disagreement yesterday. That's why I came away."

Jake's brows met abruptly.

"Hasn't he been treating you properly?"

"Oh, it's not that. I . . . I can't tell you what it was. But . . . he said he should wire to you to . . . to go to Liverpool."

Maud's hands clasped each other very tightly. She was striving with all her strength for composure. But she could not bring herself to look him in the face.

"And so you came away," Jake said slowly.

She nodded, swallowing down her agitation.

"I didn't want to meet you . . . like that. I didn't know what was in the telegram."

Jake's fingers patted her knee gently.

"And so you came back here for refuge! You needn't be afraid. Uncle Edward may go to blazes. I shan't read that telegram. And now that that matter is disposed of, you'll maybe like to go and see your mother."

She met his eyes with a feeling that she could do no less.

"You're very good," she said, with an effort.

"Then it's the cheapest form of goodness I know," he said. "Are you going to spend the night here along with your mother?"

He seemed bent upon making things easy for her. His attitude amazed her. She kept asking herself again and again if this could be the man from whom she had fled in bitterness of spirit all those weeks ago, and she hesitated to answer his question.

"Maybe you'd sooner stay here," he said, in his quiet voice. "It's up to you to decide. Guess I shan't interfere any with your movements."

His one hand still lay on her knee. It pressed upon her a little as though seeking to convey something that she was slow to grasp.

Her doubt subsided under the steady touch. She suddenly knew beyond all questioning that she stood on solid ground. Yet it was not without difficulty that she answered him.

"I think . . . perhaps . . . for tonight . . . I will stay with her."

Jake nodded, with his face to the flames.

She looked at his bent head, conscious of a new distress. How was she going to repay him for this, his goodness to her? He was trusting her blindly. He had refused to let his eyes be opened. For she knew he would keep his word about that telegram. Jake always kept his word.

Her distress grew, became almost unbearable. She saw herself in a new and horrible light, and shrank in anguish of soul from the revelation.

Jake was not looking at her. He seemed unaware of her agitation. After a moment he took his hand away and rose.

"Don't let your mother take too much out of you!" he said. "Have a meal and turn in as early as you can! Guess you're needing a good rest."

"Yes, I am tired."

Jake was silent again. Then, in a curiously hesitating voice, he said:

"I just want to tell you that you're not to be scared of me any more. Reckon you've had a hell of a time all your life, but it's to come to an end right now. For the future, you do the asking and I the giving.

"You're the boss, and don't forget it. I'm your man, not your master, and I'll behave accordingly. Guess I'll even lie down and let you kick me if it'll make you happy!"

Maud was gazing at him in open amazement long before he had finished his astounding speech. The slow utterance, half-sad, half-humorous, was spoken with the full weight of the man's strength of purpose.

There was a touch of the superb about him. But every word seemed to pierce her with a deeper pain, pain that was well-nigh unendurable.

As he uttered the last deliberate sentence, she rose quickly with a gesture of protest. She could bear no more.

"Jake, you . . . you . . . you hurt me!" she stammered incoherently.

He put out a hand to her.

"No, no! That was not my intention."

It was almost as though he pleaded with her for some species of clemency. She was sure she read entreaty in the red-brown eyes. But she could not lay her hand in his.

She could not, she could not! She stood before him, panting, speechless, shaken to the very foundations of her being.

His hands fell.

"I just want you to be happy, that's all. Happy after your own notions of happiness. Maybe there ain't room for me in the general scheme of things. If that's so, I reckon I'll stay outside."

He turned aside with the words.

"I'm going now. So long!" he said, and left her, striding away in his square, purposeful fashion without a backwards glance.

Only when he was gone did it flash upon her that this . . . this . . . was her dream come true. All unknowing, wholly without intention, he had opened her eyes. And she knew that he loved her, he loved her!

Maud went and sat with her mother, who was horrified when she told her she was going to stay with Jake and refuse Saltash's offer of marriage.

Her mother argued with her and said she was a fool not to wait until she saw Saltash, who was returning in the morning.

But above her mother's warnings, above all the trouble and the tumult of her soul, she heard a voice within, clear, insistent, indomitable.

"Love is only gained by Love. We must pour out all we have to win it, purge out hearts of all selfish desire, sanctify ourselves by the complete renunciation of self, before the perfect gift can be ours."

The perfect gift! The perfect gift! She had almost ceased to believe in it. But that night she dreamed that she had it in her grasp.

Chapter Nine

A woman's figure clad in a streaming water-proof stood on the step, and in a low voice asked for Lord Saltash.

"Will you walk in, madam?" Billings said, with a deep bow.

She entered and stood on the mat. He took her umbrella and set it aside.

"Will you permit me to remove your water-proof, madam?" he suggested.

She seemed to hesitate, but in a moment yielded.

"But I can only stay a few moments. Please tell him so!"

"Quite so, madam!" Billings was deftly removing the wet garment. "Up in the music-room, if you please, madam."

She followed him up the dim hall. They ascended the grand staircase in solemn procession, and reached the music-room door.

The great room was dim and shadowy, heavy with some mysterious, Eastern fragrance that hung in the air like incense. It was lighted by two fires that burned without flame and a red-shaded lamp that shed a mysterious arc of light far away by the piano.

"His lordship will not keep you waiting long," Billings said.

"Is he out?" Maud asked quickly.

"He has been out, madam. He came in wet through and is changing. He begged very particularly that you would drink a cup of coffee while you awaited him."

He indicated a divan, but Maud remained on her feet. The atmosphere of the place disturbed her. It seemed to be charged with subtleties that baffled her, making her vaguely uneasy.

She had come in answer to a message accompanying a great bunch of violets that had reached her that morning. She had not wanted to come; but for this once it seemed imperative that she should meet him face to face, and explain that which she felt no written words could ever express.

She had sent him her rash summons, and he had replied by that bunch of violets and the request that she would come to him, since he did not wish to risk interruption from *"Madame la mere."*

On this point she had been fully in accord with him, and she had sent back word that she would come in the afternoon just to speak with him for a few minutes.

She had hoped that he would gather from that that since the sending of her summons she had repented of her madness.

It would not be an easy interview, she was sure; but she was not afraid of Charlie. She hated the thought of hurting him all the more because she did not fear him. He would let her go; oh, yes, he would let her go. He had never sought to hold her against her will.

She stood before the fire, absently watching the servant as he busied himself over the coffee, till the aromatic scent of it suddenly brought her out of her reverie.

"Oh, thank you," she said. "I don't think I will have any. I have only come for five minutes' talk with Lord Saltash."

"His lordship particularly desired that you would take a cup, madam," the man replied. "It is a very special Egyptian brew."

She did not want the coffee, but it seemed ungracious to refuse it. She took the cup and set it on the mantelpiece.

"It should be drunk very hot, madam," said Billings persuasively. "Will you be so very kind, madam, as to taste it and tell me if it is to your liking?"

She hesitated momentarily, but it was too small a matter to refuse. She took the cup by its slender handle and put it to her lips. Instantly it was as if a warm current of life went through her, a fine, golden thread of delight.

She looked at Billings and smiled.

"It is delicious."

"The second cup is generally considered even better than the first, madam," he said.

"Oh, I won't take more than one, thank you," she said.

And Billings retired, closing the door soundlessly behind him.

Maud lifted the cup again to her lips. Its fragrance pervaded all her senses. It was unlike anything she knew, and in some subtle fashion it made her think of palms and orange groves, and the strong sunshine of the East.

It presented before her mind a vivid picture of beauties that she had never seen. She drank again; and again that strange sense of dawning bliss came to her. It was like the coming of a tropic morning after a long, black night.

She drained the cup and set it down. It seemed a little strange to her that her hand should be trembling as she did so, for all her misgivings had vanished. She had stepped as it were into a garden of delight.

A strange, unearthly happiness was here. It was as if her life had been suddenly and mysteriously filled to the brim with all that she could desire.

The only thing lacking was music. She looked across at the grand piano lighted with that one red lamp, and a haunting memory came to her. She saw the altar and the glow of the undying flame before it; but the flowers, the white lilies of purity, where were they?

A vague distress came to her, filtering as it were through locked senses, dispelling the golden rapture, dimming her dream. She moved over the polished floor, drawn by the red arc of light. She reached the piano. She stood before it. And then her dream changed.

The vision of the altar faded, faded. She slipped down before the gleaming keys. She struck a soft, sweet chord. And with it the former magic took her.

As of old, she never knew quite when he came to her. She only realised very suddenly that he was there. His dark face gleamed down at her in the lamplight. His odd eyes sent a mocking invitation into hers.

Again her vision was swept away. Her hands fell from the piano and were caught in the same instant into his.

"Oh, Charlie!" she gasped incoherently.

He drew her close, laughing at her with half-teasing tenderness.

"Queen of all the Roses!"

But she hung back from him. It was almost as if something dragged her back.

"I . . . I have something to say to you. I came to say it. What was it? Oh, what was it?"

His swarthy face was bending nearer, nearer. She saw the humorous lift of his black brows.

"You have said it. There is nothing left to say. There will never again be any need for words between us two."

He laughed at her again with a kind of kingly indulgence. His arms went round her, pressing her to him, ignoring her last, quivering effort to resist. His lips suddenly found her own.

And then it was that her eyes were opened, and her memory came back. In a flash of anguished understanding she was brought face to face with the realities of life.

She knew that she had been emmeshed in a dream of evil delight, drawn unaccountably, by some hidden, devilish strategy, to the very edge of that precipice that she had striven so desperately to avoid.

In that moment she would have torn herself free, but her strength was gone. Her body felt leaden and powerless; her throat too numb to utter any protest. Her visions had all fallen away from her, but she thought she heard the roar of the whirlpool below.

And through all, she was madly conscious of the lips that pressed her own, the arms that drew her closer, always closer, to the gulf.

She thought that her senses were leaving her, so utterly helpless had she become. An awful cloud seemed to be hanging over her, slowly, slowly, descending. Faintly she tried to pray for deliverance, but his lips stifled the prayer.

Against her will, as one horribly compelled, she knew that she returned his kiss.

Then she was lying on the low divan with Charlie beside her, holding her, calling her his queen, his captured angel, his wife.

She did not know exactly what happened afterwards, for a great darkness took her. She only knew that she was suddenly lifted and borne away. She only heard the rush of the whirlpool as it closed over her head.

Something was waking her. Someone seemed to be knocking on the outer door of her brain. She came back to consciousness as one returning from a far, far journey that yet had occupied but a very brief space of time.

An inner sense of urgency awoke and responded to that outer knocking.

As through a maze of disconnected impressions she heard a voice.

"I give you ten seconds, my lord," it said. "Just
—ten—seconds."

The words were absolutely quiet, but the deadly
determination of them smote upon her like the call
of a trumpet. She started up.

The next instant she was staring about her in
utter bewilderment.

She was in a room she had never seen before,
oak-panelled, lighted by a domed skylight. It was
furnished with bizarre Eastern luxury. The couch
on which she lay was a nest of tiger-skins.

But she saw these details vaguely. The voice she
had heard had made all else of no importance. It
had spoken close to her, but it was not in the room
with her, and she could not for the moment tell
whence it had come.

She could only listen with starting eyes fixed on
the stuffed skin of a cobra poised on a small table
nearby, as if ready to strike.

She even fancied for a moment that the thing
was alive, and then realised with a passing relief that
it had been converted into the stem of a reading
lamp.

Again the voice came. It was counting slowly,
with the utmost regularity. But it was not allowed
to continue. Saltash's voice, quick and imperious,
broke in upon it.

"Be quiet, you damned fool! If you murder me,
you'll only be sorry afterwards. I have told you I
don't know where she is."

"You have told me a lie, my lord."

Grim as fate came the answer, and following it a
movement that turned her sick with fear.

She sprang to her feet with a wild cry.

"Jake! Jake! I am here! Jake . . . come to me!"

She threw herself against the panelling of the wall in a frenzy of terrors and beat upon it fiercely, frantically. It was through the panelling that those sinister words had reached her.

But it resisted her wild efforts. She beat in vain.

"Oh, Jake!" she cried again, and broke into agonised sobbing. "Jake, where are you?"

And then she heard his voice again, short this time and commanding.

"Let her out, my lord! The game is up."

"Trust a woman to give it away!" said Saltash, and laughed a cold, hard laugh.

Then the panelling against which she stood suddenly yielded, and slid back. She found herself standing on the threshold of the music-room, close to one of the carved fireplaces. And facing her stood her husband.

All her life she was to remember the look he wore.

Saltash was nearer still, but she scarcely saw him. She went past him, sobbing, inarticulate, unnerved. She stretched out trembling, beseeching hands to the man in whose eyes she read the lust of murder. She cried aloud to him in her agony!

"Take me away! Come away! Be merciful this once . . . only this once! Jake! Jake!"

She reached him, she clung to him; she would have knelt to him. But he thrust his left arm round her, forcibly holding her up.

He did not speak to her, did not, she believed,

so much as look at her. His eyes were fixed with a terrible intensity upon the man beyond her. His attitude was strained and unyielding.

The untamed ferocity of the wilds was in every line of him, in every tense muscle. Ruthlessness, lawlessness, savagery unshackled, fiercely eager, beat in every pulse, every sinew of his frame. She felt as if she were holding back a furious animal from his prey.

But she clung to him closer and closer, seeking to pinion the murderous right hand that was thrust away out of her reach.

She heard another laugh from Saltash, but she did not dare to turn. And then came a sound like the click of a spring trap.

The tension went suddenly out of Jake. He relaxed and with a certain roughness took his hand from his pocket and grasped her by the shoulders. His eyes came from behind her and looked straight into hers. And she knew without turning her head that her own hour of reckoning had come.

They were alone!

For many, many seconds he looked at her so, with a red-hot glow in his eyes that seemed as though it would burn its way to her most secret soul. She endured it with a desperate courage.

If he had caught her by the throat she would not have flinched. But his hold, though insistent, was without violence. And at last, very, very slowly, he let her go.

"I guess that ends it," he said.

"What do you mean?" Through quivering lips

she asked the question. She felt as if an icy wind had suddenly caught her. She was cold from head to foot.

He made a slight gesture as of one indicating the obvious, and turned away. She saw his square figure moving away from her, and a terrible fear went through her.

Her very heart felt frozen within her. She tried to speak, to utter his name; but her throat only worked spasmodically, making no sound.

He reached the door, opened it, and then, as if he could not help it, he looked back at her. And in that moment, with frantic effort, she burst the bonds that held her. She threw out her arms in wild entreaty.

"Jake!" she gasped. "Jake! Don't . . . don't leave me!"

He stopped, but he did not return. There was a curious look on his face. He seemed to stand irresolute. She began to move towards him, but found herself trembling too much to walk.

She tottered to the mantelpiece for support. But she still looked towards him, still tremulously entreated him.

"Jake, you . . . you don't understand! You never will understand if you leave me now. I'm going under . . . I'm going under! Jake . . . save me!"

She bowed her head suddenly upon her hands, and stood quivering. She had made her last piteous effort to escape from the toils that held her. Nothing but a miracle could save her now. Nothing but the power of that Love.

Seconds passed. She thought that he had gone,

had abandoned her to her fate, left her to the mercy of a man who would compass her ruin.

And she wondered in her agony if she could muster sufficient strength to flee from that evil place and snatch her own deliverance down on the dark, lonely shore, where no one could ever drag her back again.

Then, very suddenly, a hand touched her, closed upon her arm. It was as if a current of electricity ran through her. She turned with a great start.

Jake's eyes, very level, quite inscrutable, looked straight into hers.

"I guess we'll be getting along home," he said.

His hand urged her steadily, indomitably. He led her, speechless, from the room, supporting her when she faltered, but never hesitating or suffering her to pause.

At last she was out in the gathering darkness and the rain was beating in her face.

It was then that her weakness came back to her, a sense of terrible exhaustion that gave her the feeling of dragging heavy chains. She fought against it desperately, dreading every instant lest he should misinterpret her dragging steps and leave her.

An overwhelming drowsiness was creeping over her, numbing all her faculties. She struggled to fling it off, but could not. It crowded upon her like an evil dream. She staggered, stumbled, almost fell.

"Reckon you're tired," Jake said.

She answered him with a rush of tears.

"I can't help it! Really I can't help it! I . . . I believe I must be ill."

She tried to cling to his supporting arm, but her

hands slipped weakly away. She felt herself sinking, sinking into a black sea of oblivion, and knew it was futile to struggle any longer. . . .

*   *   *

"Where am I?" she murmured a long time later.

Jake made answer very quietly, as if he had expected the question.

"You are here in the old parlour with me. I brought you home."

"Oh!" She gazed round her doubtfully. Her brain felt clogged and dull.

"Have I been . . . away?" she asked. "Where is . . . Bunny?"

He rose and moved across the room to the fire.

"Bunny is at school," he said, and stooped to lift off a saucepan. "Yes, you have been away. You came back from Liverpool yesterday."

She gave a quick gasp. The mists were beginning to clear a little. She became dimly conscious that something terrible had happened. She raised herself on her elbow, but was instantly assailed by a feeling of sickness so intense that she sank back again.

She was lying with closed eyes when Jake came back to her. He bent over her with a steaming cup in his hand.

"Try a little of this!" he said.

She looked up with an effort.

"I don't think I can, Jake. What has happened? Am I ill again?"

"Guess you'll remember presently if you drink this," he said.

She drew back, shuddering.

"What is it? Not brandy?"

"No. It's beef-tea."

He sat down beside her with a resolute air, and she suddenly realised that resistance was useless.

He was very gentle with her, feeding her spoonful by spoonful; and gradually as she swallowed it she revived. Her brain stirred and seemed to wake. Memory came crowding back.

Long before the cup was finished, that last scene in the music-room hung before her like a lurid picture from which she could not tear her gaze.

Quietly Jake set aside the cup.

"Maybe you'll sleep better now."

She lifted her heavy eyes to his.

"No, I don't want to sleep any longer. Jake, you . . . you are not going away?"

He seemed on the point of rising. She stretched out a beseeching hand and laid it on his arm.

"Jake, I . . . I want to tell you . . . something. Will you listen to me? Please . . . will you . . . . listen to me?"

His arm grew tense as stretched wire under her touch. She thought there was a glitter of hardness in the red-brown eyes as he said:

"There is no call for you to tell me anything unless you wish."

She sat up slowly, compelling herself to face him.

"But I want you to . . . understand."

He laid his hand abruptly upon hers with a gesture that almost seemed as if he would restrain her.

"You needn't fret any about that," he said. "Reckon I—do understand."

The vital force of the man was in that free grip

of his. She looked to see the awful flare of savage passion leap back into his eyes. But she looked in vain. His eyes baffled her. They seemed to hold her back, like a sword in the hand of a practised fencer.

The words she had thought to utter died upon her lips. There was to be no reckoning then. And yet she could not feel reassured. He did not look like a man who would forgo his revenge.

"What . . . what are you . . . going to do?" she faltered at last.

"I shouldn't want to know too much, if I were you," said Jake, softly drawling. "Not at this stage, anyway."

"Jake," she said. "I am going to tell you something that will make you . . . terribly angry; but it's something that you must know."

She paused, but he sat in silence, grimly watching her. She found her resolution wavering and gripped it with all her strength.

"When I came back here from Liverpool it was not . . . not to see my mother, as I gave you to understand. It was to . . . to . . ."

She faltered under his look, found she could not continue, and suddenly threw out her hands in piteous appeal.

"Jake . . . don't make it impossible for me to tell you!"

He rose also. They stood face to face.

"Are you going to tell me that you lied to me?"

She drew back from him sharply. The question felt like a blow.

"I am telling you the truth now."

"And for whose sake?"

He flung the words brutally, as a man goaded beyond endurance. But the moment they were uttered he drew a hard breath as though he would recall them. He came to her, took her by the shoulders.

"You take my advice!" he said. "Leave the whole miserable business alone! You've been tricked, badly tricked. You have appealed to me to protect you and that's enough. I don't want any more than that. I reckon I understand the situation better than you think.

"You are trying to tell me that it was your original intention to elope with Saltash. Well, maybe it was. But you had given up the notion before you went to him at the Castle, and he knew you had given it up.

"If he hadn't known it, he wouldn't have taken the trouble to drug you. It's an old device, old as the hills.

"He's probably done it a score of times, and with more success than he had today. Yes, that makes you sick. I guessed it would. And that's what he's going to answer to me for—what he'll ask your pardon for on his knees, before I've done with him."

"Oh, no, Jake, no!" She broke in upon him with a cry of consternation. "For pity's sake, no! Jake, I can't bear it! I cannot bear it! Jake, I beseech you, leave him alone now! Leave him alone! You . . . you can punish me in any other way. I'll bear anything but that . . . anything but that!"

Piteously she besought him, shaken to the soul

by the grim purport of his speech. She did not flinch from him now. Rather she appeared to him as one in sore straits, pouring out her entreaty with all that remained of her quivering strength.

And her words made an impression upon him of which she was instantly aware. His hands still held her, but the tension went out of his grasp. He looked at her with eyes that were no longer hard, eyes that held a dawning compassion.

"Reckon you're the last person that deserves punishing," he said at length, and in his voice she fancied she caught an echo of the old frank kindliness. "You've been the victim all through. Reckon you've suffered more than enough already."

She hid her face from him with a sudden rush of tears. Something in his words pierced straight to her heart.

"You don't know me!" she sobbed. "Oh, you don't know me!"

She drew herself away and sank down in the chair by the fire where once she had poured out all her troubles to him.

He did not kneel beside her now. He stood in silence, and as he stood his hands slowly clenched and he thrust them into his pockets.

He spoke at last, but it was with a restraint that made the words sound cold.

"Maybe I know you better than you think. I know you've cared for the wrong man ever since I first met you. Guess I've known it all along, and it hasn't made things extra easy for either of us, more especially as he was utterly unworthy of you.

"But you're not to blame for that. It's just human nature. You'd never have fallen in love with me, anyway."

He paused a moment.

"I don't see you're to blame any for that, either. Anyway, I'm not blaming you. And if—if punishing Saltash means punishing you too—well—even though he's a skunk and a blackguard—I reckon—I'll let him go."

He was moving to the door with the words. They came half-strangled, as if something within rebelled fiercely against their utterance.

He reached the door and stopped with his back to her.

"You'd better get your mother to join you here tomorrow," he said. "I'm sleeping with the Hundredth Chance tonight. He's been below par lately, and I'm worried about him."

He opened the door. He was on the point of squarely passing through when quickly, tremulously, she stopped him.

"Jake, please . . . please wait a moment! I must . . . I must . . . Jake!"

He closed the door again and turned round, but he did not come back, nor even look at her. There was a hint of doggedness about him, almost as though he waited against his will.

She stood up. Something in his attitude made it difficult, painfully difficult, to speak. She strove for self-control.

"You . . . are going to . . . to forgive me?" she said quiveringly.

He glanced up momentarily, a grim flicker as of a smile about his mouth.

"For what you haven't done, and never could do? It would be mighty generous of me, wouldn't it?"

She moved a step towards him.

"I . . . might have done it. I . . . so nearly . . . did it," she said, in distress. "I don't deserve any kindness from you, Jake. I . . . don't know how to . . . thank you for it."

He made a sharp gesture with one hand.

"If I've given you more than bare justice, put it to my credit! Make allowances for me next time!"

Something rose in her throat. She stood for a moment, battling with it. Bare justice! Had she ever given him so much as that? And he rewarded her with this blind generosity that would not even be aware of the weakness that had so nearly been her ruin.

Trembling, she drew nearer to him. She stretched out a quivering hand.

"Jake," she said, and the tears were running down her face. "I . . . will try . . . to be worthy of your . . . goodness to me."

He took her hand, gripping it with a force that made her wince.

"Shucks, my girl," he said, with a gruffness oddly uncharacteristic of him. "That's nothing. Be worthy of yourself!"

And with that abruptly he let her go, and turned and left her. She knew by the finality of his going that she would see him no more that night.

*   *   *

It was curiously like the old days to see Jake enter the parlour on the following morning with

Chops the red setter at his heels. But for Chops's delighted welcome of her, Maud could almost have felt that the intervening weeks had been no more than a dream.

She sat in her accustomed place and fondled him. Then, as Jake passed her, she put out a detaining hand.

"Good-morning, Jake!"

Her face was burning; yet she lifted it. He stood a second, only a second, behind her chair; then bent and touched her forehead with his lips.

"You're down early," he said. "Have you slept?"

She nodded, feeling her agitation subside with thankfulness.

"How is . . . the Hundredth Chance?"

Jake went to the fire.

"I think he'll be all right; but I won't trust anyone else to look after him. By the way, here's a letter for you!"

He held it out to her behind his back. She took it. Her fingers closed upon a crest.

She got up sharply, went to his side, and with a passionate movement dropped it straight into the flames.

"Shall we have breakfast now?" she said.

"Here's another letter!" said Jake.

The grim smile was hovering about his mouth; but he made no comment whatever upon her action.

She took the second letter.

"Is this all?"

"That's all," said Jake.

"It's from Uncle Edward." She opened it and began to read.

Suddenly she glanced up and found his eyes upon her. They fell instantly.

"You can read it too," she said, and held the letter so that he might share it with her.

He stood at her shoulder and read. It was a very brief epistle, written in evident distress of mind.

My Dear Grand-Niece,

Will you permit me to tender to you my very humble apology for the gross behaviour by which I drove you from the shelter of my roof? The fact that you have returned to your husband's house convinces me of the base injustice of my suspicions.

I ought to be old enough to know that a woman cannot be judged by her friends. If you find that you possess sufficient magnanimity to extend a free pardon to a very lonely and penitent old sinner, will you of your charity return, for however brief a period, and give him an opportunity to demonstrate his penitence?

Your humbly and hopefully,
Edward Warren.

"Oh, poor old man!" Maud looked up quickly. "But how did he know I was here?"

"I wired to him of your safe arrival," Jake said, "in reply to a wire from him which I didn't read. I thought he might come posting down here if I didn't."

"Poor old man!" she said again. "Thank you, Jake."

He looked at her.

"For keeping my word? I generally do that. What are you going to do?"

"I'll write to him," she said.

He moved round to his place at the breakfast-table.

"You're not wanting to go back then?"

She hesitated.

"What is it?" he said. "Money? I can let you have some if you're short of it."

"No, Jake, no!" She flushed. "I think . . . I think I'll stay here for the present. I will make him understand."

"Please yourself!" said Jake, and opened the morning paper.

A faint sense of disappointment went through her. She had fancied her decision would have evoked approval if not open pleasure from him. She poured out his coffee in silence.

As she brought it to him, he glanced up at her.

"Don't stay on my account if you feel you'd sooner go! I get along very well alone."

"Thank you," she said, and stiffened slightly. "I'll think about it."

After a time he glanced across at her again.

"Are you going to see your mother?"

She answered him somewhat listlessly.

"Yes, I suppose so."

"She'll have to decide on something soon," he observed.

Maud bit her lip. The thought of going to her mother again was wholly repugnant to her. She marvelled that he did not see it.

"I am sure she won't come and live here," she said, after a moment.

He finished his breakfast and got up.

"I may not get back before nightfall. I have to go over to Graydown."

She scarcely acknowledged his words, and he did not wait for any acknowledgment. He took up his riding-whip and went out. Chops looked round at her doubtfully, and followed him.

The door closed upon them. And suddenly Maud leaned upon the table and hid her face. This was to be her life, then, the unspeakable dreariness of a loveless home. She had thought he loved her.

And now she saw that it began and ended with mere kindness, and possibly a sense of duty. His passion for her, that fiery, all-mastering desire, had burnt itself out, and there was nothing left. An unutterable weariness came upon her. Oh, she was tired, she was tired of life!

It was then that in some mystic fashion that voice which she had once heard spoke again in her soul.

"The spark is ours for the kindling, the power to Love, the power to create Love. . . ."

Was she, indeed, capable of kindling this lamp in the desert? Out of those dead ashes of passion, could Love the Immortal indeed be made to rise?

She sat for a long time and pondered.

When, an hour later, she went down the hill to the town, the day was brilliant and the sky without a cloud.

Down by the quay a white yacht rocked at her

moorings. She marked it with a throbbing heart. Why, oh why, did he linger? She yearned to thrust him forever out of her life.

She reached the Anchor Hotel and entered. The bareness of the place smote cold upon the senses. She passed through it quickly and went up to her mother's room.

"Oh, my dear, at last!" Querulously Mrs Sheppard greeted her. "Shut the door and come in! Charlie is watching for you. He will be over directly."

Maud stood still in the doorway, every spark of animation gone out of her.

"Mother, what are you doing? What do you mean?"

Her voice sounded frozen and devoid of all emotion. Her fingers were clenched rigidly upon the handle of the door. She stared at her mother with eyes that were suddenly stony.

"What do you mean?" she repeated.

Mrs Sheppard looked up at her, smiling.

"I mean, dear, that while you go for your Mediterranean cruise, I am going back to London. Poor child, I hope that horrible cowboy person wasn't very cruel to you, But thank goodness you've broken away. You had Charlie's letter, did you? I told him I was sure you would come directly you knew he was waiting."

Maud turned stiffly, as though her limbs had become automatic.

"I am going."

Down the wide staircase she ran like a wild thing

seeking freedom, down into the bare, echoing hall. But the moment she reached it, she stopped dead, stopped as one suddenly turned to stone.

He was waiting for her, there in the sunny, open doorway, a smile of arrogant satisfaction on his ugly face, and triumph, open triumph, in his eyes.

He came to meet her like a king, carelessly gracious, royally self-assured.

"Ah, Maud of the Roses!" he said. "Free at last!"

He reached her where she stood, rigidly waiting. He opened his arms to take her. And then, as though there had been the flash of a dagger between them, he stopped. She had not moved.

She did not move. But the blazing blue of her eyes gave him check. For the space of many seconds they stood, not breathing, not stirring, and in those seconds, as by the light of a piercing torch, each read the other's soul.

It was Saltash who gave ground at last, but insolently, with a smile of bitter mockery.

"This scene is called 'The Unmasking of the Villain.' The virtuous heroine, having descended from her pedestal to expose him, gathers her mud-stained garments about her and climbs back again, confident that the worthy cow-puncher who owns her will conclude that she has never left her exalted position!" He paused, and added mockingly:

"I wonder if the worthy cow-puncher is quite such a fool as that."

Her face was quite colourless, but she heard his gibe without a sign of shrinking. Only as he

ceased to speak she lifted one hand and pointed to
the open door.

"Go!" she said.

Just the one word, spoken with a finality more
crushing than any outburst of anger! If it expressed
contempt, it was involuntary; she uttered only what
was in her soul.

He looked at her, and suddenly the derision in
his eyes flamed into fierce malignancy.

"I am going. You will never kick me from your
path again. You shall tread it alone—quite alone
except for the cow-puncher, who, no doubt, will see
to it that you walk on the stony side of the way.

"And I warn you it will be very stony, especially
when he comes to realise that his lady wife has been
his ruin. A tramp across the world with Jake Bolton under those conditions will at least destroy
every illusion. And I wish you joy of the journey."

He made her a deep ironical bow, and swung
upon his heel. But as he went, she spoke, suddenly, passionately, as though the words leaped forth,
compelling her.

"Jake Bolton is a man . . . a white man!"

Saltash laughed aloud, lifting his shoulders as
he sauntered away.

"With the heart of the beast, *chere Reine*. For
that I also wish you joy."

He went. She put up both hands to her eyes as
though to blot out some evil vision.

Presently, like a creature that has been sorely
wounded, she also crept away, fleeing ashamed by
another door, that no one might observe her going.

No, Jake was no fool. He saw only what he chose to see, believed only what he willed to believe. He had been generous to her; but he was no fool. He had refused the mute offer of her lips only that morning. Why? Why?

The answer lay in Saltash's mocking words, and all her life she would remember them. The poison-plant had born its bitter fruit indeed, and she had been forced to eat thereof.

It burned her now with a cruel intensity, consuming her like a darting flame. But she knew by its very fierceness that it could not last.

Very soon her heart, her soul, would all be burnt away; and there would be only dead ashes left, only dead ashes from which no living spark could ever be kindled again.

No, Jake was no fool. He would not blame her, that was all, because she was a woman.

*   *   *

"Why doesn't Maud come back?" said Bunny discontentedly. "It's beastly mean of her to stay away over the holidays."

"You can go to her if you like," said Jake, between whiffs at his pipe. "But I'm a fixture, so long as there's anything left to do."

Something in the last words caught Bunny's attention. He looked at him with sudden shrewdness.

"What do you mean, Jake? What's up?"

Jake was silent. He sat moodily smoking and staring into the fire.

"What is it, Jake?"

Jake puffed at his pipe for a few seconds, as if considering his reply.

"Your Uncle Edward wanted her, and I reckon that's just the silver lining to my cloud. He's a rich man, I gather. He can look after the two of you, if I go under."

"Jake! You aren't going under!" Horrified incredulity sounded in Bunny's voice. He leaned swiftly forward to look into Jake's face.

A queer, dogged smile showed upon it for an instant and was gone.

"Don't worry any. I shall come up again. I've been under before, practically down and out. But it hasn't killed me. It ain't going to kill me this time. So long as you and Maud are provided for, I can fend for myself."

"But, Jake, what's it mean? You haven't lost money?" urged Bunny in bewilderment.

"No. I've got a little money. There are plenty of poor devils worse off than I."

Jake leaned his head back against Bunny's wiry arm.

"But it ain't enough to keep me going. If it had been, I reckon I shouldn't have waited for notice to quit."

"Is that what you've got? Jake, you aren't in earnest! Charlie wouldn't be such a blackguard!"

Jake uttered an abrupt laugh; his teeth were clenched on his lower lip.

"Oh, Charlie's a blackguard all right, blackguard enough for anything. Don't you ever make any mistake about that! But I presume it's up to him to sell the stud if he feels so disposed. There ain't anything specially blackguardly in that. It's just his polite way of telling me to git."

"Sell the stud! Is that what he's going to do? Oh, Jake, Jake!" Shocked sympathy was in Bunny's voice.

"I hadn't meant to tell you on your first night. But you're such a shrewd little chap. And you've got to know sooner or later. Don't make an all-fired fuss about it, anyway!"

"All right, Jake." Bunny sounded a little breathless, but there was resolution in his voice. "It's you I'm thinking of. When—when's it going to be?"

"The sale? Early in the year, I expect. I haven't any definite instructions as to that. I'm expecting 'em every day. All I've been told officially at present is to cancel all engagements."

Jake heaved an abrupt sigh that seemed to catch him unawares, and became silent.

"P'raps he won't sell 'em all, Jake," said Bunny hesitatingly. "He couldn't surely sell the Hundredth Chance!"

"Yes," he said heavily. "I reckon the Hundredth Chance will go with all the rest."

He looked at Bunny, and there was desolation in his eyes.

"Does Maud know?" Bunny asked at length.

"No. I didn't want to worry her before I need."

Jake's eyes went back to the fire, gazing into it, dumbly troubled. "I fancy there's no doubt that the old man will provide for her, for both of you. That's what I'm counting on, anyway."

Bunny made an abrupt movement of impatience.

"Oh damn all that, Jake! What of you?"

For the first time his strong language went unrebuked. Jake's eyes remained fixed upon the fire. He spoke slowly.

"Reckon I shall go back to America. I shall find my feet again there. There's no call for you to be anxious about me. Guess I shan't starve."

"Jake!"

Bunny's arm went round his shoulders, gripping them hard. He spoke into Jake's ear a rapid nervous whisper.

"Jake, if you're going to America, I'm coming too. I just won't be left behind. I'll work, Jake. I won't be a drag on you. But I can't stay behind, not after all you've been to me.

"Jake, Jake, say you'll have me! I'm as strong as an horse. And I'd sooner starve along with you than be left without you. I—I, Jake, please!"

He suddenly bowed his head upon Jake's shoulder with a hard sob.

"Little pard!" Jake said, and pulled him down beside him. "Don't act the fool, now! That isn't like you!"

"Jake, Jake, why don't you go to Maud," Bunny said at length. "Maybe she's wanting you and hasn't the pluck to say so. Women are like that, you know."

Jake did not answer.

"Give her the chance, Jake!" Bunny urged. "You don't know her like I do. She always was shy. Lots of people thought her proud, but it was mostly shyness. Give her the chance, Jake! Just this one chance! It may make all the difference."

"Think so?" said Jake.

"Course I do. I know Maud. She'd sooner die

than show you her feelings. But she's got 'em all the same. Maybe she's wanting you, quite a lot, Jake. You can't tell."

"And maybe she's not," said Jake.

Bunny lifted a hot, earnest face.

"Don't be an ass, Jake!" he urged again. "Go in, man. Go in and win! You love her, don't you?"

It was a straight shot, and it found its mark. Something fiery, something wholly untamed, leaped into Jake's eyes. They shone like a flame upon which spirit had been poured.

Bunny pulled himself free with a sound that was almost a whoop of triumph.

"Go and tell her so! I'll bet you never have yet!"

And Jake uttered a laugh that was curiously broken.

"You're getting too damned clever, my son."

*   *   *

"It'll be real sport to take her by surprise," said Bunny with a chuckle of anticipation. "But what a beast of a journey it's been!"

They had been travelling practically all day, and they found a tall, gaunt house, standing back in a dark dripping garden, unlighted, forsaken.

"It can't be the place!" said Bunny, for the first time feeling his ardour for the adventure slightly damped.

"We'll soon find out," said Jake.

They groped their way to a flight of steps, and with the aid of a match found the bell. It rang desolately through the building.

"The house is empty!" declared Bunny.

But after a considerable pause a step sounded within, and a white-faced maid-servant opened the door to them.

"Come in!" she said, in a hollow voice. "You're very late."

"Is Mrs Bolton here?" asked Jake, as he stepped onto the mat.

She nodded as if in agitation.

"Yes, I'll tell her."

She shut the door behind them and went away, leaving them in the narrow, dimly lit hall.

There came the rustle of a dress, a footfall that was light and yet somehow sounded weary. She came through the dim hall with a slow, tired gait.

"Good-evening!" she said. "Will you come up-stairs?"

Bunny's fist suddenly prodded Jake in the back. He went forward a step, almost involuntarily.

"Maud!" he said.

"Jake!" she stood as one transfixed.

He strode forward, and somehow her two cold hands were in his before he knew whether he had taken or she had offered them.

"My girl!" he said, and again huskily. "My girl!"

She lifted a quivering face.

"Jake, thank you for coming! I . . . I hardly thought you could have got here so soon."

"You've been wanting me?"

She nodded.

"I sent for you, yes. I . . . I didn't feel as if I could . . . face it all . . . by myself."

His hold was warm, full of sustaining strength.

"You'll have to tell me what has happened. I didn't get your message."

"You didn't?" She looked momentarily startled. "Then why are you here?"

"I came . . ." He hesitated, glanced over his shoulder. "Bunny's here too."

"Thought we'd just look you up," said Bunny, emerging from the background. "Hullo, Maud! What's the matter? Is the old man ill?"

She turned to greet him.

"He died yesterday."

"Great Scott!" said Bunny.

Jake said nothing. He was watching her closely.

She kissed Bunny lingeringly, but without emotion.

"He was only ill five days," she said. "It was a chill and then pneumonia. I nursed him right up to the last. He wouldn't have anyone else. In fact he wouldn't let me out of his sight."

Her face quivered again, and she paused.

"I was expecting the undertaker when you came in. I've had to arrange everything. The funeral will be the day after tomorrow. Will you come into the dining-room? There's a fire there."

She led the way to a stiff and cheerless apartment.

She was plainly worn out, and from that moment Jake took command. He made her sit in one of the stiff velvet chairs in front of the fire, made her drink some wine, and left her there with Bunny in charge.

It must have been more than an hour later that

she was aroused by a few whispered words over her head, and she sat up to see Bunny on his feet, preparing to take his departure.

She looked up in swift distress.

"Oh, are you going? Must you go?"

"Yes, he must go," Jake said gently. "He'll get locked out if he doesn't. And the little chap's tired, you know, Maud. He's been travelling all day, and wants a good night's rest."

"Yes, of course. You must go," she said. "I wish you could have slept here, but perhaps it's better you shouldn't. Can you find your way alone? Jake, won't you go with him?"

But Bunny strenuously refused Jake's escort. He bade her good-night with warmth, and she saw that he hugged Jake at parting. And then the door closed upon him, and Jake's square figure came back alone.

He came straight to her, and bent over her.

"My dear," he said, "you're tired to death. You must go to bed."

She shook her head, wanly smiling.

"I'm too tired to get there."

"All right, I'll put you there."

"No, no, Jake!"

She stretched out a quick hand of protest; but there was no holding him off.

His arm was already about her; he lifted her to her feet. His face wore the old dominant look, yet with a subtle difference. His eyes held nothing but kindness.

She yielded herself to him almost involuntarily.

"I haven't been to bed for nearly a week," she

said. "I've slept of course in snatches. I used to lie down in Uncle Edward's room. Poor, dear old man! He wanted me so."

Her eyes were full of tears.

"I . . . I was with him when he died. We had arranged to have a nurse this morning, but the end came rather quickly. We knew his heart was weak. The doctor said . . . it was better for him really . . . that he went like that."

He entered her room as one who had the right.

"You treat me as if . . . as if I were Bunny," she said at once, smiling faintly through her tears, as he helped her undress.

"A man ought to be able to valet his own wife," Jake smiled in answer.

The words were simply uttered, but they sent the blood to her cheeks.

"I am sure I shall never sleep again," she said.

Yet, as she sank down at last upon the pillow, there was a measure of relief in her eyes.

"Now you're going to lie quiet till morning." Jake said, tucking in the bedclothes with motherly care. "Good-night. Is that comfortable?"

He kissed her lightly, caressingly, exactly as he might have kissed a child.

She tried to answer him, to thank him, but could not. He smoothed the hair from her temples, and turned away.

But in that moment her hands came out to him with a gesture that was almost convulsive, and caught and held his sleeve.

"Oh, Jake!" she said, and suddenly began to sob.

"I want you more than Bunny does. Don't go. Don't go!"

It was a cry of utter desolation. He turned back to her on the instant. He stooped over her, his face close to hers.

"Do you mean that?" he said, and in his voice, low as it was, there sounded a deep note as of something forcibly suppressed.

She clung to him, hiding her face against the rough tweed coat.

"I've no one else," she sobbed.

"Ah!" Jake said.

A very strange look came into his face. His mouth twitched a little as if in self-ridicule.

"I reckon you'd say that to anyone tonight."

"No . . . no!" Quiveringly she answered him. "I say it to you . . . to you! I'm so terribly . . . alone . . . so . . . so . . . empty. Uncle Edward used to tell me . . . what it meant to be lonely. But I never knew it could be . . . like this."

"Poor girl!" Jake murmured softly. "I know—I know."

The look of faint irony still hovered about his lips, but his voice, his touch, conveyed nothing but tenderness. He was stroking the dark hair with a motherliness that was infinitely soothing.

She was holding his other hand tightly, tightly, against her breasts, and it was wet with her tears.

"I've been . . . so miserable," she told him brokenly. "I know it's been . . . no one's fault . . . but my own. But life is so difficult . . . so difficult. I've treated you badly . . . badly. I haven't done—my duty. I've always yearned for the things out of reach. And now, oh, Jake, my world is a desert. I haven't a friend left anywhere."

"That's wrong," Jake said in his voice of soft decision. "You've got me. I mayn't be the special kind of friend you're wanting. But—as you say—I reckon I'm better than nothing. And I'm your husband anyway."

He put his arm about her as she lay, and gathered her close to him, not speaking.

She was trembling all over, and her face was still hidden. But she yielded to the drawing of his arm, clinging to him blindly, desperately.

He held her so for a little while, then with steady insistence he moved his other hand, beginning to turn her face upwards to his own. She tried to resist him, but he would not be resisted.

In the end, panting, quivering, she yielded very suddenly, and lifted her face voluntarily to his. She offered him her lips. But her eyes were closed. She palpitated like a trapped thing in his hold.

Yet when his lips met hers, she returned his kiss; and it was for the first time in her life.

* * *

When the dim dawnlight came filtering in, Jake's eyes turned to meet it with a lynx-like watchfulness as of an animal on guard. He had not slept all through the night, but had lain on top of the bed beside Maud.

His face was grim and still, and there was a hint of savagery—or was it irony?—about his mouth. For the second time in their lives, Fate had driven her to him for refuge. Like a bird out of the storm she had come to him, and she had not loved him.

His eyes grew brighter. They shone with a great and bitter hunger. He turned them upon her sleeping face. And then magically they softened, grew pitiful, grew tender. For, though she slept, the veil was lifted, and he read the sadness of her soul.

His lips suddenly trembled as he looked upon her, and the irony went out of him like an evil spirit. Whether she loved him or loved him not, she was his, she was his, till the storm-wind drove her from him.

And she needed him as she needed no one else on earth.

His arms clasped her. He gathered her closer to his breast.

Chapter Ten

"By Jove!" said Bunny, in a voice of awe. "Then Maud will be rich, will she? Just think of it!" He drew a deep breath that ended in a whistle. "It puts a different complexion on things."

"Quite different," said Jake.

"He's left her the whole caboodle! Say, Jake, what's it come to? Did the lawyer chap give you any idea?"

"No one knew what the old man was worth," Jake said, with his eyes still fixed steadily ahead. "He wasn't very great at spending money. But he owned a large factory, and had a vested interest in several others, besides some thousands in other concerns. The lawyer put it down at not less than two hundred and fifty thousand pounds."

He turned round with the words. Someone was entering the room. It was Maud. She looked pale, aloof, and very sad.

"Jake has been telling you?" she asked.

Bunny nodded.

"It's rather great, isn't it?"

"I don't think money alone can bring happiness," she said rather wistfully.

"Depends how you spend it," maintained Bunny

stoutly. "Of course, it is a downright curse to the people who hoard it—like that beast who buried his talent. But you can make any amount of happiness out of it if you try."

"Perhaps you're right, dear. Perhaps there is happiness to be got out of it. Anyhow, we'll try, won't we? Won't we, Jake?"

There was almost a note of entreaty in her voice; but she received no answer. She turned sharply. Jake had gone.

"Never mind!" said Bunny, quick to console. "He's busy. Letters or something. But you've got me. Say, Maud, you'll be able to keep Mother above water now. That's rather a mercy, anyway."

He almost forced her into the channel of his own cheery speculations.

* * *

"Home for Christmas. Motoring from Graydown. Three cheers. *Bunny.*"

The ecstatic message stood on the mantelpiece in the old parlour above a roaring fire, and Jake stood in front of it, grimly patient, while the old grandfather clock ticked monotonously in the corner.

It was Christmas Eve, still and frosty. The glass door into the garden was wide open, so that he could hear the first hoot of a motor.

It was nearly a fortnight since he had left her, and all his veins were on fire at the thought of having her here again. He yearned for her with a fierce hunger that tore at the very soul of him, a hunger that he knew he must suppress, crush down out of sight, before he met her.

Because in her desolation she had turned to him for comfort, he must not take it for granted that she needed him still. She had had time to recover, time, possibly, to be amazed, to be shocked, at her own yielding.

He dreaded to see that instinctive recoil from him which he had learned to know so cruelly well in the summer.

Those words of hers—"I can't pretend to love you. You see, I don't"—still haunted him. And he remembered how once, in bitterness of soul, she had told him that she hated him.

He clenched his hands over the memory, cursing himself for the passion that even now leaped so fiercely within him.

Someone knocked at the open door that led into the garden. He turned sharply and saw Sam Vickers's good-humoured countenance looking up at him.

"Post just in, sir," he remarked. "I was coming round, so I brought your letter along."

"Oh, thanks. Come in, Sam," Jake answered. "Shut that door. I trust you, and I'm going to tell you something."

"Hadn't you better think it over first, sir?" he suggested.

"No." Jake held out his hand suddenly. "I trust you. You remember what happened in the summer at the Graydown meeting, when I thrashed young Stevens?"

"Quite well, sir." Sam's reply came brisk and smart.

"You know why I thrashed him?" Jake proceeded.

"Yes, sir. Thrashed him and kicked him out, sir. I was never more pleased in my life."

"He's been employed at the Castle stables ever since," Jake said very bitterly. "I was a fool, a damned fool, not to expose him. But Lord Saltash knew that he pulled the Albatross. I told him so. He's now saying that he has proof that I aided and abetted, proof enough to get me warned off the Turf."

"Proof be damned, sir!" said Sam warmly. "That ain't a good enough story for anyone, with a head on his shoulders, to swallow."

"No, Sam. You're right. And Lord Saltash knows it. I can't go to him and demand to see his proof, because he's on the other side of the world. But there's no scotching a lie of that sort. It'll have spread like the plague long before he gets back.

"And, meantime, he has decided that horse-racing and breeding are no longer his fancy, and he is going to sell the stud—and me along with it."

Jake's mouth took a bitter, downward curve with the last words.

Sam's jaw dropped.

"Going to sell the stud, sir?"

"Yes, before the spring meetings. You'll be all right, Sam. Anyone would be glad to get you. The stewards know you all right."

"Oh, I wasn't thinking of that, sir. I was thinking of you." Sam's blue eyes were gravely troubled. "You've got a wife, sir."

"My wife inherits her uncle's money. She is not

dependent upon me, fortunately for her." Jake was
speaking through set teeth. "I knew it was coming.
I've known it for some weeks."

His eyes suddenly glittered afresh.

"It ain't a knock-out blow, Sam," he said. "Don't
you make any mistakes as to that!"

Sam's eyes sparkled in response.

"It's you that's the knock-out, sir," he said, with
eager partisanship. "He hits below the belt, but he
won't down you that way. You're better known
than I am. And no one will believe you're not
straight. Saltash ain't fit to employ anyone except
Dick Stevens and the likes of him. I often wondered who squared Dick that time, but it wouldn't
surprise me now if . . ."

He paused, looking at Jake interrogatively.

"Good-night, my lad!" Jake said. "I must go.

He went to the door with the words, and opened
it. There came the sound of a motor-horn without, and the gay whoop of a boyish voice. Jake's
spurs went jingling down the passage.

And Sam turned to leave through the garden
door by which he had entered. He crammed his
cap down over his eyes as he did so.

"Poor old boss!" he said. "Poor old boss!"

*　　*　　*

"Oh, isn't it good to be home again?" said Bunny. "Isn't it just good?"

They sat before the glazing fire in the parlour
after a late supper, drinking Mrs Lovelace's rhu-
barb wine and enjoying the glow.

Maud's cheeks were flushed and her eyes very
bright.

"How are the animals, Jake?" she asked. "How is the Hundredth Chance?"

"They're all going strong. You must see them for yourself in the morning."

After Bunny went to bed they sat in silence for a while and then suddenly Maud said:

"Jake, I want to talk to you."

"About your affairs?" he said.

"Our affairs, Jake," she said, her voice very low.

He jerked his head as if to indicate attention, but he said nothing further. It remained for her to proceed, and she did so, slowly, as if carefully weighing each word.

"You have left me a free hand in the settling of Uncle Edward's affairs, and Mr Craven is a very clever businessman. I know Uncle Edward trusted him implicitly. But I should like you to know everything that has been done, that is, if you care to know."

She paused a moment.

"You do care, don't you, Jake?"

"I care for your welfare," he answered. "Not being your trustee, it's not essential that I should be told every detail."

"Jake!"

There was quick pain in her voice, pain that he could not fail to note. She leaned forward, stretching a hand to him across the hearth.

"Jake!" she said again, very earnestly. "Do you think that . . . that I shall ever forget . . . that I owe you . . . everything?"

He took her hand, but with a curious doggedness he kept his eyes averted.

"I guess we're quits," he said. "You don't owe me anything."

There was no bitterness in his voice, no emotion of any sort. The clasp of his fingers was no more than kind. His mouth looked stubborn.

But a strange sort of stubbornness seemed to have entered into Maud also. She kept her hand in his.

"I take . . . another view," she said. "I don't think any man . . . has ever done . . . more for a woman . . . than you have done . . . for me."

Haltingly the words came, but she spoke them bravely.

"It's a big, big debt, Jake . . . immeasurably big . . . a personal debt that can never be repaid. I feel . . . contemptible . . . whenever I think of it."

Jake's fingers closed upon hers with a quiet strength.

"You've no call to feel like that," he said.

Her hand clung to his suddenly, desperately.

"You believe in me, Jake?"

His face did not vary.

"I guess I've proved that."

She uttered a sharp, catching sigh.

"Yes . . . yes! That is another debt. But till . . . till that night you came to me at Uncle Edward's . . . I was never . . . quite . . . sure."

"Why weren't you sure?"

He put the question abruptly, with an insistence that demanded an instant reply. But still he did not look at her. His eyes gazed ever straight into the fire.

Tremulously she answered him.

"I met Charlie . . . the morning after . . . down

at the Anchor. He said . . . he said . . . you wouldn't be . . . such a fool. That was why I went away."

"Damn him!" The words burst from Jake with terrific violence. He sprang to his feet as a man goaded beyond all bearing.

"Curse him!" he said, his face gone white with passion. "May his soul rot in . . ."

"Jake!" The name was a cry, breaking through the fierce rush of his fury.

Maud was on her feet also. She held him by the shoulders, in a vital, quivering hold.

"You're not to say it!" she said, and her face was close to his, compelling him to silence. "You are not to curse him! A curse comes back!"

She put one hand on his mouth, for he seemed on the verge of breaking forth afresh. She looked him full in the eyes.

"You're not to, Jake!" she said. "I won't have it. You who have been . . . so splendidly generous . . . can afford to leave a beaten enemy alone!"

Suddenly his arms were round her, gripping her. The naked soul of the man was looking into hers. With a supreme impulse, she took her hand away and gave her lips to his, surrendered herself wholly to the fiery passion that had suddenly blazed upon her.

But in a moment his arms were loosened. He went back against the mantelpiece as though he had been struck a blow between the eyes. He stood motionless, his mouth working but uttering no word.

She stood before him, pale to the lips, but not without a certain strength. She had offered, and he

had not taken. But yet her doubts were set at rest.
Perhaps for the first time in her life she faced him
wholly unafraid.

"So . . . we will leave him out of it," she said,
breathing fast. "He has . . . ceased to count."

Jake moved, pulled himself together.

"You must forgive me. Maybe you'd be wise to
leave me. I shall be—saner—presently."

She put one hand against his breast.

"No, Jake, no. You're going to be sane now. Sit
down again! Let us finish our talk!"

He looked at her with the red light still smoul-
dering in his eyes. After a moment he took her wrist
with a grip in which passion lingered.

"I'm trying to act fair by you," he said, with a
faint smile that somehow touched her heart. "It
seems to me you've never had a chance, not a real
chance, all your life.

"What with Bunny, and me, and—and—Saltash"—his mouth twisted over the name— "you've
been handicapped right and left. That's why I've
sworn to myself that I won't interfere with you any
more.

"You shall have a free hand. This money of yours
makes it possible. Play with it, spend it, enjoy yourself! Be happy! I won't step in to prevent it."

Maud's eyes were suddenly full of tears, yet
she laughed.

"You've sworn to give me a free hand?" she said.

"Sure." He nodded.

Her other hand clasped his quickly, pleadingly.

"Then, Jake, you won't be angry if . . . if . . . I

decide to do something that . . . that you may not
. . . altogether . . . like?"

"It's your money," said Jake doggedly.

"Yes . . . yes. And . . . I have your permission
. . . your unreserved consent . . . to . . . to do what
I like with it?"

Her voice quivered. She was clinging to him almost unconsciously.

He stood stiffly facing her. He had forced his passion down again, but there was tension about him
still.

"My girl," he said, "if you want to turn it all into
paper and make a bonfire of it—I shan't object."

"Oh, I don't want to do that," she said, and again
she faintly laughed, though in her laughter there
was a sound of tears. "I felt just at first . . . just at
first . . . that I didn't want it.

"But I've got over that, though I've come to the
conclusion that there's no fun to be got out of
money unless there's someone to enjoy it with you.
And so . . . and so . . ."

She became a little breathless and her hands
hands pressed his in agitation.

"I'm making over half of it to you . . . by deed of
gift. Please, Jake, please . . . you don't mind?"

"What?" said Jake.

He raised his tawny brows, staring at her for an
instant in sheer, overwhelming amazement; then
they came down uncompromisingly in a thick,
straight line above his eyes.

He put her hands away from him, gently but
with the utmost decision. He turned himself from

her and bent to pick up the poker. Then, as he stirred the fire, with his face in the glow, he spoke briefly, almost roughly.

"I don't know if you're joking or in earnest; but that's the one thing that I can't, and won't, consent to. So I reckon that's all there is to it."

"Jake!" There was consternation in her voice, bitter disappointment, keen pain. "Oh, Jake, you can't mean to refuse . . . like that!"

"How did you expect me to refuse?" said Jake, without turning.

"Not as if . . . as if . . . I had insulted you," she answered chokingly.

He dropped the poker and straightened himself.

"Maybe you didn't intend any insult. But you don't credit me with an over-allowance of self-respect, do you?"

He turned round to her slowly at length.

"We won't talk any more about it," he said, something of the old kindliness in his tone. "Guess it's an impossible subject. You'll know me better next time."

She struggled for utterance with lips that trembled piteously; her eyes were brimming with tears. Finally, with a small, hopeless gesture, she turned away, moved across the room blindly, found the door, and fumblingly opened it.

"Good-night!" she whispered then, in a voice that was scarcely audible, and in another moment the door closed without sound behind her.

She was gone. Jake's mouth set itself in a hard, straight line. He squared his shoulders with the instinctive movement of a man facing odds.

Then abruptly he lifted his clenched hands above

his head and swore a frightful oath that comprehended himself, the world, and all things in it, in one vast anathema.

"Say, Jake, are you going to spend the night downstairs?"

Bunny's thin, eager face peered round the door with the words. He slipped into the room, clad in pyjamas, his hair all ruffled on his forehead.

"Jake, you won't go to America now, will you? Maud is rich enough to keep us all. She wants to share everything with you."

Jake's eyes looked at Bunny, but they saw beyond him.

"I know all about that. I know just what she wants. She wants a watchdog, one that'll fetch and carry and accept all benefits with humility. She's lonely now; but she won't be lonely long.

"She'll have a crowd round her, a set of fashionable, gibbering monkeys, who will sneet at the watchdog, the meek and patient hanger-on, the adjunct at every party, who lives on his mistress's smile and doesn't object to her kick. That's what she wants. And that, my son, is the one thing she's not going to get."

"But what on earth do you want, Jake?" burst Bunny, half-startled, half-exasperated. "You needn't be that. You never could be that. Her idea was to make you independent."

"Oh, yes, I know." Jake's mouth twisted a little. "She's mighty generous. She figures to hand over half her fortune by deed of gift."

"And you wouldn't have it?" Bunny almost gasped.

"I wouldn't touch it," Jake said, with a sound that was oddly like a suppressed laugh in his throat.

"But why in wonder not?" Bunny stared at him as if he thought he had gone suddenly mad. "We've taken oceans of things from you."

"That's different," said Jake.

"How different? Make me understand, Jake! I've a right to understand." Bunny's voice was imperious.

Jake looked at him. There was actually a smile in his eyes, but it was a smile of self-ridicule.

"You asked me just now what I wanted," he said. "I'll tell you. I want a woman who loves me well enough to chuck up everything, everything, mind you, and follow me barefoot to the other end of the world."

He broke into a laugh that seemed to hurt him.

"And that," he said, "is the one thing I'm not going to get. Now do you understand?"

"Not quite, Jake. Not quite." He looked back at Jake with awe in his eyes. "You think she doesn't love you well enough. Is that it?"

Jake nodded, still with that smile of self-mockery about his mouth.

"You've hit it, my son. We're not a pair, that's the trouble. She means to be kind, but I'd sooner go empty than be fed on husks. I didn't offer either of you that. It was the real thing I gave you. But she, she hasn't the real thing to offer. And so I'll do without."

He turned squarely to put out the waning lamp, as though the discussion were ended, but Bunny stayed him with a nervous hand.

"Jake, suppose you're wrong? Suppose she does care, cares badly?" His voice quivered with earnestness. "Women are queer fishes, you know, Jake. Suppose you've made a mistake?"

"Where's the use of supposing the impossible?" asked Jake sombrely.

Yet he paused, his hand rubbing the boy's rough head caressingly.

"Ah, but just for a moment," Bunny insisted. "If she loved you, Jake, you wouldn't refuse then to —to do what she wanted?"

"If she loved me," Jake said, and stopped suddenly.

He moved abruptly to the lamp and extinguished it. Then, in the dim light that filtered through the blinds from a full moon of frosty radiance, he spoke, deeply, slowly, solemnly.

"If she loved me, I would accept anything under the sun from her. Everything she had would be mine. Everything of mine would be hers. And before God I would make her happy, if she loved me."

*   *   *

Jake was leaning on the half-door of the loose-box in which was lodged the black colt of his dreams—the Hundredth Chance. The animal's head was nuzzled against his shoulder. There seemed to be a perfect understanding between them.

But suddenly the colt started back. He was suspicious of all the world but Jake.

Jake looked round, his face grey in the failing light.

"Hullo! What is it?"

Sam came forward and gave him a card.

"Mrs Bolton was out, sir, and a gentleman asked for you; said he'd wait in the yard, sir."

Jake bent his brows over the card. It bore a name that seemed vaguely familiar to him, though in what connection he could not for the moment recall:— Monterey W. Rafford. He looked up.

"He's no friend of mine. Do you know what he wants?"

"Said he was a friend of Dr Capper, sir," said Sam.

The visitor was standing under a lamp, and he moved to meet Jake, who then recognized him as the anaesthetist who had taken part in Bunny's operation.

"I am very pleased to meet you again, sir, though no doubt you have forgotten me."

They shook hands. Jake was looking at him with steady eyes.

"No," he said, in his slow way. "Of course not."

"I've given up sending sick people to sleep," Mr Rafford explained. "And I'm after art treasures at the present moment. To be particular, I'm after Saltash's wonder in marble, *The Fallen Woman*."

"Come into the house," Jake suggested.

"No, not right away if you don't mind. There's a little light left. Will you show me the animals?"

Jake's right hand clenched on his whip.

"Have you done a deal over them too?" he said, sinking his voice very low.

"No. But I've got an idea," Rafford said. "I'll tell you what it is presently. You've got some valuable stock here, I'm told. I hope you don't object to showing me round?"

His smile was disarming. Jake swung round on his heel without another word.

"What's come to Saltash?" Rafford questioned. "He seems ready to throw up everything."

"Yes, that's him," Jake said. "But then he hasn't had the working up of the stud as I have. It's nothing to him to part with the animals. They were no more than a pastime."

"And not always a creditable pastime at that?" suggested Rafford. "I guess you're too straight for him, Mr Bolton. He's a crooked devil, but a curiously likable one."

He smiled as if at some reminiscence.

"Well, what's your opinion? Do you think he could be persuaded to sell this show privately if he got a good offer?"

Jake's reserve came down upon him like a mask.

"I can't say. You'd better go to his agent, Bishop."

Rafford was still faintly smiling.

"I've just come from him.

"It doesn't rest with me," Jake said, doggedness in every line.

"No, I know. But I'd like to feel that I've got you behind me. My patron would like to know that."

"Who is your patron?" Jake asked.

"His name is Ruse. You mayn't have heard of him, but he's quite well known in a good many circles, especially on our side. He has taken a fancy for horse-racing, and he will probably drop a lot of money over it before he's done; that is, unless he's lucky enough to retain you for his trainer."

A hot gleam suddenly kindled in Jake's eyes, and as suddenly died.

"I reckon that won't be possible," he said. "Lord Saltash will see to that."

"Saltash may not be able to prevent it," Rafford observed quietly. "Ruse will want a trainer, and when I tell him how your heart's in the job, it wouldn't surprise me if he persuaded you to keep it on. You wouldn't be very hard to persuade, I take it?"

Jake hesitated momentarily, then passed the question by.

"Is your friend in England?" he asked.

"He will be in England very soon after the deal is completed, if it is completed," Rafford answered.

"Won't he want to see the stud first?" Jake's voice was quietly business-like. He seemed to have put all personal considerations away.

"I doubt it," Rafford said. "The value of the stud is well known, and I think Saltash will get his price without much haggling. My patron is particularly anxious to prevent the stud coming on the market. He is prepared to offer something better than a market price to make sure of it."

Jake looked at him, faintly smiling.

"You have an interest at stake?" he suggested.

"Only the interest that makes me want to push a thing to success. I have full powers, though." Rafford's face reflected his smile. "When my patron got news of this thing, shall I tell you what he said to me? Just 'Clinch!' I shall carry out those instructions if I can, to the letter."

"You won't do it in a day," Jake said. "Maybe you'd like to put up at my place, pending negotiations."

Rafford's hand came out to him with impulsive friendliness.

"No, sir. You're more than kind, but I won't do that. I've seen the animals and I've seen you. That's enough. You and I mustn't get too intimate over this deal. You know what Saltash is. When we've pulled it off, I'll be delighted, if there's still time."

He gripped Jake's hand hard, looking him straight in the face.

"You've given me a real happy hour, Mr Bolton," he said. "And I shan't forget it. It was mighty generous of you, considering you regarded me as the first of the vultures. Well, I hope I shall be the last."

"I hope you will," Jake said.

Late that night when Maud rose to go upstairs, he came out of what had apparently been a doze before the fire, and spoke for the first time of his own affairs.

"Bunny told you some time ago that the stud was to be sold, I believe?" he said.

Maud stood still on the hearth, looking down at him. The question evidently startled her, for her breath came suddenly faster.

"Yes, he told me," she said.

"Why didn't you tell me you knew?" said Jake. He saw that his abruptness had agitated her, and leaped forward to take her hand.

She suffered him to take it, but she was trembling from head to foot.

"I didn't think . . . you wished me to know."

He bent his head slightly, so that only the shining copper of his hair met her look.

"It wasn't that. At least, not at first. Just at first I didn't want to bother you. Afterwards, well, I guess I'm an independent sort of cuss, and I was afraid you'd want to finance me when you knew I was to be kicked out."

"I did want to, Jake," she said quickly.

He nodded.

"I know. I was mighty ungracious over it. I've been sorry since."

"Jake!" She stooped a little, a quick dawning of hope on her pale face; but he kept his head bent.

"No," he said. "The answer is still No. I don't want to hurt your feelings any, but I can't live on anyone's charity. If there's anything under the sun that I can do to serve you, I'll do it. But I can't do the pet-dog business.

"For one thing, I'm not ornamental enough. And for another, it ain't my nature."

He paused a moment, but Maud made no attempt to speak. Only the hope had all died out of her face, and she looked unutterably tired.

"Just when your uncle died, you were feeling extra lonely, and"—his voice sank a little—"you turned to me for comfort. But I didn't flatter myself that I had become permanently necessary to you. I knew you never intended me to think that.

"That brings me to what I set out to tell you about

the stud. There is a chance, I think it's a good one, that it may be kept together after all. There is also a chance, a less-promising one, that I may be retained as trainer.

"If I am offered the post, I shall accept it. If I am not offered the post, well, I shall have to start again at the beginning. I shall have to rough it. So if that happens, you will have to go your way, and I mine."

He ceased to speak, and his hand relinquished hers.

Maud stood up. She was no longer trembling, but she was very pale.

"I hope you will get the post," she said, after a moment. "You . . . I think you would feel it if you had to part with the horses. They mean . . . so much to you."

"I belong to them," Jake said simply.

She smiled a little with lips that quivered.

"Then I hope you will have them always," she said. "Good-night . . . and thank you for being so . . . explicit."

She looked at his bent head, stretched a hand above it almost as if she would touch it, then drew it swiftly back and turned to go.

A few seconds later she was ascending the stairs, still piteously smiling, with the tears running down her face.

*   *   *

An icy wind was blowing as Maud climbed the steep road by the church. It whirled down on her with a fierceness that made quick progress out of the question. Nevertheless, she fought valiantly against it, fearing that Jake would have returned before her.

He was negotiating about some land for a new stables near to Graydown, where the American who had bought all the stud wished it to be.

Round the bend of the road the wind caught her mercilessly. It was while she was struggling round this bend that there suddenly came to her the sound of galloping hoofs and a man's voice wildly shouting.

She drew to one side, and stood against the hedge; and in a moment a horseman dashed into view and thundered past her.

He was gone like a whirlwind into the dusk, and Maud was left with a throbbing heart that seemed to have been touched by a hand that was icy-cold. She was nearly sure that the animal had come from the stables, and that the man was Sam Vickers.

He was not a furious rider as a rule. What had induced him to ride like that tonight? Something was wrong, something was wrong! The certainty of it stabbed her like a knife.

What could it be? Had Jake met with an accident? Was Sam tearing thus madly down to Fairharbour to find the doctor?

The strength of a great fear entered into her. She began to run up the hill in the teeth of the wind. She had only half a mile to go. She would soon know the worst.

But she had not gone twenty yards before her progress was checked. She became aware of a drifting mist all about her, a mist that made her gasp and choke. She ran on in face of it, but it was with failing progress, for the further she went the more it enveloped her like the smoke of a vast bonfire.

The coldness at her heart became a tangible and ever-growing fear. She tried to tell herself that the suffocating vapour blowing down on her came from a group of ricks that stood not far from the entrance to the stables.

Some mischievous person had fired them, and Sam had discovered it and gone to raise the alarm. But deep within her there clamoured an insistent something that refused to be reassured.

Gasping, stumbling, with terror in her soul, she fought her way on, till a further bend in the road revealed to her the driving smoke all lurid with the glare of flames behind.

It was here that there first came to her that awful sound as of a rending, devouring monster, the fierce crackling and roaring of fire! The horror of it set all her pulses leaping, but its effect upon her senses was curiously stimulating.

Through the roar of the furnace there came to her the shouting of men's voices and the wild stampeding of horses.

And twice before she reached the gates she heard the terrible cry of a horse. Then, as though she moved on wings, she was there in the stable-yard in the thick of the confusion, with the fire roaring ahead of her and the red glare all round.

The whole stone-paved space seemed crowded with men and horses, and for the first few seconds the noise and movement bewildered her.

Then she grasped the fact that only one side of

the double row of stables was alight, and that in consequence of the driving north wind the other side was in comparative safety.

They were leading the terrified animals out through a passage that led to further buildings on this safe side. But the task was no light one, for they were all maddened by fear, and almost beyond control.

As she drew nearer, however, Maud saw that the men themselves were grappling with the situation with energy and resolution, and there was no panic among them.

One, a mere lad, gripping a plunging horse by the forelock, recognised her and shouted a warning through the din.

She came to him, unheeding the trampling hoofs. "Is Mr Bolton back?" she cried.

He shook his head, striving to back the animal away from her. He had a halter flung over his shoulder which he had not stopped to adjust.

Maud took it from him, and between them, with difficulty, they slipped it over the terrified creature's head. Then, obtaining a firmer hold, the boy shouted further information.

"No, the boss ain't back yet. He'll be in any minute now. Sam's gone for the fire-engine. He thinks the house'll be safe if the wind don't veer. But the other side'll be burnt out before he gets back at this rate. We've got most all the animals out now, though."

"Not all?" Maud cried the words with a momentary wild misgiving.

The boy yelled back again, still wrestling with the struggling horse.

"All but the Hundredth Chance. He's gone by this time. We couldn't save 'im. It's like an open furnace along there."

She did not feel the stones under her feet. The seething crowd of men and horses became no more than shadows on the wall. Twice as she went she narrowly escaped death from the plunging hoofs.

The heat was terrific, but the smoke was all blown away from her. She felt no suffocation. But when she reached the stone passage that led to the group of loose-boxes where once she had stood horror-stricken and listened to Jake reprimanding Dick Stevens in the language of the stables, she realized the truth of what the boy had said.

It was like an open furnace.

Yet there seemed a chance, the faintest chance, that that one loose-box at the southern corner, the best loose-box in the whole of the stables, might yet be untouched by the devouring flames.

The block of buildings was alight and burning fiercely, but it was not yet alight from end to end. It looked like a lane of fire at the end of that stone passage, but she could see the line of loose-boxes beyond, fitfully through wreaths of smoke.

All the doors stood open as far as she could see. They had evidently taken the animals in order, and it had been the fate of the Hundredth Chance to be left till last.

And how to reach him? It had baffled his rescuers. For the moment it baffled her also. She stood at the entrance to the stone passage, looking through, feeling the stones under her feet hot like a grid, seeing the red flames leaping from roof to roof.

Then the driving wind came swirling behind her, and she felt as if a hand had pushed her. She plunged into the passage and ran before it.

She emerged in that lane of fire. It roared all round her. She felt the heat envelop her with a fiery, blistering intensity, but ever that unseen hand seemed to urge her. She hesitated no more, though she rushed into a seething cauldron of flame.

And ever the thought of Jake was with her, Jake who loved his animals as he loved nothing else on earth.

She reached that line of boxes. The roof was burning now from end to end, but as she tore past the open doors there came to her an awful cry, and she knew that the colt still lived.

The smoke came down on her here, blinding her, but though it stopped her breath, it could not stop her progress. It seemed as though no power on earth could do that now until she had reached her goal.

Crouching, with lungs that felt like bursting, she forced a way over those last desperate yards.

Every door was open save that one, and against that one there came a maddened wild tattoo. The Hundredth Chance was fighting for life.

She reached the door through swirling smoke. The flames were shooting over her head. She caught at the bolt. It was burning hot as the door of an oven; but she knew no pain. She dragged it back.

Again there came that fearful shriek and the

battering of heels against the wood. The animal was plunging about his prison like a mad thing. She mustered all her strength and pushed upper and lower doors inwards at the same moment.

Instantly there came the rush of hoofs. She was flung violently backwards, falling headlong on the stones. The Hundredth Chance galloped free; and she was left shattered, inert, with the fire raging all round her.

But the deed was done, the great task accomplished. And nothing mattered any more. Jake loved his animals as he loved nothing else on earth. . . .

* * *

What was that red light burning? Symbol of undying Love! Symbol of the Immortal! The lamp that burns forever before the High Altar of Heaven!

Who was that speaking? Was it the Voice that had not sounded in tempest or fire, but only at the very last, when all other things were past?

"Love is only gained by Love, by the complete renunciation of self. Love is a joyful sacrifice, to give and give without measure, not counting the cost, rejoicing only in the power to give, till it all comes back a thousand-fold—Love the Invincible, Love the Divine, Love the Perfect Gift."

Someone was calling, calling. At first it was suggestion rather than sound, a vague murmur from the old, sad world so many millions of miles away.

But gradually it grew till it seemed the echo of a cry, and at last the cry itself became articulate, a cry of anguish rising from the void.

"Come back! Come back! O God, send her back to me! Send her back!"

There came a great sound of singing as of men and angels praising God before the High Altar of Heaven. Then the darkness of earth rushed upwards like the smoke from a mighty furnace, and all was blotted out. . . .

*   *   *

Someone was holding her. Someone was whispering her name. She opened her eyes upon the old world of cloud and sunshine, and looked into his face, and it was the face of a man who has suffered agony.

"Thank God!" he said, "Oh, thank God!"

Then she remembered in what cause she had spent herself.

"What of . . . the Hundredth Chance?" she whispered.

He caught his breath. His lips were quivering.

"He's safe enough. But—Maud—what made you do it?"

She looked at him wonderingly.

"But it was . . . all I could . . . do."

He bent his head over something that he was holding and it came to her with a little start of surprise that it was her own hand swathed in bandages.

"Have I been . . . hurt?" she asked.

He did not look at her."

"Thank God not seriously," he said, speaking with an odd jerkiness. "The colt knocked you down. You were stunned. You scorched your hands over that infernal bolt. But the wind blew the fire away from you. You weren't actually burnt."

"Is the fire out?" she asked anxiously. "Tell me what happened?"

Jake's head was still bent.

"Yes, they soon got it under. There wasn't much left to burn that side. It was a good thing the wind held, or the whole show might have been gutted. It's all safe now."

Maud's eyes wandered round the panelled parlour and came back to his bent head.

"I feel so . . . strange, as if I had been a . . . long . . . long journey, and it all happened . . . ages and . . . ages ago. Is it so very . . . long ago, Jake?"

"About four hours," said Jake. "Dr Burrowes has seen you. He couldn't stay except to give you first aid. He is coming back presently."

"And . . . you have been . . . here with me ever . . . since?" she said, with a touch of shyness. "Didn't you want to be looking after the animals?"

He shook his head, gazing steadily downwards.

"Have you been . . . anxious about . . . me, Jake?" she whispered.

"Yes."

"But Dr Burrowes must have known if . . . if I were in any . . . danger," she said.

He answered her with what she felt to be a great effort.

"Burrowes was anxious too. He was afraid of the shock for you. He thought there was—danger."

She moved her hand a little, and in a moment, as though he feared to hurt her, he laid it gently down.

"I am so . . . sorry you have been . . . worried about . . . me," she said.

"It doesn't matter now," said Jake. He reached out for a glass that stood on the table. "Burrowes left this for you. Can you manage to drink it?"

He held it to her lips with a hand that was not so steady as usual. She drank and felt revived.

Her brain was becoming more active. There was something in Jake's attitude that required explanation.

"I am better . . . now. Tell me a little more! How did I get here? Who found . . . me?"

"I found you. The Hundredth Chance came tearing out. We had some trouble to catch him. And then one of the boys suddenly said . . ."

Jake stopped and swallowed hard.

"Said—said you had been in the yard, and must have set him free. I got to you just in time."

"You saved me?" she said swiftly.

He nodded.

"Jake," she said wistfully, "aren't you glad your animals are all safe?"

"They belong to the new boss," he said doggedly. "They don't belong to me."

Her face changed a little.

"I think they belong to you first, Jake. You love them so."

He made a sharp gesture.

"It's quite likely the new boss will tell me to shunt."

"Oh, he won't do that, Jake!" she protested quickly. "I'm sure he won't do that. You . . . you are one of the best trainers in England."

His mouth twitched a little; she thought he wryly smiled.

"One of the best blackguards too, my girl," he said grimly.

She opened her eyes in surprise.

"Jake, what do you mean? Are people saying hateful things against you?"

He gripped his hands between his knees.

"It ain't that I meant. People can say what they damn please. No, it's just my own estimate of myself. I'm going to chuck the animals.

"They've come near costing me too dear. I'm going to give in to you now. You can do what you like with me. I'll serve you to the best of my ability, fetch and carry and generally wait round on you till you're tired of me. Then I'll go."

"Jake! Jake!" She was half-laughing, but there was remonstrance in her voice. "But I never wanted you to give up the animals. Why, I don't believe you could live without them, could you?"

He gave himself an odd, half-angry shake.

"I've done with 'em!" he declared almost fiercely. "I can't serve two masters. If the new boss don't chuck me, I shall chuck him."

"But the horses, Jake!" she urged. "And the Hundredth Chance! You can't be in earnest. You . . . you have always loved them better than anything else in the world!"

"You're wrong!" He winced sharply. "And I am in earnest. If—if you had lost your life over the colt, I'd have shot him first and myself after. What sort of brute do you take me for? Do you think I'm without any heart at all? All animal and no heart?"

The question was passionate, but yet he did not look at her as he uttered it. He was gazing downwards at his clenched hands. He was formidable at that moment, but she did not shrink from him. Rather she drew nearer.

"Of course I don't think so. But . . . but . . . am I first with you, Jake? Am I really . . . first?"

He made a choked sound in his throat, as if many emotions struggled for utterance. Then, almost under his breath, he muttered:

"An easy first! An easy first!"

Her bandaged hand slipped onto his arm. Her eyes were shining.

"Oh, Jake, thank you for telling me that. You . . . I know you didn't want to tell me. And . . . and now . . . I've got to tell you something that I don't want to tell you, either . . . that I don't know how to tell you. Oh, Jake, do help me! Don't . . . don't be angry!"

He turned towards her, but he did not lift his eyes. He seemed almost afraid to look her in the face.

"My girl, you've no call to be afraid of me."

But there was constraint in his tone, constraint in his attitude, and her heart sank.

"I'm so . . . horribly afraid . . . of hurting you," she said.

A faint, faint gleam of humour crossed her face.

"Oh, I guess I'm down. You needn't be afraid of that, either."

She tried to clasp his arm.

"Jake, if . . . if I really come first with you, perhaps . . . perhaps . . . you'll be able to forgive me. It's because you came first with me, too . . . a very, very long way first."

Her voice shook.

"It's because I wanted you to have what you wanted without . . . without feeling under an obligation to me, or anyone. It's because . . . because your happiness is more to me . . . a thousand times more . . . than anything else in the world!"

Her breast began to heave; Jake's eyes were suddenly upon her, but it was she who could not, dared not meet their look.

"Ah, I haven't told you yet!" she said brokenly. "How shall I tell you? It's . . . it's the animals, Jake. It's the stud!"

"What about the stud?" he said.

His voice was sunk very low; it sounded stern.

With a great effort she mastered her agitation and answered him.

"It's yours, Jake, all yours. The new boss is . . . is just an invention of Mr Rafford's. You . . . you are . . . the new boss!"

"What?" he said.

He got up suddenly, with a movement that verged upon violence, and stood over her, and she felt almost threateningly.

"I've played a double game. I met Mr Rafford first at Liverpool, and then I chanced to meet him again here after . . . after you had refused to have my money. And he was kind and sympathetic, and offered to help me.

"I wanted you to have the horses. And I couldn't bear to think that you should lose them through me. Oh, Jake, don't look so . . . so terrible!"

She sank back, panting, on her cushions. That one brief glimpse of his face had appalled her. He had the look of a man hard pressed and nearing the end of his strength. She saw that his hands were clenched.

"Why have you done this thing?" he said after several tense seconds.

"Oh, Jake, only . . . only because I . . . love you."

"Only!" he said, and with the word she saw his hands unclench.

For a moment a wild uncertainty possessed her, and then it was gone. Jake dropped down on his knees beside her and took her into his arms.

"Maud," he said. "Maud!"

But no further words would come. His voice broke. He hid his face against her breast with a great sob.

Her arms were round his neck in an instant, her cheek was pressed against his hair. All doubts were gone forever.

"My darling!" she whispered. "My darling!"

And through the great storm of emotion that shook Jake, she said the soft words over and over, holding his head against her heart.

She kissed the cropped hair above his temple, drawing him nearer, even nearer, to the inner sanctuary of her soul, till at length by the shattering of her own reserve she broke down the last of his too.

He lifted his face to her with no attempt to hide his tears, and in the long, long kiss that passed between them they found each other at last, where the sand of the desert turns to gold.

Chapter Eleven

"The black colt leads! The black colt leads! He wins! He wins! He wins!"

A great shout went up from the straining multitude as the Hundredth Chance, ridden by Sam Vickers, shot past the winning-post, three lengths ahead of the horse behind.

It was a sensational victory, for it was his maiden race, and the crowd yelled themselves hoarse over it, cheering and cheering again till the black colt came forth in a welter of sweat and foam to gather his laurels, still carrying his jockey and led by his owner, Jake Bolton.

He bore himself proudly, as if fully conscious of the distinction he had won. Jake looked proud too. His hand caressed the streaming neck.

It was a popular meeting, and it was plainly a popular victory, though the favourite had not proved the winner. Jake Bolton's name went from mouth to mouth, and the throng cheered him to the echo.

He smiled his open, pleasant smile in answer. He had been looking to this moment for the past two years, he had worked hard for it; and his trust in the Hundredth Chance had been vindicated, his labour rewarded.

He knew that yet greater victories lay before his favourite. The Hundredth Chance was a born winner. He would be famous.

Back in the paddock a slim, boyish figure leaped to meet him.

"Jake, he's a stunner! Let me hold him a minute, Jake! Well done, Sam! Well done!"

Sam grinned from ear to ear as he dropped from the saddle.

"Pretty sight, weren't it, Sir Bernard?"

"Best I've ever seen!" declared Bunny enthusiastically.

He led the black colt proudly after his jockey for a few paces, then gave him up and went back to Jake.

"I'm so jolly bucked," he said, hugging his arm. "I want to dance on my head. Do you know what I heard a chap say of you just now, a chap who knew too?" he said. " 'There goes Bolton, one of the straightest men on the Turf.'

"It sounded just fine. I wanted to go and shake hands with him."

Jake laughed, a quiet, satisfied laugh.

"Was Maud pleased?"

"Oh, rather! She's going home now, I was to tell you; and say she'd save up and congratulate you in private."

Jake disengaged himself from Bunny and went about his business, but the smile lingered in his eyes for the rest of the afternoon. And it was the smile of a man who grasps his heart's desire.

There was a white house on one of the great rolling downs behind the Graydown racecourse, a low, white house with gabled roofs and dark green shutters. There were woodland trees about it, and a terraced garden bright with many spring flowers.

Behind it lay the racing-stables, also white—model stables, the pride of Jake's heart. He seldom approached the house by any other route. But as he passed between the long, orderly buildings on that particular evening after his horse's victory he did not linger.

Straight to the house he went, and straight within, pausing only in the wide, square hall to throw down hat and whip before he passed on, guided by the notes of a piano, to a room that overlooked the garden and the whole sweep of hillside beyond.

She did not hear him enter. She was playing softly, a dreamy melody that had in it something of dawning gladness and of infinite hope.

Only Chops, the red setter, lying by the open French window, looked up and wagged a noiseless welcome. Then, as he reached her, she caught the jingle of his spurs, and in a moment she had turned to meet him with a vivid smile of eagerness.

"Oh, Jake, I am so glad . . . so glad!"

He put his arms about her as she sat, staring at the flushed face upturned to his.

"What's that you're playing? A paean of thanksgiving!"

Her eyelids fluttered under his look. She laughed faintly. She offered him her lips with just a hint of shyness. He kissed her, but he continued to look at her with an intent glitter in his eyes.

"You're glad, are you? Really glad?"

Her arms clung about his neck.

"Yes, really glad, Jake. I know you call the Hundredth Chance your luck. I was horribly anxious lest . . . lest he should lose after all."

He smiled a little.

"What if he had? Think I can't stand up to a loss?"

She lifted her eyes to his for a moment, but they fell almost immediately.

"No. To use your own language, I think you're just fine. But . . . but all the same, I've been saving up a little consolation for you in case you needed it."

"Well, let's imagine I'm in need of consolation," said Jake. He spoke very softly through lips that were suddenly tender. "I'd enjoy to be consoled by you."

She laughed again, that faint, shy laugh, and, freeing one hand, began to feel over the keys of the piano, striking a soft chord here and there.

Jake stood for a moment or two, then bent, bringing his face on a level with hers. She made a light gesture of protest, and then very suddenly, as if compelled, she raised her eyes full to his. They were of that intense blueness that comes from the heart of a sapphire.

"I love you," she whispered. "I love you more every day . . . every night."

His big hand closed upon her wrist. He drew a great breath. She went on, but her lips were quivering.

"I don't need to tell you that, do I. You know it so well. I don't think I really need to tell you . . . of this other thing either . . . of this big, big gift that is coming to us. Oh, Jake, my darling Jake, I have so hoped . . . so hoped!"

He held her closer.

"My own darling! I guess you'll be happy now?" he whispered.

She smiled at him through tears.

"No, not for my own sake . . . for yours . . . for yours!"

She uttered a trembling laugh.

"I've given you lots that you didn't want to take . . . things that had cost me nothing. But this . . . this is different. And . . . it's what you wanted."

He clasped her to him almost fiercely. "My precious, I want nothing, no one, but you!"

She clung to him with a tenseness that was passionate.

"That is what I wanted to say to you, my darling. You will always be first . . . first . . . first. Dr Capper once told me that . . . that my frog would turn into a prince someday.

"And . . . dear . . . he was right. You are the prince of my heart forever. I love you as . . . as I never thought it was humanly possible to love."

"Maybe it's not—all human," he whispered, with lips that moved against her own.

"You are right," she whispered back. "It is Divine. The perfect Gift. But it only comes to those who give, without measure, not counting the cost, rejoicing only in the power to give till it all comes back a thousand-fold . . . a thousand-fold."

Her voice thrilled, and her arms clung closer.

"I once heard a Parson preach about that. And

at the end he said, 'It is then that the ploughman overtakes the reaper, for the ploughman and reaper are one.'

"Jake, I think that man spoke a great truth. You and I have done some heavy ploughing, but we are beginning to be reapers now."

Her lips suddenly pressed his closely, lingeringly. Her tears were gone.

"It's good to reap our own harvest, isn't it, Jake?" she murmured. "Yours and mine together?"

And Jake answered her in his own language, his voice very soft and slow, his eyes gazing straight into hers, seeing her soul.

"Sure, my darling," he said. "Sure!"

ABOUT THE EDITOR

BARBARA CARTLAND, the celebrated romantic author, historian, playwright, lecturer, political speaker and television personality, has now written over 150 books. Miss Cartland has had a number of historical books published and several biographical ones, including that of her brother, Major Ronald Cartland, who was the first Member of Parliament to be killed in the War. This book had a Foreword by Sir Winston Churchill.

In private life, Barbara Cartland, who is a Dame of the Order of St. John of Jerusalem, has fought for better conditions and salaries for Midwives and Nurses. As President of the Royal College of Midwives (Hertfordshire Branch), she has been invested with the first Badge of Office ever given in Great Britain, which was subscribed to by the Midwives themselves. She has also championed the cause for old people and founded the first Romany Gypsy Camp in the world.

Barbara Cartland is deeply interested in Vitamin Therapy and is President of the British National Association for Health.

Barbara Cartland

The world's bestselling author of romantic fiction. Her stories are always captivating tales of intrigue, adventure and love.

☐	THE TEARS OF LOVE	2148	$1.25
☐	THE DEVIL IN LOVE	2149	$1.25
☐	THE ELUSIVE EARL	2436	$1.25
☐	THE BORED BRIDEGROOM	6381	$1.25
☐	JOURNEY TO PARADISE	6383	$1.25
☐	THE PENNILESS PEER	6387	$1.25
☐	NO DARKNESS FOR LOVE	6427	$1.25
☐	THE LITTLE ADVENTURE	6428	$1.25
☐	LESSONS IN LOVE	6431	$1.25
☐	THE DARING DECEPTION	6435	$1.25
☐	CASTLE OF FEAR	8103	$1.25
☐	THE GLITTERING LIGHTS	8104	$1.25
☐	A SWORD TO THE HEART	8105	$1.25
☐	THE MAGNIFICENT MARRIAGE	8166	$1.25
☐	THE RUTHLESS RAKE	8240	$1.25
☐	THE DANGEROUS DANDY	8280	$1.25
☐	THE WICKED MARQUIS	8467	$1.25
☐	LOVE IS INNOCENT	8505	$1.25
☐	THE FRIGHTENED BRIDE	8780	$1.25
☐	THE FLAME IS LOVE	8887	$1.25

Buy them at your local bookseller or use this handy coupon:

Barbara Cartland

The world's bestselling author of romantic fiction. Her stories are always captivating tales of intrigue, adventure and love.

☐	THE CRUEL COUNT	2128	$1.25
☐	THE MASK OF LOVE	2366	$1.25
☐	AN ARROW OF LOVE	2426	$1.25
☐	A GAMBLE WITH HEARTS	2430	$1.25
☐	A KISS FOR THE KING	2433	$1.25
☐	A FRAME OF DREAMS	2434	$1.25
☐	THE FRAGRANT FLOWER	2435	$1.25
☐	MOON OVER EDEN	2437	$1.25
☐	THE GOLDEN ILLUSION	2449	$1.25
☐	FIRE ON THE SNOW	2450	$1.25
☐	THE HUSBAND HUNTERS	2461	$1.25
☐	PASSIONS IN THE SAND	2801	$1.25
☐	THE SLAVES OF LOVE	2802	$1.25
☐	AN ANGEL IN HELL	2803	$1.25
☐	THE WILD CRY OF LOVE	2804	$1.25
☐	THE BLUE-EYED WITCH	2805	$1.25
☐	THE INCREDIBLE HONEYMOON	2806	$1.25
☐	NO TIME FOR LOVE	2807	$1.25

Bantam Book Catalog

Here's your up-to-the-minute listing of every book currently available from Bantam.

This easy-to-use catalog is divided into categories and contains over 1400 titles by your favorite authors.

So don't delay—take advantage of this special opportunity to increase your reading pleasure.

Just send us your name and address and 25¢ (to help defray postage and handling costs).